D0068217

Katharine Galgano

THE DEVIL HATES LATIN

Published by Regina Press
A Division of Regina Foundation of Oregon

R.

REGINA PRESS

Regina Foundation of Oregon
12042 SE Sunnyside Road
Suite 486
Clackamas, Oregon 97015

All characters and events in this book are purely fictitious. Any similarity to actual events or persons, living or dead, is purely coincidental. 'Katharine Galgano' is the author's nom de plume.

Designed by Donna Sue Berry and John LaMaestra
Manufactured in the United States

ISBN 978-099-664-7908

"The most beautiful thing we can experience is the mysterious.
It is the source of all true art and science."

- *Albert Einstein, What I Believe (1930)*

-

Dedicated

To Father Richard Cipolla
Who led me back to the Faith of our ancestors,
a treasure greater than rubies.
With love, respect, and admiration.

PROLOGUE

The Cardinal inhaled sharply. The view from the papal apartments over St Peter's Square revealed a stark late winter's tableau that was pure magic. Before him lay a painting executed in grays and whites, the work of Italian genius etched against a ferocious sky.

The heavy black snow clouds had been massing over Michelangelo's famous dome all morning, discouraging all but the hardiest tourists from waiting in the queue which normally snaked around Bernini's magnificent Colonnade.

In recent weeks there had been huge crowds of tourists there, eager for a glimpse of the new pope. The sudden death of the previous pontiff had spurred the usual hoopla surrounding a papal election, though this time the many billions following on social media had ramped the chaos up to unprecedented levels.

Reporters unfamiliar with Catholicism scrambled to untangle it all -- conspiracy theories speculating wildly about the pope's unexpected demise, leads leaked from chanceries around the world, even astute remarks from *san pietrini*, the Romans who had maintained the Basilica from time immemorial, and whose accustomed stance was one of dignified silence.

When the white smoke finally rose, the world's media was utterly wrong-footed. They had speculated approvingly on the potentialities of a cigar-chomping, Harley-riding German liberal with massive funding, or a handsome Filipino with an infectious grin and smooth delivery. Uncertain about how to spin the narrative on a tiny, fierce Cardinal from an African backwater, most media had simply ignored him.

Now, the tall, lanky American Cardinal found himself on his knees, kissing the papal ring of the first black man to sit on the throne of Peter.

The new pope was a reserved man, and no longer young. He was, however, extremely focused, and intent on his purpose. After the briefest of pleasantries, he came immediately to the point.

"You have an exorcist in your diocese of Boston, a Dominican," he stated flatly. "Would you say he is capable of organizing training for a large number of priests?"

"If you mean Father Corinth," the Cardinal replied carefully, "he is highly intelligent, and very serious. His ministry has, however, been limited mainly to the cases to which my predecessor directed him, so they have been few."

The pope nodded.

"Your predecessor was not a believer in the power of exorcism." Another flat statement of fact.

"I cannot say for certain," the Cardinal replied diplomatically.

"...but you are." The pope was unsmiling.

The Cardinal nodded, albeit a bit reluctantly.

"Why is this?"

"I have seen the rise of popular interest in the diabolical in recent years," the Cardinal sighed. "Consistently, more and more cases of obsession and possession are brought to us from families desperate for help after medical intervention has proven unsuccessful."

"To what do you attribute this?"

"To be honest," the Cardinal took a breath, and then plunged ahead. "I believe this is emanating from some of the Western elites," he finished forthrightly.

"What are your grounds for believing this?"

"An unrelenting focus on sexual depravity in the media, the huge amount of money being spent for legalizing this agenda, and the unrelenting pressure to normalize this and to teach these things in the schools." The Cardinal was clear and concise. "And, personal experience in my own ministry."

"What has been your experience?"

"I have heard anecdotally – and usually from their distraught family -- about the tastes of the super-rich and famous in America," the Cardinal said. "And then, there's been the murders."

"Murders?"

"We had a very kind man in our archdiocese, a good Catholic man of means. He was responsible for bringing the Latin Mass to the Boston area, under my predecessor. This man was recently murdered in cold blood by his own 22 year old son. The boy approached his mother and father as they were leaving a restaurant after Sunday Mass, and stabbed his father repeatedly to death in full view of his mother and others."

The Pope inhaled sharply and paused, his eyes fixed on the Cardinal's.

"And why do you believe this was satanic?" When it came, the pope's question was delivered calmly.

"The boy was found to have been involved with Satanists, a participant in their Black Masses. And, there was the experience of the exorcist."

"Father Corinth?"

"Yes, he was asked to bless the house of the deceased on the day of the funeral. As he walked around the perimeter, praying and sprinkling holy water and blessed salt, some women screamed. This caused him to jump quickly aside to avoid being struck by a large black snake which seemed to launch itself from under the eaves, directly at Father Corinth."

"And how do you know this was diabolic?"

"Well, it's unlikely that it was a natural phenomenon. There are no large snakes native to the area, and certainly not snakes which climb," the Cardinal explained. "And, though several people saw the serpent fly through the air, *no one saw it hit the ground. It disappeared.*"

The pope nodded, and looked away for a moment without speaking. For a moment he seemed lost in thought. The he roused himself and spoke matter of factly.

"This phenomenon which you have observed in your diocese is widespread," he said sadly. "We have reports of this and far worse. We wish to put the resources of the Holy See to work providing the proper training for priests to combat this."

The Cardinal nodded.

"The office of exorcism has been neglected for more than 50 years. The few that we have are in their 80's, brave men and good who have been nevertheless treated by the Curia as pariahs, embarrassing vestiges of the Middle Ages. We need young men to take up this work. Tell me, how did Father Corinth come to be an exorcist?"

The Cardinal sighed.

"He told me that he was a farm boy in the Midwest, and as a teenager became involved in the occult through popular 'heavy metal' music. This was before the internet, so the spread of this was more limited. Apparently, though, at university he witnessed horrific sexual violence connected with the occult, and was so thoroughly repulsed that he ran straight into the arms of the Dominicans."

"Yes, we know of their good work and their growth in America."

"He worked on the streets of Boston with the homeless after ordination, which is where he started to see the effects of occultism, mixed with drugs and organized crime."

The pontiff nodded grimly.

"He came to my attention when I asked the religious superiors in my diocese to identify the most prayerful men in their communities. I interviewed them all, and chose three to begin training with a Dominican priest in his 90's who has been quietly working in this field since before the Council."

The pope's expression lightened.

"Is that true, Cardinal?"

"Yes, I am happy to report that it is," the Cardinal smiled back at the pope. "Father Donovan is now 100 years old, as sharp as a tack. The demons, I am told, hate him."

The pope smiled broadly.

"And now we have this young man who was trained by a master exorcist. Cardinal, please bring Father Corinth to Rome as soon as possible."

The meeting was clearly over. The Cardinal rose to take his leave. As he turned, however, the pope spoke again.

"And do give our best regards to Father Donovan," he said.

The Cardinal bowed his assent, and left the magnificent chamber.

CHAPTER 1

Truth be told, when he saw the strange customer waiting outside his shop, Marco was a bit annoyed. He'd been looking forward to his morning espresso – a necessary indulgence before his often-grueling, nine hour day commenced.

Marco considered himself to be the consummate hairdressing professional. This, in a Rome full of serious hairdressers, was a mark of pride, like his *bella figura* and amiable demeanor. Marco never lost his temper with a customer, no matter how irritating or demanding or yes, deranged they might be.

This, too, was a matter of necessity. Italians of a certain age visit their hairdresser once a week, a key to maintaining the necessary *bella figura*. Toiling long hours in a neighborhood of gossiping *romani*, Marco had worked hard to achieve his reputation of gentility.

But the man waiting outside his shop was a stranger. Marco wondered if he might be a visiting relative, or even a new arrival to the close-knit middle-class neighborhood. As the man approached, he noted the closely-shorn haircut and the foreign cut of the clothes of – a priest?

Marco sighed. He'd been hoping for that twenty minutes with his espresso, but it was unlikely now. There was no rescheduling a priest, even if he was just a stranger without an appointment.

Half an hour later, Marco sat nursing his espresso with a rather bemused expression on his handsome face. The interlude with the strange priest had left him unsettled.

It wasn't what the man had said, though his American-inflected Italian had been quite good, probably a product of his years studying in Rome.

"*Don Signore*, where are you from?" he'd asked, using the formal honorific. The slight, pale priest settled into Marco's chair. Marco noted that he was the kind of American –rare these days—who aged well. The priest was in his forties, with fine lines etched around his blue eyes and sensitive, long-fingered hands.

He'd been friendly enough, not peremptory or arrogant or overly familiar, as priests could be. In fact, there was an unusual quality to this priest – a kind of depth, a seriousness that Marco was unused to. It was almost un-nerving.

"These are your children?" the priest had asked, a typical enough question. But the American had taken note of the pain in Marco's eyes when he'd attempted to answer jovially in the affirmative.

Not that he'd said anything untoward. But Marco saw that the priest perceived his pain, which was both embarrassing and oddly infuriating. Feeling suddenly defensive, he found himself, to his great annoyance, talking about his divorce. How angry he was, how little control he had. How he was alone at Christmas, because that bitch – sorry Padre, but you know what I mean – refused him access to his own children. All of this, mind you, before his espresso.

What he didn't say, of course, because it was none of the priest's business, was that the divorce had come because of his affair with Flaminia, the personal trainer at his gym, who'd left him with an empty wallet and a sexually transmitted disease which he had neglected to mention to any of his subsequent lovers. He declined to mention his online porn habit, or that he was keeping three sets of books at the shop – one for the tax man, one for his greedy ex-wife and the real one, for him alone.

Marco didn't go into the fact that when his son no longer wanted to see him or even speak with him by phone, he began to hate everyone and everything. That the Devil had bitten deeply into Marco and was steering his life was something that Marco didn't see.

But the strange priest did. For, unbeknownst to Marco, who sat watching the retreating figure of the priest making his way up the busy street, Father Paul Corinth was not a typical cleric.

Indeed, Father Paul had a highly unusual job. He was the Pope's exorcist, newly arrived back in Rome. And that morning he was on his way to start his new job, one that he wasn't at all sure he was capable of handling.

CHAPTER 2

Gina Pirisi looked at her reflection critically in the mirror. Her thick, long hair had once been smooth -- a dark, chocolate brown. Today its luxurious Italian length was streaked with permanent chemicals, the frazzled ends bearing a strong resemblance to straw.

Gina's hair was just one casualty of the days she had been with Marco. Gina often thought that he fancied himself to be living the life of the MTV he watched obsessively, where American mega-stars and Italian crooners took turns singing the virtues of hedonism and passion on flat screen TVs mounted a few inches from the noses of his neighborhood clientele.

He saw women all day long, Marco told Gina in the beginning. But none like her.

Gina had golden skin, fiery hazel eyes and the quick wit of her forebears, *romani* since forever. Her body was still young and taut, though she'd passed her 30th birthday. Truth be told, it looked more and more like there would be no ecstatic day of the *sposa* for Gina. Southern Italy's 40% unemployment rate meant very few young men could think about starting a family. That left the gay ones, and the divorced ones, like Marco.

Gina was a practical girl. She had devoted herself to learning her trade, and by her mid-twenties had won herself a coveted job at an upscale Roman salon, where rich women paid many times the going price of a neighborhood hairstylist to be flattered and cossetted by a sympathetic staff. Working there required talent, hard work, tact and diplomacy, as well as a fierce competitive streak in order to develop 'a following'. Though she would have never admitted it, her job was exhausting, and demoralizing, and this is probably why she had fallen so easily into Marco's clutches.

Because she lived so near to his salon, and because they were both hairdressers, it seemed easy to talk with him. He was handsome, in his way, and seemed very experienced in the ways of the salon world. After awhile she would come to him after work, asking his advice about the latest treachery she'd had to endure – offhand slights, whispered innuendo, stolen clients. He would listen, nod sagely and ask her to dinner.

One thing led to another and then another, and before six months had passed Gina was pregnant. This proved to be unacceptable to Marco, already the father of two expensive children.

It was early one Tuesday night when she told him, in his shop. She stopped by while his staff were sweeping up. As the lovers' voices rose from the back room, the two hairdressers exchanged glances, quickly excused themselves with a jaunty "ciao!" and fled into the Roman dusk.

It wasn't much of a battle, actually. Marco did not want this child. Gina wanted Marco. The child had to go. The certain knowledge of this dragged the normally ebullient Gina down as she left Marco's shop that night. He had to meet with his lawyer, again. The discussion, he said, was closed.

Gina stumbled out of the shop, wiped her tears with the back of her hand and ducked into her parents' place nearby. Mumbling that she didn't feel well, she went quickly to bed.

She slept fitfully that night and was not quite herself when she greeted Mrs. Dyson White for her usual Wednesday morning appointment at the high-end salon in the *centro storico* where Gina worked. Gina was Mrs. White's favorite, as her light hand didn't irritate Mrs. White's delicate scalp. And after ten years as a stylist, Gina knew how to soothe imperious ladies.

The fifty-something Mrs. White, however, was sharp as a tack.

"Whatsamatter with you?" she demanded to know as Gina was helping her into the salon's gown in the dressing room. She was short, buxom and feisty. "You get up on the wrong side of bed?"

Gina's boss had told her the Whites were very rich. To Gina's experienced eye, Mrs. White had at first looked like any number of aging divas who frequented the expensive salon, with one exception. Mrs. White was an Italian-American who spoke a horrible Brooklyn version of Italian; also, she wore a crucifix. Apparently Mr. White was some sort of American tycoon who had spent time in jail. Gina wasn't sure for what, though it was hard to imagine the redoubtable Mrs. White involved with anything criminal.

Throughout the wash and blow-dry, Gina tried her best to fend off Mrs. White's persistent questions. After all, a professional shop was no place to be discussing one's personal problems, especially with her boss keeping an eagle eye on this valuable client. In the end, however, she relented, and surreptitiously accepted Mrs. White's card.

"Call me," were Mrs. White's last words before her Italian chauffeur swept her out of the shop. Gina nodded and smiled mechanically, pocketing the card as she watched the back of Mrs. White's coiffured head slip into the Mercedes Benz.

Gina had heard that pregnancy hormones made women more emotional. Perhaps that is why the rest of the day seemed interminable; all day, she dreaded her commute home. As she stepped out into the gathering evening, she eyed a couple embracing passionately outside the salon. The slender young girl slipped onto the back of her lover's Vespa, which then nosed out into the chaotic Roman traffic.

Hot tears sprung immediately to her eyes and as she turned determinedly away, Gina almost ran into a woman a few years older than she. The woman was walking a dog – one of the legions of such women throughout Rome and indeed Italy. In Gina's lifetime, the land of *la famiglia* had morphed into the land of pet owners, everyone walking at top speed to preserve their *bella figura*, everyone keeping their options open.

Dejected, Gina hunched her shoulders and strode purposefully on, but despite all her efforts, the tears welled up again and began coursing down her cheeks. Where could she go? To her mother? Valeria was certain to be broken-hearted; she and her father had sacrificed so much to raise Gina and her brother. Now her brother had given up his dream of a university education and was working a crummy job. And Gina was pregnant by a cad.

Her *telefonini* buzzed, and she slipped the earpiece on without breaking her stride. The number was unfamiliar, but feeling desperate, she answered anyway.

"Gina?" It was Mrs. White, in a business-like, American tone. She got right to the point. "I got your number from your boss. I hope you don't mind me calling."

"N-no," said Gina. It came out in a kind of choked whisper.

"Honey," the older woman began kindly. "You've been doing my hair for two years now, and I know when something's wrong. Are you pregnant?"

Gina nodded into the phone, the tears falling down her face like rain. To make matters worse, she found herself stopped at the gate of the neighborhood playground. The tiny *bambini* running around, the mothers chatting -- it was too much. She began to sob, oblivious to the stares of the passers-by.

"Honey, I'm sending Carlo to pick you up," Mrs. White snapped. "Where are you?"

"Oh, no, Mrs. White," Gina protested through her tears. "That's not necessary."

But Mrs. White was a force to be reckoned with, and before long Gina found herself ensconced in the creamy leather interior of the Benz. The driver, Carlo, solicitously handed her a box of Kleenex before he shut the car's solid door.

Mrs. White was waiting at the door of the underground parking garage to their luxury pre-war apartment building. Within an hour Gina had unburdened herself of her secret, while Mrs. White listened sympathetically.

"So, no chance this Marco will marry you?"

Gina sighed and sipped her tea. It seemed that Marco was unequal to the responsibility of marriage, and barely competent to raise the children he had. When she'd timidly told him that she was pregnant, his reaction had been catastrophic.

"Oh *mama mia*," he'd rolled his eyes. "This is impossible."

He continued to shake his head dolefully as she'd tried to explain how it happened.

"Gina, this is your fault," he'd said, finally. "You played with fire – now you need to take responsibility."

He would be generous, he sighed, and pay for the abortion. But she'd better be quick, he warned, as these things get more expensive as time wore on.

"And you have already been way too irresponsible, *bella*," he'd said, winningly. One hand caressed her chin as the other ran through his thick, long mane.

"Oh Jesus, Mary and Joseph," Mrs. White fumed. "This guy's a real jerk."

Gina nodded dully. It was true.

"Blaming this on you is the first sign of a true jerk. The second sign is this phony crap about caring for you. He cares about his pocketbook. Period." Mrs. White was indignant.

Gina nodded again. She could not defend him.

"Gina, tell me something. Do you *want* a family?"

"Y-yes. N-no. It's impossible," Gina stuttered stubbornly. "I must work. Who will care for this baby? My parents work too. Rome is expensive," she finished helplessly. How could a woman of Mrs. White's wealth know how hard it was just to have a decent life?

Come to think of it, why *did* Mrs. White care so much about her? Gina's eyes narrowed as a thought came to her. She'd heard about people who made money on human trafficking. Healthy white babies were valuable commodities, it seemed. Is *that* how these people got so rich? Is *that* why Mr. White had gone to prison in America?

She gazed around at the elegant furnishings and the expansive view of the bend in the Tiber with new eyes. Was this woman about to offer her money for her baby?

She stood up, suddenly full of purpose.

"I need to leave now," she told the astonished Mrs. White.

"W-why?" Mrs. White gasped.

"Because I am late," Gina answered decisively. She stood up. Her tears were dry now. "My family will be expecting me."

Despite Mrs. White's protests, Gina remained firm, though in the end she reluctantly agreed to let Carlo drive her home.

Unfortunately, Gina's brother happened to be parking his Vespa outside their apartment building when the Benz pulled up. One eyebrow shot up in surprise as Luca watched his sister emerge from its posh interior, assisted by the burly Carlo, who handed her gently out of the car.

Once inside the building, Luca refused to let her disappear upstairs without an explanation. His wiry body on the alert, his normally affable expression drawn into a mask of worry, Luca stood his ground. When evasions and protests proved fruitless,

Gina finally broke down and agreed to explain, but only outside, away from prying ears.

"Oh Jesus," Luca said, when she finished in tears. He was smoking. They were across the street, hidden behind the huge, filthy recycling containers, invisible to the building residents.

Gina sighed. Her little brother was good and loyal, but clearly not able to help. She was, however, unprepared for his response.

"So why won't you just have the baby for money?" he said casually, though he was watching her intensely.

"*What*?!" Gina was shocked. "No!"

"Why not?"

"Whaddya mean, why not?" she sputtered furiously. "I'm not a *putana*! What do you think I am? I'm not *selling* my baby!"

The two looked at each other in the dim light. Gina was breathing hard. Suddenly, the garbage reek and Luca's cigarette smoke was making her ill. A wave of nausea swept over her.

"I don't feel so good," she whispered, her hand on her belly. She attempted to swallow, but felt something stick in her throat.

"Santa Maria," Luca breathed, and stabbed out his cigarette on the grimy sidewalk. He regarded his sister soberly. "You hear yourself?"

Gina nodded morosely, wondering how far along she was. Suddenly, she felt tremendously tired, and thought longingly of her bed upstairs in the family nest her parents had created for them in the heart of the Roman metropolis.

"I said," Luca repeated, "do you *hear* yourself?"

Gina looked at him uncomprehendingly.

"You just called it 'my baby,'" He stated flatly. His face was emotionless, but his dark eyes were watching her intently.

Gina shook her head. Yes, she had. She knew what her brother was thinking – if she wouldn't give her baby up for money, then she had to admit that 'it' really was a baby. Her baby. A swell of emotion hit her, along with another wave of weariness. It was all too much to think about. The tears started to course down her cheeks again.

"I got no right," she whispered weakly, thinking of how her parents would react to the news. "Who's gonna take care of it?"

In the end, Luca agreed to keep her secret, "but just for a week," he added darkly. "You can't screw around with this."

CHAPTER 3

The young nun swept down the hallway in a state of high excitement. The summons to the Mother Prior's office had not been unexpected. Rumors had been flying around the Boston convent for about a week of a new establishment, a 'daughter house' to be founded in Italy.

This would be the Sisters' second European venture. The first, in Scotland, had come at the behest of an embattled bishop there, who had gladly made a huge, 19th century church property in a depressed industrial suburb of Glasgow available to the four American Sisters, members of a newly-established Order dedicated to the 'support of the family' just ten years before.

"I'm old enough to remember the Westerns," he'd announced in his thick Glaswegian accent. The reception for their arrival was crowded with a polyglot of Catholics – Scots of Irish extraction, converts and newly arrived immigrants from Poland and India. The bishop's old face was creased in a broad smile.

"In the films, when all would seem darkest, the American cavalry would come charging over the hill. Well, I'm here to say that our cavalry has arrived," he turned a beaming smile on them. "Sisters, welcome to Scotland, with all our hearts we welcome ye."

The four sisters, all in their early 30s, had since settled happily into their new lives in Scotland. They were there for the poor, after all. For the tired women their own age with alcoholic, unemployed men and intractable teenagers. For the pregnant young girls without hope, headed for the abortion mills to erase the consequences of their 'mistake.' For the Catholic families that were simply not forming.

Of course, it wasn't just the Catholics. Scotland's native population was actually declining, a fact mostly hidden behind the statistics which showed a 2% growth rate. A little digging would reveal the truth –Scots were dying later, and the shortfall in births was made up by immigration, largely from Eastern Europe and the East.

It seemed as if the Scots had entirely lost interest in the humble joys of married and family life. Middle-aged Scots were divorcing in record numbers. Among the working class young, interest in love and marriage was being replaced by casual sex, incited by internet porn and binge drinking bouts. On the university campuses, homosexuality was all the rage. At all levels of society, easy access to drugs and booze cushioned the impact of lives led on the knife's edge of a hopelessness.

After two years in Scotland, however, the sisters were optimistic, with no thought of returning to their bursting motherhouse back in Boston. This wasn't just because there was simply not enough room for them there.

For, unbeknownst to the vast majority of American Catholics, a whole new generation of women were 'discerning' their vocations as religious. They were drawn by the traditional life of the Sisters, who lived in community, wore floor-length habits and prayed the Divine Office. Hundreds of young women found their way to the Order's doorstep every year, and Mother Superior's major problem was how to find room for them all.

Her solution to the overcrowding was the traditional Catholic one – founding daughter houses in other places. In a decade, they had begun eight houses in America, plus the house in Glasgow. Everywhere, the teams of sisters were kept busy taking in pregnant women and helping them through the birth and early years of their babies' lives.

"We really can do so much good here," Sister Mary Grace explained via Skype to her Superior. The Scots, for their part, were flabbergasted at the appearance of these young Sisters. Most had never seen a habited Catholic sister in their entire lives.

"Sometimes it's like we stepped out of the movies," said Sister Mary Grace, laughing as she described the Scots staring open-mouthed at the Sisters, always in twos, good-humoredly learning to navigate left-side traffic roundabouts and puzzling Glaswegian dialects.

Everywhere they went, however, they were received with cordiality. A minority of stern old Calvinists and new-style atheists alike were simply too shocked to react to their warm, uncomplicated presence. Most had assumed that the Catholic Church was down for the count, as the media trumpeted parishes closing and empty seminaries. A predatory homosexual Cardinal had been relieved of his See by the Pope just a year before; persistent rumors of similarly-disposed prelates dominating the Scottish Church had frightened off many would-be vocations. The media seized the opportunity to scourge the Church whenever possible, and Scottish Catholics avoided discussing what little faith they had left.

Most congregations in Catholic churches in working class Glasgow were thinning groups of old ladies, determinedly singing the forever-1960s anthems of the post-Vatican II generation. Like their Church of Scotland counterparts, wealthy Catholics in posh neighborhoods kept their churches open as necessary outlets for their social and charitable hobbies.

Most had no idea about the American sisters and their quiet work of saving Scottish babies and their mothers, one at a time. Sometimes, Sister Mary Grace doubted if many of the Irish-Scots Catholics would approve, if they knew.

She sighed; her own wealthy Irish-American family had deeply disapproved of her choice to enter the convent ten years before. But she had never looked back from the day she took her final vows, though her own mother, a prominent divorce lawyer, was not in the church to see her daughter clothed in the simple white habit of her Order.

Her father, divorced from her mother when she was a child, was a mostly-unsuccessful artist remotely of Italian extraction. He stood respectfully, hands folded when not nervously running through his shock of unruly gray hair, in the last pew. As his daughter lay prostrate before the Bishop, dressed in the white, floor-length habit, he, however, remembered the 'Our Father' of his childhood, and prayed for the first time in decades. When he glimpsed his daughter's face immediately after she took the veil, he was shocked at her expression of pure, unadulterated joy.

The years since had flown by as Mary Grace blissfully immersed herself in the ordered life of the convent. Eventually, she became the Novice Mistress, charged with the formation of the young girls who seemed to gather in an ever-increasing flood at the convent doors. And now, the same was beginning to happen in Scotland, though the young girls attracted to her convent were mostly unformed, 'Catholics in name only' as the phrase went in America. Nevertheless, the happiness of the sisters was contagious, and curious young Scots girls were taking notice.

Meanwhile, the Sisters in the Boston mother house were moving ahead with their plans to open another daughter house, this time in Italy. Sister Mary Benedicta, the young nun who swept into her Superior's office halted when she saw the other three sisters seated there.

A smile spread across her intelligent face. This was most certainly "it."

CHAPTER 4

Dyson White regarded his wife stoically as she moved among the pots on their rooftop terrace. It was a spring morning in the Eternal City, and Michelle Orsini White was in a good mood. An avid gardener, his diminutive, dark-haired wife had managed through sheer persistence to interest her husband in the tomato vines growing up through her trestles, and the pots of mint and basil interspersed between her glowing spring flowers. Every morning, he knelt by her side, carefully weeding, watering and re-potting. The fresh smell of the earth and the herbs rose from the pots; spring sunlight glinted off the cloudy green Tiber far below.

It was critical that Dyson take an interest in *something*, to Michelle's mind. Since his release from a US federal penitentiary in Texas two years before, the tall, laconic 57-year old ex media and publishing tycoon hadn't reacted much to anything except for a rather desultory concern with high papal politics. Nothing else about his business empire interested him; he was resolved to stay in Rome and 'keep an eye' on the Papacy. One thing was certain, however. He'd sworn never to set foot in America again. The Whites were staying in Rome as expatriate employees of his British media arm.

This was unfortunate because it meant that they couldn't see their daughter Sophia, now Sister Mary Benedicta of the Boston Order. Sophia had practically flown into the convent after graduating from Christendom College, a small Catholic school in Virginia renowned for its orthodoxy. There, her roommates had sustained the girl throughout her father's ordeal at the hands of a Washington, DC federal prosecutor, who had filed 30 counts against him alleging everything from racketeering to conspiracy, insider trading, fraud and obstruction of justice.

In the end, it cost Dyson five years of legal maneuvering and tens of millions in legal fees to get 28 of the 30 counts dismissed. Michelle, who had no head for legal technicalities, couldn't understand why her husband of 30 years had to serve a four-year prison sentence.

"What did you do wrong?" she asked for about the hundredth time on the night before he was to report to prison. This turned out to not be a very easy question to answer, even for the normally adroit, articulate Dyson. He had to admit that his wife's Brooklyn characterization of the legal assault as a 'shakedown' was apt; what was clear was that the charges were politically motivated.

America was on shaky ground in 2009, threatened by a near-collapse of her banking system and debilitated by a war against terror on two fronts. A radical new Administration had swept into power, borne on the enthusiasm of young people fueled by social media-based promises of a peaceful, progressive new era. In reality, a few opportunistic businessmen with a net worth north of a billion dollars had paid for the new President's ascent from obscurity. The very last thing they wanted was another media voice in the United States raising questions about how this President had been elected, or what tactics his Party was using to stay in power.

Hence, the lawsuit. Though White's lawyers had appealed the case all the way to the Supreme Court, it declined to review the two counts that remained against him. A few days later, Dyson White entered the American underworld of a federal penitentiary.

Michelle moved into an apartment in nearby Dallas, and twice a week rose at dawn to visit her husband in his purgatory. She was immensely gratified when his four-year sentence was commuted to two years on the basis of his exemplary behavior, and the day he was released found them both on a corporate jet winging its way to Fiumicino airport outside Rome.

White wanted to go to Mass, he told his wife, at St. Peter's Basilica.

But first he was going to Confession.

There was no line. Tourists were scarce in this part of St Peter's; only the faithful were interested in the quaint old Sacrament. Michelle watched her husband emerge from the Baroque wooden confessional in the gloom and walk slowly over to the pew where she was saying her own penance.

She'd told the priest about her sins – her fury at the mistreatment of her husband, her temptation to follow her wealthy women friends' taste for the occult, her secret wish that something terrible would happen to the vile prosecutor who had persecuted Dyson. But when her longtime friend, now deeply involved in New Age practices, suggested that an 'accident' might 'be arranged' if Michelle could be persuaded to work hard to visualize this, Michelle had been taken aback.

"Y-you're kidding, right?" she had replied, nonplussed. "Y-you want me to put a hex on this guy -- kinda like my grandmother and the 'evil eye'?"

Her friend had been condescending.

"You have to assert control," she had said, severely. "The universe will respond to your will, but only if you take control of this."

As desperate as she had been, Michelle had declined the offer. When she had later jokingly told Dyson about it, he'd turned unexpectedly grim.

"Devil worship," he had snapped. "Stay the hell away from it. And stay the hell away from that person, if you know what's good for you – and us."

If she hadn't just lived through the last horrendous months of Dyson's trial, Michelle knew she would have bristled at his suggestion. In all their years together, Dyson had known better than to comment on Michelle's choices – on anything, really.

In truth, up until the charges had been filed, Michelle's world had been a cozy, secure one, centered on their parish school in their affluent suburb. Michelle was Catholic because she was born and raised that way. There had been no 'choice' involved; likewise, she had no interest in proselytizing. The Faith had always been there, part of her family's way of life, and she saw no need to explore it, or to deepen her attachment.

But that was before the months and months of agony had pried open Michelle's closed world. Once she disclosed her agony, she found that her friends either made themselves scarce -- or shared their own. That was how Michelle learned about the cancers – physical and spiritual – that were eating away at the fabric of life all around her.

There were the living widows. That's how she thought of the wealthy women whose husbands had deserted them for porn habits, prostitutes and other lovers, both male and female. Both sides stayed in the marriage for fear of the ruinous consequences of divorce, at least for a time, rendering their elegant homes a living hell. Then there were the children lost to cults, strange sexual proclivities or lonely lives lived on the internet, with dogs and cats as their offspring. And everywhere, there were the drugs – the recreational drugs, plus the prescriptions handed out like candy to a population that was trained to ask for them for every possible reason, real or imagined.

And as the stress of this life ramped up, so did the cancer rates. She had been attempting to counsel yet another woman friend with a breast cancer diagnosis when the news appeared abruptly over her cellphone.

The text was brief: Dyson had been convicted. Game over.

The night he'd left for prison, she'd taken her rosary beads outside into her garden. As the dusk gathered, she'd sat on the lawn, knees drawn up to her chin, telling the beads and trying to regulate her too-rapid breathing.

That night, she'd brought out her grandmother's crucifix with the candles and the holy water. She had lit the candles, and opening the plastic bottle filled with holy water, had proceeded to methodically sprinkle the water, murmuring a blessing, on every single object in her bedroom. It took her about twenty minutes to accomplish this, during which time a small part of her stood apart and wondered at what she was doing.

Once it was done, she lay on her bed and presently fell into a deep slumber. The very next morning, she enrolled in an online catechism course. Before long, she had found an orthodox Catholic priest to be her spiritual director.

When she'd moved to be closer to Dyson, he had recommended a good Catholic parish in Dallas. There, in that unassuming church filled with families speaking with an unfamiliar Texas drawl, she had heard the first Latin Mass since her youth. Entranced, she became a regular figure in the pews, for devotions, for benedictions, for a constant 54 day novena to our Lady of Pompeii that she recited, begging for her husband's early release and for protection for her family.

This was how Michelle survived Dyson's imprisonment.

Now that the ordeal was over, Michelle's tears had splashed onto her knees on the hard wooden kneeler in the confessional at St. Peter's. The priest had responded with deep sympathy. *"Coraggio, signora. Coraggio."*

Later, as she knelt saying her penance, Michelle basked in the emotional release -- a cleansing, really – that she'd experienced by opening her heart to a humble priest as an anonymous sinner. She actually felt she could trust his judgment, unlike shrinks or friends or even family, for whom she was always the tycoon's wife.

People were funny about rich people, she had learned long ago. Mostly, they told Michelle what they thought she wanted to hear. It had a coruscating effect on her opinion of other human beings, leaving her wary of the motivations of basically everyone. Except Dyson and her children, of course.

In addition to Sister Mary Benedicta, there was their eldest daughter Stacey, married to a senior intelligence officer stationed in East Anglia. Their youngest was Patrick Edward, who like his father had early on shown signs of a maverick's distaste for boarding school education amid the privileged lives of America's elite. Unfortunately, this phase of Patrick's life had coincided with his father' public humiliation at the hands of the Washington prosecutor. Though most of his school friends were blissfully ignorant of the goings-on outside the confines of their co-ed school in verdant New England, a few were not. Of these, most remained staunchly supportive of Pat.

One or two, however, were members of a student political group which had recently morphed from a radical Marxist to a Sexual Left position. It was their leader, a girl whose mother was the most prominent breast cancer surgeon in America, who decided to mock Pat in public for his father's predicament.

The contemptuous words 'fascist fuck' were barely spat out of her mouth before Pat lost control of himself, lunging for the girl in a blind fury – and this in full view of horrified teachers and students. In the resulting melee, Michelle was told, her son had accused the girl's mother of being a 'ghoul, profiting from the hapless victims of Big Pharma' and called the girl herself names that Michelle was sure were not normally bandied about in those elite environs.

Net, net, Pat had been expelled. When he arrived in Dallas, Michelle was too overwhelmed to argue with her son about finding another private school.

For his part, he'd had it, Pat said grimly. Returning home, he'd immersed himself in a Catholic homeschooling program which concentrated on the Great Books and refused to listen to his mother's arguments in favor of more conventional schooling.

He could do this schoolwork anywhere, he'd argued, pointing out with some justification that their luxury apartment residence in Dallas was a temporary one. But he'd been unable to bring himself to visit his father in the prison, despite his mother's entreaties. It made him too angry, he told her.

Dyson soothed her distress about this when they met at the prison in a bare room outfitted for a 'conjugal visit.' On her first visit, Michelle had stared in disbelief at the queen-sized bed made up with prison-issued regulation linens. Dyson watched her face register shock and comprehension.

"Is that what I think it's for?" she stage-whispered as a guard with a carefully-composed expression took his leave of them.

Dyson nodded soberly.

"Are they outta their *minds*?" she spoke her question aloud without thinking. Dyson grinned at her and after a moment, they both laughed. It was the first time that Michelle had any inkling that they might actually survive this ordeal.

She placed the books she'd brought Dyson on the bedside table. The guards hadn't registered any emotion as they checked through them: St Augustine's *The City of God* and his *Confessions*, and a collection of the *Lives of the Western Fathers* edited by Christopher Dawson. As a low-risk prisoner with no history of violence, Dyson was permitted plenty of leeway, including religious reading material.

"I'll bet you're the only one reading," she'd said slyly, handing him the *Confessions*.

"You'd be surprised," her husband responded shortly, leafing through the second-hand copy. "The *Koran* is widely read here."

It was all part of his education, he told her in the days and weeks following his release, as they trekked through Rome, searching for an apartment. Two years spent among what he called

'America's walking dead' had given him a lot of time to think about where the West was headed.

"If the greatest democracy the world has ever known can fall this far in just a few short years," he told her suddenly the night before as they sat on their terrace drinking Orvieto Classico, "just what is next?"

Michelle didn't know, but it was clear that somehow Dyson felt that Rome was central to the drama now unfolding before their eyes.

CHAPTER 5

The two prelates faced each other across the long table. This same table had hosted decades of Board of Directors meetings for a once-mighty American computer hardware company, now a shadow of its former self. The Community had acquired the property in suburban Boston fifteen years before, announcing their intention to use it as a seminary.

That was, however, before the swirling tropical storm of the US sex abuse cases had swept through, unfortunately first exploding into the headlines in the Diocese that was hosting them. Suddenly Catholic families with impressionable teenaged boys became deeply suspicious of the intentions of an Order which featured glamorous Latin American priests, handsome and perfectly coiffed, driving shiny German cars.

As such, the plans for the seminary were quietly shelved but the Community hung on to the property as it continued to serve very well for its original intended purpose of money laundering for the drug cartel which underwrote its existence. And when the Community's founder came under deep suspicion brought about by a global outcry against the Community's well-documented predatory homosexual environment, his 'suicide' was quietly arranged for by the cartel. (As an old poisoner, the Founder should have been more careful about what he ingested, Community insiders pointed out.)

For its part, the Vatican issued press releases about the need for the Community's accounting procedures to be reformed and dismissed its senior level of prelates. Within hours the world media had moved on to juicier stories.

Now, there was a new Cardinal in the Diocese. This was a concern to Father Pilar, who had maintained a cordial relationship with his predecessor, a smooth-talking Redemptorist brought in to calm the city after the news broke that his predecessor had aided and abetted sex abusers.

Together, they had worked to quell the rumors, stoked to a fever-pitch by law firms scenting blood in the water.

When it was all over, the Archdiocese had paid out more than $40 million in hush money to the 'victims' on the law firms' class action complainants lists. The Redemptorist was not dismayed, however.

It was all merely a stepping-stone to the One True World Church, he explained in confidence to a skeptical Pilar. His years in Germany had shown him this – it was all part of God's plan to bring all Christians together, regardless of sect. The most important thing was that the Gospel was preached.

And the Catholic Church's obsession with sexual sin had to be made a thing of the past. What right had the Church to limit the God-given right to sexual pleasure to a small minority of married, heterosexual Christians? Perhaps these lawsuits would finally bring the Church around, he sighed.

To his credit, Pilar refrained from succumbing to outright laughter in the face of the American prelate, now a Cardinal. Why were these *norteamericanos* so obsessed with ideology, he wondered for the umpteenth time. For some reason, they had to throw themselves into torments of justification for what seemed to Pilar were very simple, elementary facts of life. Sex was sex. Business was business. Beyond this, Pilar was not prepared to venture.

Nevertheless, he smiled agreeably at the Cardinal and arranged for the agreed-upon reward for his cooperation. Once the Cardinal retired to his unprepossessing house with excellent security in Belize paid for by the Community, life went on quietly for Father Pilar.

Unfortunately, the Cardinal's replacement was one of the tiresome new crop of prelates with 'orthodox' views, made even more toxic by his status as a convert from Protestantism. The man had read the early Church Fathers, it seemed, and following in the footsteps of John Cardinal Newman, the 19th century Anglican who had created such a fuss in England, and 'crossed the Tiber.'

Father Pilar sighed. If there was anything worse than a liberal churchman twisting himself into knots to justify his tastes, it was an intelligent bishop who actually *believed*.

Across from him, Alexander Cardinal Portland smiled. He had deliberately chosen to meet the Community on its own grounds, waving aside their offer to pay a ceremonial call at his Residence shortly after his appointment to the Boston See.

He had been curious to see what they were doing with the 1970's facility sprawling along the side of Interstate; in the event it seemed the answer was just about nothing. Groundskeepers kept the place neat, of course, but there were few cars in the parking lot. The interior of the old corporate complex was sparsely furnished in what he recognized as rented business furniture, though the private offices of the priests were sleek and modern. Clearly, only the best would do for these men's personal use.

"So good of you to come to visit us," Father Pilar began in his cultivated Mexican accent, somewhat faded after fifteen years in New England. His thin face was wreathed in smiles. "You must be horribly busy."

The Cardinal nodded, returning the smile politely. "I'm just getting the lay of the land, Father."

He was a tall man with a somewhat reserved manner. His Midwestern frankness reminded Pilar of the manner of some of the older, patrician investment managers with whom he'd had to deal on questions of which bond funds the Community was interested in. These *norteamericanos* with their over-sized suits and bland faces were such dunderheads, really.

"Ah, yes, it's *such* a learning curve at first, isn't it?" Father Pilar remembered to be solicitous.

They spent the next thirty minutes engaged in small talk, followed by a short tour of the facilities. The Cardinal asked some polite questions, but Father Pilar was not at his ease as he stood watching his visitor drive off in his unremarkable, mid-size Japanese sedan. It had been barely an hour's visit.

Pilar was a product of the Community, of course, which had been always careful to maintain its façade of complete orthodoxy and faithfulness to the Church's precepts. At the same time, they were absolutely modern in their beliefs and liturgical practices. In this way, they stayed above the fray generated by the traditionalists and modernists in their global cat-and-mouse game; in contrast, the Community engaged in an elaborate dance carefully choreographed to deflect any untoward curiosity. After all, religious politics was a relatively unserious pastime. From their perspective, there were far more important concerns to focus on.

The new Cardinal, however, was playing his cards close to his chest. As he watched the sedan disappearing down the long corporate driveway, Father Pilar was sure of it.

CHAPTER 6

Stacey White Toffler sighed, and leaned back in her airplane seat. A petite blonde, at 33 she was the mother of two young children, well cared-for by the military's elaborate benefits for senior officers on foreign assignments. The RAF base they were assigned to was nestled in East Anglia's low, flat lands across the Channel from the Netherlands.

Every day, outside the window of her Grade A-listed, rented home, the enormous US Air Force tankers and AWACS would suddenly appear, dropping out of the cloudy English skies like machines from a science fiction future. The contrast with the environs of the 17th century village in which they lived couldn't be more pronounced.

Stacey loved her village. She loved walking the children in their double 'pram' into town on sunny days. She loved browsing in the English shops, and having tea and cakes with the other officer's wives. She loved Philip, too. They had been married for almost ten years now, and she was proud of him and his career -- most of the time, that is.

In the last two or three years, however, a change had come over Philip. He was increasingly irritable, she noticed. Little things began to bother him: the babies' crying, dinner being late to the table. In truth, he treated her with growing impatience, and after a while it seemed like she was always walking on eggshells. He spoke to her only rarely, and when he did his voice was edged with impatience, verging on contempt.

At the same time, his sexual demands seemed to ramp up significantly. At first, she responded, hoping that a few exotic sexual moves would satisfy him. But these only seemed to heighten his desire for more sex, so much so that she struggled to contain her feeling of growing resentment. She kept her counsel, however, not wanting to exacerbate the situation.

It all came to a head when she miscarried their third child. Phil didn't even leave her in peace for a month after the D&C; the minute he could, he was demanding that she give him sex. For the first time in their marriage, she told him no.

Stacey was a patient woman by nature, but she honestly didn't know which way to turn when Philip's biting sarcasm and little cruelties began to accelerate even more in the weeks after the miscarriage. One day, she found herself sobbing in the office of the military chaplain, a young Polish priest assigned to the intelligence community.

"I-I can't stand it any longer," she told the priest. Her eyes were rubbed raw from crying, and she kept twisting a Kleenex in her hands.

He nodded soberly. He knew that Stacey was a cradle Catholic who had rediscovered her faith upon the birth of her children. She was a daily communicant, normally quite cheerful, with an ironic sense of humor.

She told him everything then, and he nodded again. These military officers could sometimes be cold and unfeeling toward their wives, so absorbed were they in their responsibilities. Perhaps she should consider a short vacation – a visit with her family?

Stacey considered the idea. Her parents and little brother were in Rome these days; she had flown there to greet them when Dyson had been released from prison, but had not returned since. Perhaps a couple of weeks there with the children would be a good thing; time with the grandparents would benefit all the generations, and the Roman sunshine would no doubt improve her mood and her health. Perhaps when she returned things would be better with Philip.

Phillip shrugged indifferently when she told him about the idea. He really didn't have much to say, in fact. The next morning, he was suddenly called away early for a meeting, and so it was that she stumbled upon the horrible video he'd forgotten to erase from the computer's history. The thing had morphed far beyond sex, she shuddered, as hooded naked figures inflicted violent debasement on each other.

Shaken to her core, Stacey didn't trust herself to confront her husband. Instead, she steadied herself by making hasty travel plans; when she called, her parents were delighted that they were coming. The next day, Philip left for work as usual. She drove herself and the kids to Stanstead Airport, and left the car in long-term parking.

As she settled the excited children into their seats, her mobile rang. It was Philip.

"I found your note," she heard him say in a flat voice. "I would have liked to have said goodbye to my own children."

Stacey fought wildly to suppress her biting retort, and managed to whisper a weak, "yes, sorry there was no time" into the phone.

"But this trip will be good for the kids," he continued, unconcerned.

She wondered if he was trying to be conciliatory.

"Yes it will," she replied quietly, and waited.

"Any idea when you'll be back?"

"Not right now," she said, forcing herself to keep her tone light. "Well, we're getting ready to take off, so I gotta go now."

As the Airbus 320 lifted off into the sunny afternoon skies and circled over the green fields surrounding London, she closed her eyes and breathed a sigh of relief. It would be so good to get away from him.

CHAPTER 7

Luca Pirisi considered himself to be *fortunato*. At 25, he had a job. Not a great job. Not a job in his field. But unlike almost every other guy he knew, he had steady employment.

Slight of build, with dark brown hair and pale skin, Luca had been a good student, particularly with languages, which is why the apartment-renting firm had taken him on. So for the past few years he'd happily done battle with Rome's fiendish traffic on his Vespa, chatting up the English-speaking clientele and making sure the mostly Latin American cleaners did their jobs.

His company liked him; he was tidy and responsible, and unlike many young people in Rome, not addicted to drugs or night life. With his slight build and non-vainglorious manner, most Italian girls considered him to be an unexciting option, however. After his few attempts at finding a girlfriend in the neighborhood had been rebuffed, he'd given up. Occasionally a foreign cleaner would make overtures, but he understood these for what they were – attempts to get Italian citizenship. Though why anyone would want to live in the Mafia-ridden hellhole that Italy had become was beyond him.

Luca preferred to vacation with his friends in Eastern Europe; it was cheap and the girls in the bars were impressed with Italian men. But Luca couldn't get serious with these girls; it was clear that they expected him to provide a glamorous life for them in Rome, which he certainly couldn't afford.

Luca thought he would have made a good teacher of young children, but the reality was that those jobs were all taken by a generation that refused to give up its prerogatives of jobs-for-life. His mother Valeria was one such as this; a clerk in one of the Italian State's numberless bureaucratic cul-de-sacs, she basically supported the family on her modest paycheck.

Luigi, his father, was a not a success. Brought up in a village near the Lazio mountain fastness of Montecassino, he had learned the trades of a peasant from his father – farming, masonry, the repair of farm machinery. In Rome, however, he was a street cleaner – another job for life, albeit with a tiny salary.

Somehow, however, Valeria and Luigi had made a life together. Schooled in the deep traditions of their forebears, they'd bought an apartment when prices were low, scraped and saved and dedicated themselves to the children.

Now, in their fifties, they were faced with the cruel enormity of the economic reality that almost all Italians knew: there would be almost no future for the next generation. What little money they made, Luca's and Gina's peers spent almost immediately in an obsessive pursuit of the chimera of a *bella figura*. Italy had become a land of impoverished consumers, all longing for the unattainable –the prestige of the good life, embodied in the elegant luxury goods touted obsessively in every street ad and TV program. A generation raised by Baby Boomers had become deeply disillusioned with Italy's immemorial bulwark against all ills: the family.

Hopelessness, cynicism and disappointment bit deeply into the fabric of Italian life, and like some airborne malaise, drifted through the windows of the Pirisi's third floor apartment. It affected everyone, but for some reason, Luigi least of all.

"Ah," he would wave his hand dismissively at the television game shows and soap operas his wife and daughter were addicted to. Shaking his head in disapproval, he would set to work in their tiny garden patch, where the family Madonnina looked down benignly from her perch on the wooden platform he'd wired for her into the chain link fence.

She was the last vestige of the faith of his fathers, this Madonnina. He had grown up in a world of parish festivals marking off the time of the liturgical year, but by the time he was an adult, it was over. The old men who ran the village church confraternity died off, and along with most of his village, he moved to Rome in search of work.

Up the street from the Pirisi's apartment building was 'Our Lady of the Angels' – a 1960's cubist experiment in church-building which had failed abysmally. Inside, he found his own generation of priests; they ridiculed the rosaries and haughtily waved aside the devotions of the peasants. Later, as his children grew, he watched as this new way of life took hold in the home. The women of his generation spurned the long hours of cooking for family Sundays. For First Holy Communion celebrations for the grandchildren, there were elaborate restaurant dinners.

Only now there would be no grandchildren. He was sure of it.

Luca was a good boy, but where were the good girls who would persevere by his side, help him build a family? And Gina, she was lost in the glamorous world of that downtown salon where she stood on her feet for 12 hours a day to make those old women think they looked young again.

Though of late there was something wrong with her, Luigi could tell. She didn't look right. Distracted, like there was something on her mind.

And whatever it was, Luca was in on it. He could tell by the way they looked at each other. There was something not right.

CHAPTER 8

"Benedicta, you need to explain to me why I should break one of the rules of the Order and let you live under your family's roof on a permanent basis," Mother Superior was kind, but firm.

Sister Mary Benedicta stifled a sigh. How could she convince Mother that she didn't simply want to go to Italy in order to see her family, but because she felt a deep calling to the young people there?

Her decision to enter the convent five years before had shaken her parents, though not as much as she'd feared. Michelle had silently speculated that there might be the signs of a vocation in her daughter early on. It seemed that her middle child had an early penchant for prayer and religious reading and an almost complete lack of interest in fashion, dating and 'being cool.'

After high school, the willowy, winsome Sophia had reluctantly agreed to attend college, but only if it was a 'truly Catholic' college such as Christendom. Michelle had no idea what her daughter was talking about, but after she and Dyson visited the school, they were impressed enough to grant her wish. Little did they imagine that the close friendships fostered by the College's religious ideals would prove to be so critical to their sensitive daughter's stability and well-being.

It started in her freshman year, when Sophia's father was indicted on a breath-taking array of charges, enough to send phalanxes of reporters camping outside the White's palatial New Jersey home. Michelle thanked God that her two youngest were away at school, and that a pregnant Stacey was safely ensconced in officer's quarters at an Air Base across the country.

Then, in the weeks and months leading up to Dyson's trial, the White's world upended. Suddenly, their house was full of documents and strategy meetings. Their lives telescoped onto the charges, the trial, the opposing side's strategy. They talked of nothing else. Dyson, accustomed to tense business negotiations, withstood the strain better than Michelle. She fell prey to deep bouts of worrying, and her rage rose against the unfairness of it all, the perfidy of lawyers, the bias of judges.

Worse, before Sophia would graduate, her parents' world would simply slip off its axis, with a crash. Ultimately, the tall, laconic businessman was jailed on a technicality. Deeply affected, Michelle sold their beloved New Jersey home and moved to an apartment within driving distance of the federal prison in Texas.

This is when her devout daughter taught her how to pray the Rosary. On Skype. Though Michelle had ostensibly learned the great Marian prayer when preparing for her first Holy Communion 40-odd years before in Brooklyn, that had been a lifetime before.

"I need to do yoga," she told Sophia, who nodded sympathetically across the miles.

"Okay so while you're doing 'down dog' you need to be saying a Hail Mary," Sophia answered her wryly, holding up her rosary beads to the computer monitor.

Michelle had no idea what that College was doing to keep Sophia on an even keel, but whatever it was, it was working. She and Patrick attended Sophia's graduation ceremony alone; Dyson was in prison and Stacey was about to deliver her first baby.

It was when they were helping her load the car outside her college apartment that Sophia dropped the bomb; she was slated to enter the Boston convent as a postulant in September, she said. She stood looking at her mother, her eyes full of bright tears.

Michelle sighed and embraced her daughter; this move wasn't exactly a surprise. Patrick looked uncertain, but said nothing. After his expulsion from boarding school, his reading had taken a serious turn under the guidance of the homeschooling curriculum he'd chosen. He knew in his heart that his sister's vocation was real.

He was worried, however, that he might have one too.

Fast forward five years, and Patrick was still uncertain, though nearing the end of his own university experience rounded off by a senior year abroad at St. Andrew's University in Scotland, a three hour drive from the new Scottish daughter-house of the Boston convent.

Now 27, his sister Sophia was Sister Mary Benedicta, with five solid years of convent life under her belt. She thrived under the schedule of prayer, meditation and active service to their Community's charism – caring for the women who came to them, pregnant and unwilling to abort their children.

Every last one of them had been advised to abort by their own mothers. Most were pregnant by erstwhile 'boyfriends'; very few had men who would stay by their side. Those few that did were blessed with good guys who suddenly found themselves in way over their heads, but who nonetheless were determined to stand by their new family.

Usually, neither of them had any idea where to turn. Most were recommended to the Sisters by what they would later recognize was sheer Divine Providence, as virtually none of them were Mass-attending Catholics.

The Sisters were guided in their work by dedicated volunteers, almost all experienced mothers and grandmothers. Sister Mary Benedicta worked easily under the direction of these good women, learning the ins and outs of caring for pregnant and lactating mothers, and all about babies. It was her pragmatic, hands-on approach and merry personality that had led her Mother Superior to select Benedicta to head up the four sisters to be sent to the Order's new foundation in Umbria. That is, until she learned some critical details about the new Cardinal of Boston's crazy idea.

"Look, Benedicta," she said carefully. "It's not that I don't think you would be perfect for this foundation."

Benedicta nodded.

"But this, er, arrangement is highly irregular to begin with," she explained with a sigh. Mother was a traditional Sister and as such she didn't know what to think about this experiment, at all.

It wasn't that she disagreed with Cardinal Portland's analysis of what was sorely needed in Italy – exactly the skills and charism of her Boston community. Italy had become a society where divorce, contraception and abortion were threatening to cut off the very existence of the next generation of Italians. Furthermore, she agreed with his prescription – maternity homes in the countryside, far from the corrosive effect of the big Italian cities and their drumbeat of materialism, cheap sex, widespread drug abuse, cynicism and despair.

It was his contention that her Order had to go further and function as the nucleus of wholly new communities, nestled in the Italian countryside in the now largely-abandoned villages in Umbria -- *this* was the problem.

"Mother," he'd argued in his patient voice, "the time to act is *now*. Italy doesn't have another generation to lose."

She agreed with him on that point, but she had serious reservations about extending the charism of her Order so far.

"We take care of mothers, and babies," she explained. "We provide them with a stable environment. We teach them how to care for themselves, and their families. This includes cooking, cleaning and basic medical knowledge."

"Yes, Mother, I know," the Cardinal smiled. This Order was a runaway success story, and he knew that Mother would hesitate to tamper with their winning formula.

"Along the way, we impart the Faith to them," she went on. "Eventually, they learn to set up a life for themselves, often with their new husbands..."

" – and often, around your convents, right?" the Cardinal finished her thought for her.

"Well, yes," she replied. "But that's not so surprising, is it? We become their spiritual home, sometimes their extended family home, too. Often, their families take years to accept that they have chosen to have families of their own, though I can't imagine why..."

The Cardinal smiled ruefully.

"Perhaps because their mothers had 'high hopes' for what their daughters would become?" he teased gently.

Mother didn't take the teasing well. "What's wrong with having a family?" she demanded. "That's a pretty big accomplishment, if you ask me. That's the trouble with this world -- no respect for the family. No respect for anything except the almighty dollar bill, or euro, or whatever."

"You're preaching to the choir, Mother," the Cardinal soothed her. "That's why it's so important that we let your Order do what it does best – help people start families."

Mother sighed. The Cardinal had started a foundation in Boston, where wealthy Catholics were donating money to support these new 'villages' with traditional Orders at their core. The original idea had been to create these in the United States.

However, an unusual opportunity had presented itself. The Diocese of Spoleto owned an entire hamlet in the heart of Umbria centered around a medieval bishop's residence. They would rent it to the Foundation for 50 years –plus provide the local workmen to convert the buildings to modern use, for a reasonable price.

The American Dyson White had agreed to underwrite this project, on the condition that his family was permitted one of the buildings there, for their private use. Mother, who originally had settled on the intelligent and energetic Sister Mary Benedicta as the local superior for this new foundation, was dismayed to learn that the White family would be financing the project.

"I won't be staying under their roof," Sister Benedicta protested. "I will be in the convent, attending to our work. Plus, my family will hardly be there. I know my parents – they won't be able to stay away from the big city that long."

Mother was unconvinced, however. After another day of prayer in the chapel, she made her decision.

"Sister Mary Grace will be the local superior in Italy," she told the four assembled sisters in her office. "Three of you will go there under her care. I will send Sister Benedicta to Scotland."

Benedicta's eyes filled with tears. She fought them gamely, however. Obedience she had vowed, and obedience she would practice. A few minutes later, she squared her shoulders and took a deep breath. Mother Prior watched her silently, and smiled.

Meanwhile, in Boston the Cardinal overcame his original wariness about dealing with an Italian diocese. Most were not noted for their innovative approaches, or their appetite for getting involved with family issues.

But apparently the bad news had finally gotten through, at least to the Spoleto bishop: there were very few Italian families being formed. Those that were, were incredibly fragile. There were almost no priests in the village churches, and a terrible vacuum had meant that the local Italians had taken up Buddhism, yoga or New Age Gnosticism.

No families, of course, meant no future for Spoleto. No families, of course, meant no future for the Faith.

Somebody had to take the first step.

CHAPTER 9

When a week flew by with still no sign from his sister about what she was planning, Luca decided to take things into his own hands.

Waiting outside her salon at the end of her work day, Luca was surprised to see the white Mercedes there too. It was Michelle's monthly three-hour hair-coloring appointment, and Carlo had, as usual, paid one of the locals to keep the place open for him immediately in front of the salon. When he finished paying the guy, Carlo turned to find himself confronting the skinny kid he'd seen outside Gina's apartment the week before.

"*Salve,*" said Luca, nervous but determined.

"*Buona sera,*" Carlo returned ceremoniously. He smiled inquiringly.

"Can I ask who you're working for?" Luca burst out abruptly. He jammed his hands into his pockets and stared defiantly at his adversary.

Carlo was surprised at this. The kid looked like he came from a decent home. What would make him act so rudely? Was he a drug addict?

Carlo knew all about drug addicts. In fact, he'd been one himself, before he'd been rescued by the Dominican Friars of the Renewal in Boston ten years before.

Like many young people in Italy, he'd emigrated in search of work. He'd been living with his American cousin at first, but soon found himself a job as a cook in the Italian North End. The work was hard but the money was easy, and he liked the club life. He picked up English quickly, and was quick with the ladies, too.

But the club drugs hit him a little too hard, and drinking to cushion the impact made matters worse. Within months he'd lost his job and found himself living on the hard streets of Boston. Winter was coming; nevertheless, he was so ashamed that he wanted to die when the bearded young friar in the white habit approached him one frosty evening with a smile and a cup of hot coffee.

He was a Catholic, yes, of course. But he had never seen religious men act like these guys. When he came to live in their shelter, he watched in amazement as they celebrated the Mass with deep reverence. Their basic seriousness underlay everything, though in conversation they were often light-hearted. Carlo was reluctant to admit it, but soon he was in awe of their joyousness. After awhile, all he wanted was to be around them, to drink in their atmosphere of hope and joy.

That was what had started his long return – first to sobriety, then to sanity and finally, with deep emotion, to the Faith. All of this had happened ten years before, of course. It had been a long, hard climb back –to his mother's apartment in Rome, to a job as a taxi driver, and then his lucky break as a driver for an English Cardinal who before his retirement had passed Carlo along to Dyson White.

Today, at age 36, Carlo had excellent English, a clean driving record and a modest lifestyle which included Sunday Mass with his mother, who still prayed every night for a good woman for her son, and grandchildren. Carlo thought this unlikely, but deep inside hoped against hope that his mother's prayers would be heard. In the meantime, he was living his life *interregno,* carefully and safely remaining uncommitted to any course of action that would endanger his precious, hard-won equilibrium. Life was best when you lived day-to-day, with little thought of the future. One day at a time, he told himself philosophically.

And now he was face-to-face with a scared young kid who wanted to know who he worked for. He was about to answer when the salon door burst open, and out came an amused Gina being led by the hand of a solemn little girl. The child was about five, dressed in a red cotton dress, with a cap of shining chestnut hair.

"Carlo," said the child in American-accented English. Her expression was one of deep seriousness. "Tell her she has to come home with us for dinner. Go ahead. Tell her in Italian."

"Ah, bella! But of course she must come!" Carlo smiled at Gina, all Roman gallantry. He bowed slightly and gestured towards the Benz. "Your wish is my command!"

Gina nodded politely, but her expression changed quickly to one of alarm when she caught sight of her brother.

"Aspett'...Wait..." said Luca, holding his hands up to forestall his sister's firestorm of questions. Brother and sister regarded each other for a tense moment, before the child spoke up again.

"Who's *he*?" she asked, tugging on Gina's hand and pointing to the hapless Luca.

"I am her brother," volunteered Luca in English, looking unhappy.

"Oh," the child said simply and looked up at Gina again. "He can come too. Grandma has a big table."

"That's right, I do!" Michelle's Brooklyn accent boomed out from behind them. "And my grand-daughter is absolutely right. You both need to come to us for dinner tonight. I want you to meet my son and my daughter, who is down from England with Katy, here and my lovely grandson, too."

"He's not lovely, Grandma," Katy corrected her primly. "He's a boy. Boys can't be lovely."

In the end, for some reason that Luca didn't understand, Gina relented. Carlo drove Gina, Michelle and Katy the few blocks to the Dyson's townhome with Luca following on his Vespa, wondering what on earth was going to happen next.

He was greeted at the door by their son, an amiable American in prep school clothes -- very expensive and very much admired by Italians. But Luca was surprised to see that Patrick lacked the hauteur that Luca associated with young, wealthy Italians. Instead, there was something intensely interiorly-focused about him.

The White's apartment ranked among the most elegant he'd ever seen, obviously outfitted by a designer for the highest end of the market. He followed Patrick through the restrained, discreet lighting designed to showcase the terrazzo and the lights of Rome beyond. Soon, they entered an enormous rustic-style kitchen centered on a thick slab of old oak topping a sturdy trestle, which served as a kitchen table to seat a dozen.

Michelle and her daughter bustled about, cooking and pouring wine for the visitors who sat, obediently chopping vegetables. Dyson White lounged about unconcernedly at one end of the huge table with his grandchildren. Even Carlo the chauffeur joined them, albeit a bit self-consciously. Luca looked in wonder at Stacey, Patrick and Dyson, but none of them seemed to think that having a chauffeur at the table with them was unusual in the least.

Dinner was a casual affair of pasta in fennel-scented tomato sauce, with grilled red peppers and spicy sausage. But before they ate, to Luca's astonishment, the family prayed -- the Catholic grace of the Americans. Neither Gina or Luca had ever witnessed this before, outside of films. At home, Luigi merely crossed himself before meals, a habit his children had assumed was an idiosyncrasy derived from his village peasant past. Yet here they were, *a tavola* with American billionaires, who prayed.

Maybe it was the wine, but a bit later Luca just had to ask, "Um, I have heard that Americans are much more religious?"

The Whites looked at each other and laughed ruefully. Gina glared at him. Carlo, next to her, grinned.

"*Some* Americans are," Dyson replied with a smile. "Not all of us."

"America's a big place," Michelle pointed out practically, as she passed the plate of fragrant roasted peppers. "All different kinds of people there."

Luca nodded somewhat dreamily. America was a place he'd always wanted to visit – Florida and California, New York and Las Vegas– places he'd seen in films all his life. He was thoroughly confused now as to whether the Whites wanted to buy Gina's baby. Why else would they put on such a big show? But somehow the children and the grandchildren didn't fit in. Did human traffickers have families of their own?

Across the table he could see that Gina was relaxing under the ministrations of Michelle and Stacey, laughing and patiently answering a battery of intent questions from Katy. Was she an Italian princess, Katy wanted to know.

"Oh no, I am *not* a princess," Gina smiled, reddening slightly. "But I *am* Italian."

The conversation turned from there to parlous state of Italy. What was it really like, Stacey wanted to know. As bad as *The Economist* reported?

"Things are very bad," Luca said, shaking his head dolefully. Gina and Carlo nodded their agreement. Unemployment was rampant, and the country was on their third 'caretaker' – an unelected leader who took the place of a democratically-elected leader in an electoral system that no one trusted.

Dyson suddenly looked up from his meal and recited a litany of economic statistics about the perilous state of the Italian economy. The Italians listened, but added nothing.

"But of course you know all this already, don't you?" Stacey piped up. "I mean, this is your country. You *live* here."

The Italians looked at each other, unsure about what to say. Luca wondered where this was going. Were they going to make an offer for the baby right here, at the dinner table?

"Italians have lost the family," Carlo suddenly heard himself say, and everyone turned to look at him. Gina observed that he was a well-built man with medium-brown hair, closely cropped. His voice, usually warm and teasing, was now measured and sad. "We have lost trust in the family. It will be the death of us."

Here it comes, Luca thought. This chauffeur is leading the charge. They are setting us up for some kind of conversation after dinner, and they have me here because they think I can persuade my sister to sell her child.

Suddenly he was angry. Who did these rich Americans think they were? Was everything for sale for these people? Well, Gina may be addled enough to think about this, but he sure as hell wasn't going to stand by and just let this happen.

Luca stood up abruptly. "Gina, we need to go."

Shocked, Gina's face drained of all color.

"Luca!" She whispered, clearly embarrassed. "We're still eating!"

Everyone at the table turned toward him, but Luca didn't care. He could see where this was going. This was some kind of perverse American sales pitch, and he wasn't going to let it happen.

Michelle put down her fork. "Luca, what's the matter?"

"He doesn't trust us," said Pat to his mother, from one end of the table. He looked serious. "He thinks something is up, though I don't know what."

Michelle turned to Luca, "What is it, honey? What don't you trust?"

The entire table turned towards him. Gina was white-faced.

"What is the matter with you?" she said in rapid-fire Lazio dialect. "How can you be so rude?"

"Rude?" he replied sardonically, also in Italian. He didn't care if the beefy chauffeur understood. "I need to get you out of here before you sell your baby to these ghouls."

At this, Carlo's eyebrows shot up, and he shook his head. The Whites exchanged glances. Michelle's Italian wasn't good enough to navigate the rapid-fire dialect.

"What? What did he say?" Stacey asked Carlo but he shook his head again and remained silent, instead watching Gina intently.

"That's not what they want," Gina said, regarding her brother intently. And then, in English, to the others at the table. "I'm sorry, my brother has a wrong understanding of something. Will you excuse us? I need to talk with him privately."

Stacey obligingly led Gina and Luca into an unused bedroom in the sumptuous apartment, and left them there alone, closing the door quietly behind her. Luca whirled on his sister.

"Gina! Let's get outta here!" he cried fiercely. "Get your coat and let's go! Why the hell you think these rich people are so interested in you, huh? You're her *hairdresser*, for God's sake. Don't be so damned naïve!"

"That's not it," Gina answered him calmly. "I was wrong about that. About them. That's not it."

"Oh yeah, that's right," he said, sardonically. "Rich people like them hang around with their hairdresser and their chauffeur all the time. What's the matter with you? Those hormones go to your head?"

"That's what I thought, too," Gina sighed, and sat on the bed. "But really, Luca, that's not it. They don't want to buy the baby. What they want is to help me *have* the baby, and keep it."

"*What*? Why? What do they care?" Luca said, disbelieving. He stood regarding his sister, hands on his hips.

"They're Catholic," Gina replied simply, her hands spread wide.

"What the hell does that mean?"

"It means they don't believe in abortion. And they want to help me, help us."

Luca's eyes narrowed. "That can't be all there is to it. What's in it for them?"

Gina sighed.

"Michelle and I had a long talk today. She says that she and her husband have lived through too much crap. When the American government persecuted her husband, she said they had two years to think about who they were, and how they were living..."

"...and what did this guy go to jail for, anyway?" Luca interrupted.

"Insider trading," Gina answered. "For his own company. It's really complicated; Michelle didn't understand it. She said it amounted to a set-up. They didn't like his politics, so they wanted to keep him and his media company out of the country. Anyway, the hell they went through brought them back together, she said. And together, they came back to the Church."

"*What*?!" Luca regarded Gina incredulously. "What kind of shit is that?"

Gina shrugged, and smiled. "I believe them."

Luca thought fast.

"What guarantee do you have that they won't just take the baby away?"

To her brother's shock, Gina laughed outright at this.

"They can't just 'take the baby away.' We could get them for kidnapping. Do they *look* like the kind of people that go in for kidnapping?"

Luca let out a strained breath. He had to admit they did not, but somehow he remained unconvinced.

"This whole *thing* is funny," he said, when another thought struck him. "Look, if you want to keep this baby so much, we don't need these people. We'll go home, explain everything, and it will be okay."

Gina looked thoughtful, and folded her arms in front of her. Luca said nothing, and waited. There was something different about Gina, he thought. His sister seemed transformed, lighter somehow, as if a great weight had been lifted from her slender shoulders. Finally, she looked up at him, her face clear.

"Y-yes, you're right," she said slowly, exhaling. "I *do* want to keep my baby...and Michelle and her family have given me the courage for this. And of course I will go home and tell Mama and Papa about this."

"You mean it? *Vero*?" Luca exclaimed in great relief.

Whatever the story was with these rich Americans, their parents would be shocked, but they would recover. Valeria and Luigi could be counted on. They would know what to do.

CHAPTER 10

The new Bishop of Spoleto answered the call impatiently. He recognized the US area code that came up on his smartphone, but not the number. It was not the Diocesan offices; he was familiar with their numbers through his long acquaintance with the former Cardinal there. No matter. He assumed that whoever was calling him from Boston would somehow be connected with the Diocese.

"Excellency," the voice was not quite familiar, however. Whoever it was spoke good Italian, albeit with a Latin American accent. "I regret to disturb you."

"Ah, of course, Father Pilar!" the Bishop responded heartily. "How are things?"

They had met at one or two of the Community's events in Rome, before all of the embarrassing revelations about their founder had surfaced and the Community had ceased holding receptions for Italian prelates and provincials. That had been several years before, however; the bishop was curious to know why Pilar was contacting him now. Just because he was newly appointed to the See of Spoleto would not occasion a call from the likes of Pilar, normally.

"Ah yes, Bishop Agnolotti died quite suddenly," the Bishop responded to the polite inquiry sadly. "Yes, a heart attack and it's probably just as well. After more than thirty years here, it would have broken his heart to have to close all of these churches."

He sighed. Spoleto of course was no different from any other Italian diocese – the problem was epidemic everywhere in Italy. No faith. No families. No money to support centuries-old churches, which stood empty and forlorn for want of priests. The Roman Catholic faith was dying in its heartland. And it was his unhappy lot in life to be the agent of its demise in this part of Umbria.

"I have a proposal for you," said Father Pilar, in a business-like tone. "We would like to help the finances of your Diocese."

The Bishop's interest was naturally quite piqued by what Father Pilar had to say. It seemed that the Community would like to locate its seminary in Umbria. Did the Bishop know of anything suitable, in terms of size and location? Of course, Pilar said he quite understood that in all likelihood given the state of abandoned properties in Umbria there would have to extensive renovations undertaken, an expense the Community was prepared to shoulder.

The Bishop sighed. If only his predecessor hadn't promised that *localita* near Trevi to that Order of American nuns and their benefactor. He could have marketed that place to Pilar at a substantial markup, enough to restore the worn-out palazzo he'd inherited near the Cathedral at Spoleto.

Father Pilar was sympathetic to his plight. Money really was no object, he explained to the Bishop, thereby only increasing his fellow prelate's frustration.

The Bishop sighed again and thought fast.

The property he had in mind was really something that needed to be seen, he told Pilar regretfully. He knew Father Pilar was frightfully busy, but was there a possibility he could fly over, just to see what was available? Of course he would be sure to compile all the necessary information regarding prices and renovation costs, so that his visit would be most productive.

For his part, Father Pilar sighed and said that yes, although he was terribly busy, he could see that this would require his personal attention. He would have to consult his schedule and would be back in touch very soon indeed.

When they rang off, the Bishop stared thoughtfully at the screen of his smartphone. Perhaps there was a chance that the Americans could be dislodged from that prime real estate and gently re-located somewhere else. After all, there were numerous other abandoned villages scattered throughout Umbria.

But, he wondered, why was the Community suddenly so interested in re-locating their seminary in Rome to Umbria – far from the intrigues of the Eternal City? And why was it Father Pilar who was inquiring, from Boston – the very same diocese that this American order of nuns came from?

The Bishop sighed heavily again, and bent to his task of reviewing the spreadsheets of predicted savings that would result from his program of parish closures. Possibly there was a way he could access the funds both of the Community and the American billionaire. This way he could renovate his palazzo and maybe even keep at least some of these ancient churches open.

Though he couldn't actually see why, as the Italians in the Spoleto diocese had long since ceased being church-goers. Like most of Italy's clergy, he assigned the blame for this vaguely to the changing mores of modern society. Then of course there was the long-standing effect of anti-clerical leftist politics in the region, as everyone knew.

He was deeply shocked by the claim of some traditionalists that somehow the post Vatican II church was implicated in all this, in particular the Novus Ordo liturgy. Such claims struck him as deeply pharisaical, though he couldn't quite articulate why.

He was indifferent to the liturgy, really. As a modern priest, his concern was far more about the realities of people's lives; like most of his fellow priests, he was a regular attendee at Caritas meetings where these things were endlessly discussed.

Over the years, he had noted the advancing age of his fellow Catholic priests, however. For his own part, he would have been delighted to share the heavy load of his responsibilities with younger priests. But they weren't forthcoming.

His initial visit to the diocesan seminary had been the last straw, however. There were exactly three seminarians there. Only one appeared to be there of his own volition, a clever young man with ambition written all over his face. The other two were clearly embarrassments to their wealthy families – one so fey that he couldn't control his constant giggling, the other with some form of retardation.

Something would have to be done about that. The Bishop sighed. Possibly he could market the seminary as a luxury hotel? That might raise enough funds to renovate his palace.

CHAPTER 11

"So how do they want to 'help' you?" Luca wanted to know. He and Gina were seated at the Pirisi's miniscule kitchen table. Their father was outside in his garden; Valeria was due home any minute from her job.

Gina smiled. "They got a whole plan and it involves some nuns and the bishop's summer place in Umbria. Mr. Dyson wants to buy it; have a look."

Luca gave a long, low whistle at the aerial photo on his sister's smartphone. What looked to be a palatial country estate comprised of several houses situated atop a high hill, surrounded by broad lawns. A white road meandered up through olive groves to the entrance, and then shot straight up through an alley of trees to the gravel courtyard fronting the house.

"A palazzo!" Luca said, admiringly. "Their new country place?"

"Actually, they say it don't look so good up close. Been abandoned for a few years. They want to fix it up, make it a home for pregnant woman who can't afford to have their babies," Gina explained.

"So they can sell them?" Luca quipped, but Gina wasn't laughing.

"Don't be an idiot. They got a Cardinal working with them on this – it's all part of the Church.'

Luca rolled his eyes. Like most Italians, his opinion of the modern Church was low – a place full of fools, thieves, and sex freaks.

"The nuns who are doing this are from America," Gina went on doggedly. "One of them is the Dyson's daughter."

"She's a nun?" Luca echoed, wondering why in the world a rich man's daughter would want to become a nun. He was about to say as much when he caught the warning glint in his sister's eye.

"Look, I want to do this," she said, watching him intently.

"What about Marco? He won't be so happy," Luca asked.

His sister shrugged.

"He's worried that he'll be on the hook for child support," she sighed, and looked unhappy. "I can't think about that now."

Of course Luigi hadn't meant to overhear them. Apparently whatever it was they were talking about was so intense that they couldn't hear their own father in the hallway. He thanked the Madonnina for that, offering up a silent prayer.

Then he heaved a heavy sigh.

So this was the problem; he might have known.

That Marco was a slick idiot, though Valeria had shushed him when he tried to say something. He sighed again. His daughter was too old to listen to her father, anyway. All he could do was talk to the Madonnina in the garden. And now here he was, about to be a grandfather, maybe.

Luigi's sigh was audible, however, to his children, who eyed each other in a sudden panic. Luca pushed open the kitchen door to find his father slumped against the wall outside, tears in his eyes.

"Papa," he said, and took a step towards him.

Luigi waved him off, wiping his eyes with the back of his sleeve, an embarrassed gesture. He sighed again and righted himself. He had to face this, with the help of the Madonnina. She wouldn't let him down.

He looked at his daughter.

"Ginaluche," he said softly, using his old baby endearment. "Ginaluche, *anima mia*." He held out his arms to his daughter.

With a strangled cry, Gina started from her chair and threw herself in her father's arms. Father and daughter clung to each other as thick tears squeezed out of Luigi's old eyes and ran down his worn face. Gina sobbed heedlessly into his flannel shirt, beyond caring what her brother thought of her.

Luca watched them, surreptitiously wiping his own tears with the heel of his hand.

"Oh my God, who died?"

The three jumped at Valeria's sudden question. She stood in the kitchen doorway, her arms full of shopping. Valeria was a typically Roman handsome woman, now growing a bit stout. Her thick mahogany hair was still cut fashionably, but her raincoat was ten years old. Her brow was knit with deep concern, and there was fear in her eyes.

"What happened? Who's got cancer?"

"Mama," Luca stepped forward in an attempt to comfort her. "Mama, nobody's got cancer. Nobody's sick. Everybody's okay."

He embraced his mother, who looked unconvinced.

"Luigi, what's going on here?" she demanded.

Her husband shrugged. "It's okay, *cara mia*, it's okay. Nobody's dying. It's actually good news," he looked at Gina, who blew her nose with some finality and looked squarely at her mother.

"Mama, I'm going to have a baby," she said, finally. She held her breath.

Valeria sat down suddenly on the kitchen chair, letting her packages fall beside her.

"Oh my God," she declared in a low, shocked tone. "A baby?"

Luigi stepped behind the chair and put his hands on his wife's shoulders.

"Bella," he began, but Valeria wasn't listening.

"How could this happen?" she asked her daughter incredulously. "What's Marco say about this?"

Gina looked grim.

"He told me to get rid of it," she said shortly, eyeing her mother closely. "He don't want another kid."

"Oh *Madonna*," Valeria responded in exasperation. She looked from her husband to her son. "He don't want to be bothered."

Luigi and Luca looked apprehensively from mother to daughter. Gina folded her arms and regarded her mother carefully, waiting.

"So how do you think you're gonna do this? Have a baby on your own? How you gonna *do* this?" Valeria asked, shaking her head dolefully.

Gina shrugged.

"You got no idea what's involved with raising a baby," her mother told her. "It's hard enough when you got a husband, but alone? Oh, Madonna!"

"She won't do this alone," Luigi interjected carefully. Gina and Luca looked at their father with surprise.

"Oh, please," Valeria waved him off dismissively. "Of course she's alone! Marco won't..."

"...Marco don't have to do nothing," Gina interrupted her. "I don't care about Marco, what he wants."

"I don't understand you," Valeria said to her daughter accusingly. "You got a good job. You look good. What the hell you want to go running around with an ass like Marco for? Why couldn't you find a decent man, not this piece of garbage?!"

Gina shrugged sullenly.

"I didn't know!" she said lamely, finally.

"You didn't know *what*?" her mother retorted, unimpressed. "That he's a piece of garbage?"

"How would I know?"

Valeria shook her head in exasperation.

"We didn't like him," she said, intently looking at her daughter. "Your father didn't like him."

Gina shrugged again, the tears welling up in her eyes. How could she tell her mother how impossible it was to find a man with a decent job who wanted to get married, in Rome? Most were still living with their mothers, playing videogames and being alternately scolded and petted while they held down part-time, temporary jobs. Marco at least had a *business*, and Gina had thought that meant he was responsible.

Her mother read her thoughts.

"Just because a man got a business doesn't make him *good*," she told Gina.

"Okay, I know that now," her daughter retorted.

"*Now* you know that," Valeria echoed bitterly, shaking her head. "Great."

"If you didn't like him, why didn't you *say* something?" Gina burst out. The hot tears were starting to roll down her face again.

"Because you wouldn't have *listened*!" her mother cried. "Your father wanted to say something but I told him no, because I *know* you. You think you got it all under control. And now look. You got *nothing* under control. *Look* at you!"

At this, Gina whirled around furiously and made for the door.

"I don't *need* this!" she threw over her shoulder. "I *thought* you would understand. But you understand *nothing*."

Valeria stood up and made as if to follow her. Alarmed, Luigi hastily stepped between his wife and his daughter.

"You gotta stop this," he said to his wife with quiet intensity. "Don't you see you're making her desperate?"

Valeria, however, ignored him.

"So, who's gonna be there for you?" Valeria snapped at Gina. "Your father and I have worked all our lives to give you a home. You realize there's no more new clothes, right? And vacations?"

Gina shook her head sadly.

"You think I don't know this? I know this."

Valeria, however, wasn't finished.

"What are you gonna *do* in the middle of the night, when you need your sleep because you're dead on your feet from standing all day at the shop? Babies cry, you know."

"I'll get up," Luca said suddenly, and stood by his father. His sister and mother looked at him, shocked.

Next to him, Luigi was nodding vigorously.

"We'll *all* get up," he said calmly, and put his arm around his wife's shoulders soothingly. "We done this before, you know."

Valeria stared at her husband and shook her head in disbelief. Her head ached suddenly.

Gina and Luca eyed their father incredulously. The corners of his mouth had begun to turn up. Valeria exhaled loudly. She sat down again in the kitchen chair and massaged her temples.

At this, Luigi sighed, turned around, and began rummaging in a cupboard. He found four simple kitchen glasses, and set them carefully before his family. Then he ambled off into the darkened dining room.

"Where's he going?" Gina asked no one in particular. Valeria shook her head dolefully, refusing to look at her children.

"Luigi!" she called, irritated, "What are you doing in there?"

Luca bent down to recover his mother's fallen packages, and set them on the counter. He peered into one of the bags.

"You get fresh burrata?" he wanted to know. He removed a baguette of freshly-baked bread. "We got tomatoes, I think."

Luigi emerged from the gloom with an open bottle of excellent wine from Montefalco.

"I been keeping this for a special occasion," he told his family, and ceremoniously poured the ruby red wine into the kitchen glasses.

While his family eyed each other in silence, Luigi presented the first glass to his wife, the second to his daughter and the third to Luca. Finally, he straightened up and raised his glass.

"To the Madonnina," he said carefully, tears choking his voice. His family all obediently drank.

As the berry-red wine warmed her veins, Gina thought of the battered Madonnina on the garden shelf outside. It had been years since she noticed the little statue, actually.

She felt better, however. She took a deep breath.

Now she needed to tell her parents about some nuns.

CHAPTER 12

"You are absolutely certain about this?" the new Cardinal was intent on getting an answer. Portland looked at the unhappy faces of husband and wife in the dining room of his secretary's two-story clapboard house in Quincy, Mass.

Outside, the blue darkness gathered over the Mc Kenny's snowy yard as the February evening settled in over the Boston suburbs. Portland had been invited for a family dinner in celebration of his appointment to Cardinal, a gesture he appreciated very much as it showed the loyalty and goodwill of Carol Mc Kenny, his private secretary.

Carol had been the mainstay of his predecessor, and he was hopeful that he could count on her expertise to smooth the thousand problems which inevitably crop up when a new Diocesan ordinary takes over, especially in a huge metropolitan See with a stormy, political past like Boston.

To be sure, it had been a strange transition, as Carol had treated him with extreme formality from the moment he had arrived. Always completely correct and astonishingly efficient, the 50-something secretary had worked hard to make her new boss happy. But there was no warmth in her conversation, and after several months he was a bit puzzled by her continuing stiff demeanor.

Carol was a seasoned private secretary, he'd learned, and had worked faithfully for his predecessor, who had hired her from the banking world ten years before. She was married to a mid-level compliance officer at a regional bank, and they had three grown children.

The Cardinal had been a bit taken aback by her invitation to dinner at the Mc Kenny's house, therefore. But in the interest of peaceful relations, he'd accepted, never once dreaming of the real reason he'd been invited.

"My wife feels that you are an honorable person," Sean Mc Kenny was saying. The remains of dinner were before them, and Carol and her husband were gazing tensely at the Cardinal, who wiped his hands on the linen napkin before carefully placing it on the polished mahogany table.

"This is why we invited you here tonight," Carol said. Her eyes reflected her worry; her mouth was set in a grim line.

It all came out then. How his predecessor had no idea that Carol had had a whole career in branch banking before the stress drove her to become a private secretary. How her banking experience had alerted her to certain, er, irregularities in his transactions on behalf of the Diocese. This in turn had led her to wonder about his relationship with the Community, which was in the habit of depositing quite large sums of cash into the accounts of the Diocese, mostly without the formality of a Cash Transaction Report being filed by the branch.

"The branch manager had been in her job for many years," Carol explained to her new boss. "She was the final signoff on CTRs, so if they were never filled out or turned in, it was her responsibility."

The Cardinal knit his brow. "So you're telling me that the Community simply deposited large sums of money into diocesan accounts? For what, do you know?"

Carol shook her head and sighed. Apparently the funds were rather quickly invested in another institution, usually through the agency of a local bond broker with a prestigious clientele. Whoever deposited the funds was not a signer on the diocesan account, and the investment transactions had been approved by his predecessor, all electronically.

"No one ever questioned this?" Portland wanted to know.

"Not until the branch manager moved away to get married, and her replacement started making a big deal about accepting the deposits without a CTR," Carol explained. "That's when I heard

68

about it, because she called our office, just a couple of weeks ago. Honestly, I would have never been suspicious unless I had spent all that time working on the banking floor."

She looked at her husband, who leaned forward with some urgency.

"This went on for years, apparently," Sean told the Cardinal. "Carol really didn't know what to do about it when she spoke to the new branch manager. She came home and told me, because this is my field."

"You work for the same bank?" Portland asked.

"No, no," Sean shook his head. "But this is a fairly typical scenario for money laundering. The bad guys get a prestigious account holder to, er, cooperate by allowing them to run the cash through their accounts. They pay off the bank manager to keep quiet. Everybody keeps their jobs."

"But doesn't the institutional investor have to have a paper trail – something to show where that money is coming from?" The Cardinal wasn't a banker, but he wasn't a fool, either.

"Yes, it's standard operating procedure to audit new clients very carefully, sometimes for years after they are brought on," Sean explained. "But if the Community was an older client, and if their account is actually domiciled somewhere else – say in Latin America – and if the bond broker is just the middleman collecting a fee from the transaction, well let's just say the incentive isn't there to be too fussy about compliance issues."

"And what did my predecessor do about this?"

At this, Sean let out a mirthless bark of laughter. Carol looked uncomfortable.

"He was a Redemptorist, you know," Sean told Portland in a voice heavy with unaccustomed irony. "Money wasn't his 'thing.' He let Carol handle the day-to-day transactions."

His wife let out a troubled sigh.

"I-I didn't know what to do," she told Portland pleadingly. "I need my job. It's not easy to get hired again, not at my age."

The Cardinal nodded.

"So why are you telling me now?" he asked.

Sean looked deadly serious.

"Because Carol thinks you're the real thing," he answered slowly, glancing at his wife. "To be honest, at first I told her to keep out of it, that it wasn't worth the risk."

At this, Carol nodded, and reached for her husband's hand. They both looked at the Cardinal.

"But she kept after me about this," said Sean carefully. "So here we are."

Here we are indeed, the Cardinal thought wearily. He would have to check with this investment company, but if he were a betting man, he would place a solid wager that his predecessor was still a signer on this account.

Before the week was out, it seemed, he would be making an unexpected visit to the premises of that once-mighty American computer hardware company.

And, he thought grimly, he would not call ahead this time.

CHAPTER 13

Standing in her mother's Roman kitchen, Stacey felt her blood run cold at Philip's Facebook message on her smartphone.

"Maybe you shouldn't come back," it read. "I want a divorce. I'm fucking sick of this."

She suddenly felt disoriented, her entire world telescoped onto the tiny screen in her hand. Everything around her – the children's complaints, her mother's voice – receded as if to a great distance.

She was abruptly quite short of breath.

"What's the matter?" Michelle had a nose for trouble like a bloodhound. She was immediately there, anxiously peering into her daughter's face.

Stacey felt the blood drum in her ears as, light-headed, she sat down. A feeling of unreality surged.

"Oh Jeez, now what?" Michelle was ready for the worst. Just that morning, she'd spent hours trying to convince Dyson not to renege on his offer to support the maternity home in Umbria when he'd gotten the call from the priest working for the Bishop of Spoleto.

"I don't like this at all," Dyson had said to her. "He's trying to pull a fast one."

"He's a bishop," Michelle had responded exasperatedly. "My God, have a little trust. If we can't trust a Bishop, who can we trust?"

Dyson felt anger and cold despair run through his veins. Michelle had good instincts, but her old Brooklyn upbringing meant she had a soft spot for the clergy, whom she naively

71

believed could do no wrong. He had a much more nuanced approach – and he'd learned to trust his own instincts when someone backed out of a sweetheart deal, which is what the bishop of Spoleto was clearly trying to do.

It had all come through an interpreter of course, a local priest. His Grace regretted this very much, but he was wondering if Mr. White would perhaps be open to a more suitable site for the maternity home?

"You would think His Grace would be grateful for the investment in his diocese," Dyson growled. The Italian priest was a bit taken aback, but in the manner of his culture attempted to smooth over any ruffled feathers that the wealthy American might have.

"Ah yes of course, but you know there are much better bargains to be had, places where we could offer these young mothers so much more," he replied easily. "Perhaps they would not have such a spectacular view, but there would be so much more space, so much more to work with," he explained.

In the end, Dyson agreed to drive up to Umbria, though winter was not a particularly agreeable time of year for a sojourn into the foothills of the Apennines. He rang off feeling disgruntled, and decided that now might be an excellent time to hear five o'clock Mass at San Trinita dei Pellegrini. It would be a Low Mass in Latin -- the consolation of reverence and serenity. By the time he returned, Michelle and Stacey would have dinner almost ready. He could relax with a glass of Orvieto, overlooking the Tiber.

But dinner turned out to be a casualty of Stacey's Facebook conversation with Phillip. When Dyson arrived home, he found his wife and daughter in a huddle over the big kitchen table. The kitchen was cold, bereft of its normal delicious warmth of the late afternoon. Uncharacteristically, his grandkids were parked in front of the TV, wolfing down a pizza.

"What's up?" he wanted to know, but his wife merely shook her head dolefully. Stacey smiled abstractedly, but looked away. Dyson thought she looked as if she'd been crying.

"We're having pizza," Michelle announced with a warning look.

"Great!" said Dyson automatically. In minutes, he found himself ensconced on the sofa next to Katy and Josh. Their movie was a cartoon rife with wise-guy asides and double *entendres* which he found mildly amusing, if occasionally a bit shocking. The evening progressed until Michelle packed the kids off to bed.

Dyson found his daughter on the terrace, a glass of red wine in her hand. She hadn't eaten.

"Hi Daddy," she said to him glumly.

He opened his hands inquiringly.

"You want to tell me what's going on?"

That's how it all came out.

"You know," she began, sighing, 'or you probably don't because your generation wasn't addicted to this stuff..."

"...Phil is addicted to something?" Dyson looked incredulous. "How can that be? Don't they test officers regularly?"

"Daddy," she interrupted him, her eyes dry but her voice shaky. "I-it's porn. Online porn. He's addicted to it."

Dyson's face was a study in conflicting emotions, as disbelief and scorn fought for control over his expression.

"Come on, honey, you're a big girl," he said finally, shrugging in an embarrassed way. "Men, are, well, men."

"This isn't *Playboy*, Daddy," she asserted. "This isn't static pictures of airbrushed models telling guys what they want them to do to them."

Dyson reddened. This was an odd conversation to be having with one's daughter.

Stacey didn't seem to notice. She took a large gulp of wine to steady herself, and set her glass down carefully. She looked her father in the eye.

"This is a guy who plays with himself constantly, any chance he gets. Every second he can get alone, online." Her father screwed up his nose with distaste, but Stacey regarded him calmly. "And he's not getting off just on videos of naked, grown women, anymore."

Dyson took a deep breath, but Stacey cut him off.

"H-he's getting off on kinds of perverse stuff – people getting hurt, homosexual stuff, stuff with kids..." at this she broke off, unable to go on. Suddenly, the tears were running down her face.

Dyson reached out instinctively and took his daughter in his arms. As he folded the sobbing Stacey into his chest, he noted that she felt smaller, less substantial. Had she been eating?

"A US Air Force senior officer, willing to give up his wife and kids, for dirty pictures," Michelle stood in the doorway to the terrace, disgust filling her voice.

"Give up his wife and kids?" Dyson echoed, incredulous. He held Stacey out at arms' length, searching her face. He noted that his daughter's upper arms were alarmingly thin. "What? Why?"

As the tears welled up in her eyes, Stacey suddenly broke away from her father, turned her back and took another large gulp of wine.

"He's told Stacey he wants a divorce," Michelle snapped.

Dyson looked at his daughter.

"Is he crazy? You'll get half his earnings, and his pension." Dyson was fully versed in the military's financial rules.

Stacey wiped her eyes with the back of her hand and shrugged. "Apparently, he doesn't care. He says I'm crazy to be so upset at him, that this is a-all in m-my head. And that he doesn't want to live with me anymore. He says I 's-suck all the air out of the room.'"

Dyson shook his head, confused.

"Do you know what he said to me?" Stacey looked at her father intently. "He called me the 'c-word' in front of the kids. And can you imagine why? Because his dinner was late."

Dyson had to admit that was extreme, but he was still confused.

"But, what does this have to do with, er, porn?"

Michelle sighed, and put a supporting arm around her daughter, faced her husband.

"Dyson, this, this 'addiction' has made Phillip into an *animal*. He's nasty, impatient, short-tempered. All he wants is his 'fix.' And he keeps getting worse, Stacey says. That's why she came here, she says. To get away from his disrespectful mouth."

"And to get away from his little 'accidents,'" Stacey added bitterly.

Dyson and Michelle looked at each other apprehensively.

"What do you mean, honey?" Michelle asked gently.

"Oh, strange phone numbers on his mobile bill. Horrible photos I can't get out of my head that accidently appear when he forgets to clean up his search history, " Stacey sounded exhausted. "Living with this, worrying the kids will stumble on it – and knowing they eventually will – walking on eggshells so no one makes him angry and turns him into a ranting, raving crazy man."

Dyson was appalled, but resolute.

"Has he hit you?" he asked, his mouth set in a grim line.

Stacey shook her head and sighed.

"A couple of times he looked like he was thinking about it, but he's too afraid of what would happen if his commander found out."

Michelle shook her head and let out a sigh of relief. "Well, thank God for the military on that account."

What she didn't say, and what she knew Dyson was thinking, was that Stacey now had even more humiliation and pain in store for her. Their daughter would have to be tested for AIDS and a whole host of other sexually-transmitted diseases.

Later that night as they were preparing for bed, Dyson looked at his wife.

"What the hell is the matter with this guy?" He shook his head incredulously. "Here's a guy with self-discipline, a smart guy with a great military career, with a wife and kids – and he's gonna throw it all away for his *right hand*?"

Michelle sighed, the practical woman of the world

"Let's hope that's all it is," she responded and then asked rhetorically. "How many hookers you think they got working the gate at that Air Force base?"

Dyson sighed deeply. Everywhere he looked, there was corruption.

"Hookers. Online porn. I thought Phil had a little class. What the hell is *this*?"

"*This*," said Michelle grimly, "Is the Devil. And the Devil is dancing all over Phillip right now."

Before they went to sleep, they prayed a Rosary together, a habit they had gotten into in Rome.

CHAPTER 14

Carlo could not quite believe his eyes. As he emerged from the deep brown-and-gold Baroque gloom of San Trinita Dei Pellegrini, the first thing he saw was the aquiline profile and tall, slight form of the American Dominican who had saved his life fifteen years before.

"Ciao, Father Paul!" he cried in delight.

Corinth turned at the sound of his name, and on seeing Carlo, his face lit up. The two men embraced warmly in the ancient Roman piazza, now choked with cars belonging to the *carabineri* stationed across the way.

Fr Paul Corinth had been a young friar almost fifteen years before when he'd stumbled on a hapless Italian kid attempting to live on the streets of Boston. Paul had worked assiduously to gain Carlo's trust – which actually hadn't been too difficult, given Carlo's desperation and youth.

Carlo had been his first 'conversion.' Paul could see—because he was gifted in this way, and because his years at the North American in Rome had given him good Italian – that Carlo was not a bad boy. He could also see that Carlo was afflicted by what he privately thought of as the 'demon' alcohol – which, he could admit was a funny way to think about what was obviously a medically-diagnosable syndrome.

His experience with Carlo wasn't unusual. All his life, Paul somehow couldn't shake the almost-visceral feeling that those enslaved to alcohol, or any number of addictions, were actually being 'ridden' by tiny-but-powerful demons. It seemed these days that almost everyone in America had their own demon, too.

In any event, Carlo had been a 'success' story for Paul. After a year with the Dominicans, he was sober and Catholic, and Paul had seen him off on an Alitalia flight out of Logan, back to Rome.

Shortly afterwards, his deep prayer life and steady personality had led the new Cardinal Portland to ask Paul to be trained as an exorcist. Exorcists were suddenly in demand. The decline of Catholic life and the internet-fueled spike in sex trafficking, New Age Gnostic practices and occultism had opened the door to evil, plain and simple. Sensational news reports focused on Satanic Black Masses on Harvard's property, but the truth was that the Cardinal was contending with many events and 'infestations' that the reporters never caught wind of.

Paul was not at all sure that he was the right man for the job, however. Raised indifferently by his mother and her boyfriend on a tumble-down farm in the hinterlands of Pennsylvania, he had never had any kind of structure in his young life. No religion, which his mother considered to be purely a matter of personal choice. No sports, as the boyfriend wasn't interested. Thus, he had drifted more and more into the neglected white-boy camaraderie of heavy metal music and the occult.

From this, Paul was rescued simply by God's intervention, he believed. In his freshman year of college, he had been impressed by the dramatic white habit and black cloak of a Dominican assigned to the Newman Center on his campus. Out of sheer curiosity, he'd stopped by for a brief chat. It wasn't much, but it was enough so that he had known where to go when the crisis came.

It happened at Halloween. He'd been invited to a party off campus, in an apartment rented by a long-haired, heavy-set, middle-aged woman who called herself a 'campus chaplain'. The place was filled with very drunken college kids. He didn't know that the gang rape – there was no other word for what he stumbled onto – was happening in a back bedroom. Instinctively, he'd backed away in horror, indifferent to the jeers that followed him as he ran, faltering, down the rickety back steps, into the night.

Despite the late hour, the Dominicans answered his desperate knocking. That had been the beginning of his conversion, reinforced by a habit of regular prayer which he picked up from the Order. Un-nerved by the indifference and immorality he encountered daily on campus, he ended up spending much of his waking day at the Newman Center, and when he graduated, he immediately entered the Dominican seminary. He was amazed to find that he was not alone, however, as by the late-1990's the Order had again begun attracting many young aspirants.

Paul excelled at his seminary studies, and was sent to the North American College in Rome, where in addition to uncovering the astonishing patrimony of the Church, he discovered a strong affinity for Italian. Suddenly, he was no longer the awkward farm boy from the wrong side of the tracks, and the delights of Italy's cuisine and culture opened an entirely new, wholly Catholic world to him. He read voraciously on his own – all of Chesterton and Belloc, Jungmann and Pius X.

After ordination, he was assigned to Boston, where the friars ran a soup kitchen and outreach for the homeless. It was there that Paul saw Christ in the faces of human wreckage. Drug-addicted, alcohol-ridden, often mentally and physically ill, these were 'hard cases' – people for whom no amount of social work, drugs or psychiatry would suffice, or even help very much.

The work was deeply frustrating for Paul, and he was careful to avoid the cynicism and black humor of many of the old-timers who worked for the Dominicans. Privately, he began to think of the men and women who he fed everyday as plagued by demons, and to pray for them, diligently, by name. It was this habit of deep prayer that his superior noted, which brought him to the attention of Cardinal Portland and his elderly exorcist.

"You have the energy and the intelligence, my boy," Father Donovan told him when they met. "But this is hard work, and it requires knowing your weaknesses – because that's where the demons strike."

Paul nodded, unsure what to say. The aged priest had an engaging manner, acquired in his long years of service as a Navy chaplain, which disguised his astuteness.

"What's your weakness, Father?" Donovan asked suddenly, in his old-timey Bostonian Irish accent.

The question came out of the blue and Paul stared, at first unable to respond. Father Donovan made a tent of his blue-veined fingers, and waited, eyes downcast.

"I-I never had a father," Paul finally responded, haltingly.

The exorcist nodded, but said nothing.

"My own father was an alcoholic, and he disappeared when I was about seven," Paul said. "My mother went through a series of boyfriends, and finally settled on one when I was about 14."

"And this man, your mother's boyfriend, what was your relationship with him like?"

Paul shrugged indifferently.

"By that time I was deep into my teenage world of the occult, Father," he admitted. "I wasn't interested in him, and he wasn't interested in me."

"Did he know what you were involved in?"

"No," Paul shook his head. "My mother and him were in their own world – working, I guess. In any case, he didn't last long, either. By the time I went to college, he was gone, too."

Father Donovan sighed. "So, what is your weakness, Father?" he repeated, softly.

"That's just it, Father," Paul said, staring intently at the floor. "I'm afraid. I'm full of fear."

"What are you afraid of?"

"That I am not good enough," Paul told him, with blunt honestly.

Father Donovan nodded, and waited.

"That I don't have what it takes," Paul continued, miserably. "I don't have what it takes to succeed, or to be considered valuable, or to be respected."

Father Donovan nodded again.

"All I can do, really, is pray," Paul whispered, sheepishly regarding his interviewer. "Pray and speak Italian."

"Know anything about Latin?" Father Donovan came to the point.

"Er, just a smattering from what I got in Rome."

"Good," the old priest reached, unsmiling, for his pen. "I think you will do nicely for this job. That is of course," he regarded Paul from under his bushy white eyebrows, "if you want it."

Despite Donovan's confidence in him, Paul's first case had been a resounding failure. The 15 year old suburban boy was the adopted son of non-practicing Protestants in the midst of a prolonged, bitter divorce. The ne'er-do-well husband had won custody of the son in the divorce agreement, along with a million-dollar settlement from his ex-wife, who had inherited an old New England family fortune.

When the boy began spending most of his time online, the ex-wife suddenly had a 'bad feeling.' Her son's newest companion, acquired in an internet chat room, was of Italian extraction, and claimed to be 18, though he looked much older. It had been her observation that these swarthy southern European types matured quickly. Nevertheless, she consulted a Catholic neighbor, who agreed that there was 'something suspicious' about the new best friend. The neighbor brought in Father Paul, but the sight of a Roman collar was too much for the boy's mother.

"I'm sorry," she told the Catholic neighbor firmly. "And I am sure he means well. But I just can't have a Catholic priest in my house. And I'm sure my ex feels the same way."

For his own part, the boy's father hadn't concerned himself too much. At age 55, he was suddenly a sought-after bachelor, and was engaged in squiring a woman many years his junior around Boston when his son suddenly went missing. This in itself wouldn't have been so worrying, except the kid stole a credit card.

The FBI traced the transactions to a service station on I95 in South Carolina the next morning, where the cameras caught the slight, pale boy with the pretty face on video, in the front seat of a black Cadillac SUV. A computer search revealed that the driver was actually a 28 year old Satanist from a Boston-based coven, on the lam from a court appearance where he was to be sentenced for child procuring.

The state police gave chase, the Cadillac crossed the meridian at 80 mph and slammed headlong into an oncoming 18-wheeler. Both the driver and his passenger were killed instantly; the 48 year old driver of the truck escaped with his life, barely.

Recovered from the back of the Cadillac was a laptop with extensive videos of homosexual child pornography. Apparently, the boy was on his way to be sold into sex slavery.

The once-Catholic parents of the Satanist told Father Paul that their son's demise was 'society's fault' and that they didn't believe in his mumbo-jumbo, before they shut the front door in his face.

The incident taught Paul the deadly reality of the threat he faced. But he persisted, and under Father Donovan's tutelage, began to grow in confidence and knowledge. By the time the Pope enlisted his services, he was a battle-scarred veteran who'd had his own conversion, of sorts. It wasn't exactly because he was weak, though he fought the constant temptation to think that he was. He understood the need for constant spiritual training, in order to stay fit and able to withstand the onslaught of evil.

Today, Father Paul said Mass in Latin exclusively. For exorcisms, he likewise used the ancient tongue of the Church. Father Donovan had quietly taught him everything he needed to know.

"The Devil hates Latin," The old priest had told him at the beginning of his training.

Father Paul was a bit taken aback. Could this be true?

"Consider the fact that in 1986, the Church of Satan promulgated a new black Mass, the Missa Niger, which is said entirely in Latin," Father Donovan had explained. "As in all things Satanic, the logic behind this is both twisted and keen. Insofar as the Devil gains his power only in the hideous reflection and inversion of what is Good, Beautiful and True, he has no interest in false things."

This was logical; Father Paul understood. Satan consistently imitates, derides and manipulates only what is True. And now, after almost ten years as an exorcist, Father Paul was convinced of it.

But today he was back in the Eternal City, with a new haircut and, quite suddenly, an old friend. He stood in the sunlight in the piazza and smiled at Carlo.

"I don't have to be back at work until this afternoon, so of course I will come with you for *pranzo!*" he declared gladly. "Where shall we go?"

This is how Father Paul came to be the guest of Michelle and Dyson White.

CHAPTER 15

As Father Pilar stepped off the plane in Florence on that wintry day, he breathed a sigh of relief. Regardless of the cold weather, it was always good to get back to civilization. The Americans could be so exhausting, so easily offended, with their puritanism and their petty snobberies.

It was inevitable, though, he supposed. The American secular religion of freedom and capitalism created this obsessive concern with 'fairness' dictated and enforced by the lawyer class while simultaneously making greed into a virtue, at least for the bankers he did business with. For fifteen years, it had been the perfect arrangement for the Community, of course – all they wanted was a place safe to leave their funds, with no questions asked.

And they had been left in blessed peace. The local wealthy Catholic Bostonians, once they got wind of the fact that there was little in the way of prestige to be gained from the Community, left Pilar and his small coterie of priests quite alone. No fundraisers. No 'silent auctions,' whatever they were. Pilar wasn't a religious man, but if he had been, he would have thanked the Lord for small graces.

Now, suddenly, it was over. Within weeks of his beloved Cardinal's retirement, that silly cow of a branch manager had suddenly run off to marry some man she'd met at an online dating service – Pilar shuddered at the horror – and had left him high and dry.

There were funds that simply had to be transferred, accounts that had to be funded, and here he was without a willing branch manager to approve these transactions. Worse, one of his priests – the best-looking and most charming, detailed these last few years to make deposits at the bank – had returned with some alarming news.

The teller hadn't been *positive*, but she was pretty sure that there was something funny happening with their account. The new branch manager had told his staff that all CTRs were to be filed, without exception.

Pilar's priest had not made his customary deposit that day.

For the truth was these deposits were the penultimate step stop in a complex, virtual 'underground railroad' for laundering drug money that the Community had constructed throughout the North American continent over the previous 15 years. Vast amounts of money generated by meth labs and recreational drugs were 'processed' through this system, for which services the Community commanded a hefty commission. The drug lords who were their clients weren't happy with the Community's extortionate transaction fees, of course, but saw little alternative. They were savvy enough to understand the virtues of 'business focus' and that outsourcing necessary money laundering services was probably best left in the Community's expert hands.

Of course, truth be told, Pilar knew that he'd become a bit lazy of late. For seven years, his fat little branch manager had been so accommodating, and the bribes he'd had to pay her were so minimal, mostly 'complimentary' weekends away at fancy spas. Infuriatingly, she'd kept this budding romance from him, and he'd been broadsided with the bad news of her departure from the banking business – apparently to focus on her new life as a maker of stained glass In Vermont.

It was all so grotesque, but it meant that they simply would have to find someplace else to park these millions.

The Community's Head was sympathetic to Pilar's problem, and suggested that a conversation with the Dean of their seminary in Rome might be in order. The new pontiff was a puzzle for the media, whose 'progressive' Church contacts were in a tizzy. Dark warnings about the pope's 'hardline stance' were grabbing headlines, though of course their clerical sources declined to be identified. For the moment, the Community was grateful that the media had far juicier stories than poisoners and the now-boring narrative of sexual abuse to focus on.

In the confusion, perhaps now might be opportune time to quietly acquire a 'summer seminary' in someplace out of the immediate orbit of Rome, he suggested. Almost-ruined palazzos were quite plentiful, and with a willing Bishop in dire need of funds, arrangements could be made to transfer the necessary millions for purchase and renovation in euros through the accounts of a small but respectable rural diocese in Italy. A bit of checking around had turned up the Bishop of Spoleto – faithful, essentially weak and new in his job. He fit the bill, perfectly. Now if only the Dean would be waiting for him at the gate, as planned.

A quick hand raised in the waiting crowd reassured him. The Dean and his two seminarians commandeered his luggage and they were soon ensconced in their comfortable-but-conservative BMW, on their way to Spoleto.

To Pilar's surprise, the seminarians were brand new, both Americans with no command of Italian.

"And this is because they won't be able to understand the conversation with the bishop?" he asked the Dean, masking his awkward question with a ready smile. The seminarians gawked out the windows in the back of the BMW, manifestly oblivious to the content of the conversation.

The Dean chuckled amiably as he steered the BMW onto the *autostrada*.

"Their innocence will comfort the Bishop, don't you think?" he smiled broadly. "Besides, one of them is the son of an American billionaire who has recently moved to Rome. It is well that we show him a good time, no? Though I do think you'll find the other one more to your liking."

Pilar ignored the jibe. His predilection for young men was a common-enough peccadillo in Community circles. He wasn't going to dignify this Dean's coarse sense of humor with a reply. Instead, he smiled politely and asked him how his seminary was faring.

As the two priests lapsed into rapid-fire Italian, Patrick White shifted in his cassock in the back seat of the BMW. He'd been in the Community seminary exactly one month, attracted like many young men to their military-like charism and apparent orthodoxy. His parents had been so pre-occupied by the problems of his sister Stacey and the constant needs of their grandchildren that they were taken completely by surprise when he'd made his announcement suddenly, one night last month.

"R-really?" Michelle whispered, in shock. She and Dyson were stunned into unaccustomed silence by their only son's announcement. The very next day, Patrick was gone, all of his possessions stored, military-like, in a duffel bag slung over his shoulder. Leaving their Roman apartment building, he squared his shoulders and thought with determination about his future.

The world was huge, and as he was coming to realize, a deeply corrupt place. He would be needing the Community to protect him, to guide him, and to give him a home in Christ.

A month later, however, a sixth sense told Patrick that something was wrong. Perhaps he'd inherited his father's business sense; at any rate, he was thinking it was definitely odd that he and this other American kid would have been chosen to check out some real estate for the new 'summer seminary.'

As the BMW exited the *autostrada* at Trevi, he wondered if this place was anywhere near his parents' planned refuge for pregnant Italian women.

CHAPTER 16

For their 'come to Jesus' talk, Dyson brought Boston's new
Cardinal to his favorite Roman trattoria. Carmela, the wife,
greeted him with her customary warmth and, deftly noting his
visitor's pectoral cross, ushered them to a quiet corner table
away from inquisitive eyes and ears. When she had brought
them their bottles of *Lacrime di Nero* and *acqua frizzante*, she retired
promptly to the kitchen with their orders.

"I always admire the *romani*," Cardinal Portland ventured with a
slight smile. "They can read minds, it seems."

Dyson nodded in amiable agreement.

"We've been living here for a year," he replied with a tight smile.
"It's been quite an education."

"I'm sure it has. Too bad their entire civilization is threatened,"
the Cardinal almost growled. He was an ex-rugby player at his
New England prep school, the great-grandchild of Irish
Protestant emigrants from Northern Ireland. His conversion to
Catholicism had shocked his not-overly religious mother and
deeply delighted his father, who had inexplicably converted in
the wake of World War II.

"Though of course it wouldn't be the first time," the Cardinal
observed, wryly. He had seen many impossible things happen.
He also had the reputation of not suffering fools gladly.

Dyson, for his part, was also a pragmatic man. He had spent his
life working in business, the son and grandson of men who'd
held seats on the New York Stock Exchange. He had only the
sketchiest education in history. But his two years in
incarceration had been well-spent in this regard; he'd found a
treasure trove in the prison library -- full of the classics of
Western literature and history virtually untouched since they

were originally stored there in the 1940s. The prison library did not have a big budget.

"I read," he began somewhat tentatively, "that there was a time in Rome when the city's population dwindled to less than 10,000 people. They lived in Trastevere, hauling water up from the river, among the ruins of a city that had once had 2 million inhabitants."

The Cardinal appraised his luncheon companion frankly. Rich donors were seldom interested in ancient history.

"If you don't mind me asking," he began, "what exactly is your interest in our project? I mean, there are many good causes out there...'

Dyson sighed. How was he going to explain himself? Fortunately, Carmela arrived with their *insalate caprese*, allowing him a brief time to collect his thoughts

"Cardinal, my education and background prepared me to run businesses," he said when Carmela had withdrawn. "And that's what I did, pretty successfully, for most of my life. Religion and history were not my primary concerns, though of course I always respected these, er, disciplines."

The Cardinal nodded, and surveyed the luscious tomatoes, fragrant basil leaves and creamy white *mozzarella di buffalo* arrayed on the elegant dish in front of him. He thought reflexively for the thousandth time about how one of the benefits of being Roman Catholic was, no doubt, the food.

"But then you got arrested," he said, looking up at his companion.

Dyson responded instantly without thinking.

"Then I was targeted," he shot back.

"Right," said the Cardinal equably. He smiled at Dyson. "Shall we say grace?"

Dyson cast a quick glance around the crowded trattoria and shrugged. After all, if he couldn't say grace in public in Rome, with a Cardinal at his table, when could he? They bowed their heads, and Dyson was somewhat surprised to hear the Cardinal intone the words in Latin.

"So," Portland resumed, as they began to eat. "You were starting to tell me why you were interested in investing in our project."

Dyson sighed. "Corruption," he replied shortly.

Portland raised an eyebrow. "What about it?"

"Italy, like the entire West, is drowning in a tidal wave of corruption," Dyson said. "There is a huge lake – an ocean really – of money that literally has no place to go in order to gain a return."

The Cardinal nodded.

"Yes," Dyson confirmed. "For the last ten years, central banks have kept interest rates very low in the OECD countries. Money flows to where it will gain the highest return for the least amount of risk – this eliminates countries where there is no reliable rule of law, including much of Asia, Africa and the Middle East. This leaves very few options for investing. Now, some of this money has flowed into legitimate projects in borderline economies such as Russia, Brazil, etc. But where has the rest gone?"

The Cardinal shook his head wordlessly. He was listening intently, his expression serious.

"Where can you get good rates of return, with almost no oversight or, importantly, taxes?" Dyson asked, his voice an intent whisper. "I'll tell you where, because I have seen it: organized crime. The drug business. Internet porn. The prostitution and human trafficking that both of these things fuel. Plus, all the associated rackets – phony religions, cults, you name it. All of these things have mushroomed in recent years."

The Cardinal nodded again, but said nothing.

"These are eating away at the fabric of our civilization, your Excellency. None of these crimes are 'victimless' because behind every filthy percentage point of return there is a destroyed family – a woman betrayed, a man's self-respect thrown away, children shunted from one to the other, or to the State. Today, our younger generations have zero trust in themselves, in marriage, and in family, as a result. To them, the lifelong bond between a man and a woman, and the rearing of children, the care of the elderly all seem impossible.

"And this has come upon us swiftly," Dyson continued. "In our lifetimes, your Excellency, we have seen this happen. Can you imagine what you would have thought at age 18 if someone had suggested that the Italian family – the bulwark of this civilization for more than 2000 years – was facing extinction, within a *generation*?"

The Cardinal cleared his throat.

"There are those," he began, 'who believe that this is due to feminism, or to the homosexual rights movement. Are you in agreement with this?"

Dyson shrugged indifferently. "Only to the extent that these ideas have aided and abetted people's decisions to 'partake' of, er, 'lifestyle choices' which then can be marketed to them. From the point of view of the sleaze marketers, homosexuality is a great thing because it expands the market for their services.

Feminism in general is a good thing for them because it loosens the bonds of family. Unchecked immigration is also good because it weakens the social fabric and drives down wages.

"It all works together. You'll notice that, politically, all of these 'issues' are lumped together under the banner of 'human rights.' I submit that if the finances of the lobbying organizations which support these politicians were examined, you would find that they derive from some pretty suspect funding sources."

Dyson sighed and looked across the crowded, chattering room. Portland regarded him thoughtfully.

"Hence how circular the arguments are in the 'cultural wars,'" the Cardinal said quietly. "Liberals champion individual 'rights' to every imaginable thing, and use the State to their social engineering ends. 'Conservatives' believe that this is all destroying our civilization, and that the State should be severely restricted to prevent it being used to restrict freedoms. In reality, both sides are serving the god Mammon, on a global scale."

"Yes," Dyson nodded vigorously. "And they are delusional in their fixation on the power of the state. What neither side seems to realize is that the sovereign nations seem helpless in the face of this destruction – probably because they have been heavily corrupted -- and that there are a global few who are getting unimaginably rich on human suffering while both sides argue about the *wrong things*."

"And so this brings us to why it is that you want to support a maternity home for Italian women," the Cardinal wiped his hands carefully on the blue-and-white checked napkin.

"I saw the victims of all this while I was in prison," Dyson said suddenly. "Every last one of those men had no father. Most of them had impregnated many women. All semblance of civilization had broken down in their world. They were predators, or, mostly, prey.

"After I was released, I fled to Italy because after that toxic, unbelievably depressing experience I needed to drink at the fountain of our civilization. I needed to be someplace where people understand what civilization *is*."

"And did you find it?"

"Yes, but it is as you say deeply threatened," Dyson sighed. "The corruption here has reached epidemic proportions. Italy is teetering on the edge of being a failed state. And once again, it is the weak who are victimized."

"The unborn," Portland stated flatly.

Dyson, however, nodded vigorously. "We have a neighbor, a doctor who works in the Italian health system, whom my wife befriended. I couldn't believe it when she told us what the abortion rate here is – twice what it is in Croatia, next door! And behind every one of those stories is a woman who has no support for having her child. In Italy, only the rich and the old can have children – and they, in effect, buy those children through artificial means. There are doctors with yachts who will perform fertility services illegal in Italy once they are out in international waters, for a price. Meanwhile, the young must destroy their own children; they are given no choice."

Portland folded his arms across his chest and waited as Carmela took away the remains of their lunch.

"This has all happened before, you realize," he told Dyson. "In late antiquity, Rome and its empire became decadent and corrupt. We all learned that in school, but what we didn't learn is that the entire reason why Christianity and Judaism both emerged from that time was because only devout Jews and Christians deeply respected life. While the pagan Romans and Arian Christians exposed their infants or practiced homosexuality, the orthodox Christians and Jews raised families."

"Exactly," Dyson nodded. "And I believe that this is why devout Christians and Jews hew so closely to their religions today – because it protects them and in many ways teaches them the critical skills they need to raise the next generation.

"But the Church has broken down here in Italy to the point where it can no longer perform these vital tasks. Old clergy still parrot the exhausted ideas of the sixties, speaking mainly to the elderly in fast-emptying pews. There are no vocations. The few committed Catholics here are isolated in the ghettos of their various 'movements' which help them find work and, sometimes, raise their children among like-minded people. But they have very little influence on the larger culture. If you are unlucky enough to be a pregnant young woman in a 'normal' Italian family, you will probably choose to abort. The evil is everywhere, Your Excellency."

Dyson's voice was tight. He didn't need to tell the Cardinal just closely it had struck his own family. "And we have reason to believe the Pope knows this. We met his new exorcist just the other day, a Father Paul Corinth."

At this, the Cardinal's eyebrows rose. He said nothing, however, and simply reached for his glass.

"You seem startled, Eminence. Do you know him?"

Portland took a sip of his red wine, and set his glass down carefully. He grinned broadly at Dyson.

"Know him?" he smiled. "I should say so. I brought him here."

"Really?" It was Dyson's turn to be surprised. When Carlo had arrived with Father Paul for *pranzo* the other day, the priest had made no reference to the Cardinal.

"I'm told by people who know these things that he's one of the ten best exorcists in the world," the Cardinal replied quietly.

"Why the sudden interest in exorcism?" Dyson asked. They both knew that he was referring to the Pope.

"Well, you know he's publicly referred to the Satanic several times," Portland said quietly.

"And he's made no secret of his contempt for the Curia," Dyson added.

Portland sighed. "Apparently, there are some in the Curia who are deeply involved with dark forces. The Pope wants Father Corinth, unofficially, 'on call' so to speak, and he wants him to teach."

"So, the Curia is corrupted," Dyson said shortly. "Where's the connection to the diabolical, for His Holiness?"

"I'm not sure," the Cardinal said, carefully. "I don't know the people involved, but the rumor is that whoever it is in the Curia has roots in Latin American drug gangs and Gnostic New Age practices. But then again the corruption does seem significantly centered here in southern Italy. And today's Mafia is very different from the old days. Drugs and prostitution used to be untouchable businesses, but that all changed in the 1970s."

Dyson laughed mirthlessly. "Yes, and it appears the Mob has lost their religion, just like everyone else here. Italy is suffering mightily from a toxic brew: the combination of Mafia corruption of literally every major enterprise – public and private – and the loss of their traditional respect for at least the outward forms of religion and the family."

The two men were silent for a moment.

"Perhaps in addition to the Curia, the crime bosses are dabbling in the diabolical?" Portland asked.

"If there's money in it, they'll dabble in anything," Dyson answered practically. "But tell me,
what official reason did His Holiness offer for bringing Father Paul here?"

"He's here to teach," Portland replied briefly, "and to train teachers."

"Teachers who will be training other exorcists?" Dyson asked. "That's a change of direction."

"Obviously," Portland said quietly, "there is a great need."

CHAPTER 17

Luigi sighed and dusted the snow off the Madonnina with his work-roughened hands. Maybe this year he should bring her inside. With all the trouble in the house, her benevolent presence would maybe help a little.

Valeria was still mad, though he knew her well enough to know that his wife's anger would dissipate once their daughter started to 'show.' Both Gina and Luca had gone back to work their jobs. No one had seen anything of Marco in the last month, after Gina had curtly informed him that she was keeping the baby.

"Don't I get a say in this?" Marco whined.

"Yeah, after all, it's your baby too," Gina retorted sarcastically.

"That's not what I meant," Marco responded, confusedly.

"Are you *listening* to yourself?" Gina shouted into the phone. "*Egoiste*! I don't have to take to this from you."

Luigi sighed. He could see Marco's plan, like it was laid out in front of him. Entice Gina back to him, make her get the abortion and then drop her as fast as possible, probably while she was still on the table. It was the only way to avoid twenty years of dunning payments to support a child he did not want. And there were plenty of other lonely women in Rome eager for a little cheap romance.

But Luigi had to give Gina credit for one thing: she seemed determined to keep her baby. Hence, they were all waiting for Gina's nuns -- Americans coming to set up a kind of a home for pregnant girls in Umbria someplace. Luigi didn't know what to think about that. Couldn't she just stay home with her family?

For her part, Valeria had other ideas. She paid all the bills in the house, and she was not too happy about the idea of Gina quitting her job. Good, steady employment was hard to find in Rome. And, she explained patiently to Luigi, they needed everyone's paycheck to pay for, well, things. Rome was expensive. Everyone knew that.

So when the day came that Gina came home with the nuns, Luigi was initially quite taken aback. They were all escorted by Carlo, the White's driver, who politely wiped his feet outside their door. Once inside, he shook Luigi's hand, bowed slightly to Valeria and nodded gravely to Gina.

The entire family gaped at the nuns in a most un-Roman way. Unlike Italian nuns, the two American women were young, in their early thirties. And unlike the foreign nuns from the less developed world who thronged Rome's streets, they were improbably garbed in almost the same flowing habits Luigi remembered his teachers wearing when he was a child in his mountain village.

Most of all, although they spoke virtually no Italian, they radiated a joy that vaulted high over the language barrier and directly into Luigi's heart. They were in Rome, Gina explained, to learn Italian as a first step towards beginning their establishment.

"*Vengo di una famiglia italo-americano,*" ventured one of the sisters, after the introductions were complete. They were sitting in the dining room over coffee, with Luca and Carlo translating.

Luigi regarded her doubtfully. If she was Italian, it was mixed with something else, something northern, though he didn't venture to say so. She was too tall and fair-skinned.

The nun read his mind.

"My mother is Irish," she smiled, which Luca translated.

To her surprise, all the Italians burst into laughter.

"That's funny? In my family, we always said it was a disaster!" the nun laughed too. "My Lord, can you imagine the combination?"

Everyone laughed again, and Luigi decided then and there that he liked this Sister Mary Grace.

"*Un po' di vino?*" he asked, and rose to find the wine glasses.

The nuns spoke about their training, and their Order's charism, which centered on helping young women have their babies and teaching them how to raise them. Sister Mary Grace had just come from Scotland, and the Italians listened in fascination as she told them about her work there.

"On average, we have about two or three girls come to us a month," she explained in answer to Valeria's question.

"And who pays for their keep?" Valeria wanted to know.

Sister Mary Grace explained that the Diocese had donated an old convent for their use while a few very wealthy Catholics provided most of the financial support.

"And everything else comes from volunteers," she said, explaining about the middle-aged Scottish women who gladly donated their time to teach the girls to cook and clean, and to care` for their babies' needs.

"They don't know how to cook?" Valeria shook her head.

Sister Mary Grace was surprisingly quite serious on this point.

"Most of them come from homes where nobody cooks," she said quietly. "And nobody took care of them when they were children, either."

The Italians nodded.

"They are all quite young, right?" Valeria asked, refusing to look at Gina. Her daughter knew exactly what her mother was thinking – *"not like Gina, who is older and should have known better."*

Gina opened her mouth automatically to protest but Carlo caught her eye and shook his head. For some reason, she obeyed the White's driver and kept a grudging silence.

"Actually, no, *signora*," Sister Mary Grace said seriously. "We have women in their late thirties coming to us."

"You *do*?" Valeria shook her head in bewilderment. "Why would a woman that age need you?"

Sister Mary Grace shrugged. "It's a tough world out there. Many women who come to us have already had abortions when they were younger. Mostly because they were forced to..."

"Forced? Who forces a woman to have an abortion?" Valeria was incredulous.

Sister Mary Grace was calm.

"When they are very young, it is often their own mothers who bring them to the abortionist. Or a friend. It's rarely the father of the child, though of course they often lay down an ultimatum – them or the child. The child almost inevitably loses."

Gina carefully kept her face expressionless. Valeria looked as if she were going to say something, but thought better of it.

"So," Sister Mary Grace continued gently, "by the time they find themselves pregnant again, many older women already know that there is no 'perfect' time to have a baby. They know this may be their last chance to ever have a family. And they may not be lucky enough to have a 'partner' who will stay by them."

"What is this 'partner'?" Valeria wanted to know. "Where are their husbands?"

"In Scotland," Sister Mary Grace responded quietly, "only the well-off marry. The vast majority of Scots no longer marry. This is the same for Catholics as it is for Church of Scotland people."

Luigi shook his head.

"*Como sclavi*," he said quietly, in Italian.

At the sisters' quizzical look, Luca translated.

"He says, '*like slaves*,' though I don't know what he means," his son explained.

The other nun, who had remained quiet until now, spoke up.

"He means that in Europe in the pagan Roman Empire, slaves didn't marry," Sister Beatrice explained. "Marriage was for the landed gentry, because it was designed to hand down property to the next generation. Slaves had no property, therefore no reason to marry."

The others looked at her with interest.

"It was Christianity that taught that marriage is a sacrament, necessary for all," she went on. "Of course this gave a sacred foundation to everyone's family, no matter how poor they were. You could say it elevated the idea of family to the sacred, as a separate matter from property-owning."

Carlo translated her words for Luigi and Valeria, and then added his own comment.

"We can't simply look down our noses at the barbarian Scots, you know. This is happening in Italy too."

At this, Gina, who had been silently listening to the conversation, stood up suddenly. There were tears in her eyes.

"When Italian men today are such spineless *animali*, what do we expect?" she demanded heatedly, her gaze sweeping defiantly over Carlo. "When Italian men no longer have *honore*, there *is* no more *famiglia*, no more *futuro*..."

"... and even if the man *is* decent, it's too expensive to have children in Italy," Valeria interrupted her daughter impatiently. "Who will take care of them when everyone must work?"

In response, Carlo simply shook his head wordlessly. But he continued to regard Gina with a searching gaze.

"We work for the wrong things," Luigi piped up suddenly. He was looking intently at his wife. "We have fallen into a great trap."

But Valeria shook her head vehemently at her husband.

"Ah, Luigi," she dismissed him with an airy wave of her hand. "Things aren't like they were in the old days. People have changed."

Gina sighed and sat down heavily. Next to her, Sister Mary Grace smiled warmly and reached out to cover Gina's hand with her own.

"*Coraggio*," she urged. But Gina responded to the nun with a worried glance, and shook her head again. For the truth was that in recent days, she had begun to have deep doubts.

The silent thoughts whirled through her brain. Increasingly and secretly, she found herself longing for the old days with Marco – the dinners out, the romantic walks, the deep feeling of security she'd felt under his possessive gaze.

It would be so easy. All she had to do was call Marco. He would be tender, and kind. In an hour the whole thing would be over. This entire nightmare would end. She could go back to her old life, her lover, and her little luxuries.

She had told no one about this, of course. What would everyone say if she changed her mind at this late date? After getting all these people involved? She looked at the nuns unhappily. Up until their arrival in her family's apartment, everything had seemed so unreal.

Now, however, their very solidness made the reality of her situation undeniable. If she was going to change her mind, she needed to make her move, and fast.

By the end of the evening, however, Luigi had a surprise for Gina and his entire family.

"I will go with these sisters," he announced solemnly, as he shut the front door behind the nuns and Carlo, with finality. Valeria and his children looked at him, dumbfounded. Gina felt her heart start to race.

"W-what do you mean, Pop?" Luca wanted to know.

"I mean," Luigi said simply, "that these sisters will need someone to look after things, out there, *en la campagna*. I will go and look after things for them."

"But what about your job?" Luca said it before his mother could.

Luigi was unruffled.

"I can take, whaddya call it, 'early retirement.' They'd be glad to see me go. I don't move so fast no more."

Valeria looked at her husband with wide eyes.

"How will we pay the bills around here?" she asked, disbelief and alarm in her voice.

"Our bills are not so high. This place is paid off," her husband responded calmly. "We don't need half the junk we buy. We don't need to go on no more cruises."

"But we need those to relax!" his wife protested.

"Nah!" Luigi smiled at her and waved his hand dismissively. "You can come to me in the country when you need a break. We'll have fun."

Gina and Luca said nothing, watching their parents closely. Valeria continued to shake her head distractedly.

"*Cara mia,*" Luigi sighed, and sat down beside his wife. He put one arm around her.

"I been living here all these years because, well, it was necessary. Now, it's not necessary. You got another two years left to go at work, right? So, this will probably take a few months to get off the ground. I'll go to take care of Gina and the sisters, and you'll come on the weekends. We'll make it work.

"Someday, God willing, Luca will need this apartment for his family. It's time we started to make some room. It's time we started to think about the next generation."

Luca looked startled, and then grinned shyly. Valeria looked at her son and then her husband.

"You got a girlfriend I don't know about?" she demanded of her son.

"No, no, Mama," Luca soothed his mother. "I got no girlfriend."

"*Now* he don't have a girlfriend," Luigi said, smiling. "But maybe, God willing, he will have one, and a family someday."

Luca looked at his father, feeling confused but oddly hopeful.

"I don't like all this change," Valeria whispered.

Luigi smiled.

"What change? I'm going to look after our Gina and our grandchild, that's all. You'll be there too."

At this, Gina finally spoke up.

"Papa, are you sure about this?"

Luigi reached out and ruffled his daughter's hair with both his hands, an old intimacy. "*Ginaluche*, we'll work it out. These nuns got the right idea. We'll work it out, somehow."

Gina tried to look comforted. Her *telefonini* rang and to her irritation, it was Carlo.

"Yes, yes of course," she told him, trying hard to disguise her impatience. How did he get her number? "We'll be there. *A le undice e dopo, per il pranzo, a gli famiglia White. Si, grazie.*"

She rang off and faced her family.

"We're invited to Mass on Sunday at eleven," she sighed. "At Trinita Dei Pellegrini, in the *centro storico*. Afterwards, for pranzo at the White's."

Valeria was shaking her head in distress again.

"Why'd you tell him we'll be there? We don't know this church or these people..."

"*I* know this church," Luca spoke up quietly, with conviction. "*I* know these people. I am going."

"And Mama, you need to come too," Luigi told Valeria calmly. "I need you to come. Your daughter needs you there."

At this, Valeria looked at her daughter.

"Is this true?" she demanded. "Do you want me to come?"

"Yes, Mama," Gina answered with a heartiness that she did not feel. To cover herself, she began to busily clear the table.

Valerie said nothing, but narrowed her eyes and watched her daughter thoughtfully as she retreated from the room, arms laden with plates.

What Luca said next, however, threw Valeria into utter shock.

"And Mama, you need to wear a veil. This Mass is in Latin."

CHAPTER 18

Patrick White slumped, terrified, in the narrow seat of the Boeing 737-800 as it bounced around the windy winter skies over Glasgow. His anxiety, something he usually preferred to keep tamped down safely under a carefully cultivated exterior of calm, spiked dangerously.

His heart pounding in his ears, his body rigid, his fingernails dug deeply into the palms of his hands, Patrick prayed silently for a swift end to his agony.

"Land the plane," he prayed fiercely, addressing a God he was no longer sure existed. "Just land the plane."

It was moments like this that, oddly, convinced Patrick that he had not completely lost his faith, though he had come very close. In fact, it was for this very reason that his sister – now Sister Mary Benedicta -- had urged him to come to this freezing cold northern city. She had just arrived a few weeks before, the replacement for Sister Mary Grace.

Of course he could stay in the convent guest floor, she explained. But she could also ask at the rectory for him.

"No," he said, cutting her off. "I don't want to stay with priests. If it comes to it, I'll just go to St. Andrews. I know people there who I can stay with."

This last confused Benedicta.

"St. Andrews is hours away," she said. "I thought you wanted to stay here."

Patrick had to admit to himself that she was right. St Andrews would be too obvious a place to look for him; few would suspect he was staying in a convent.

A few years before, Benedicta would have questioned him closely over their Skype connection. But her experience in her Order's charism had taught her a new approach to dealing with people in crisis.

"Okay," she said calmly. "At least let me send someone to get you."

"Fine," he said tersely. "As long as they aren't priests."

Clearly, something bad had happened to Patrick. He had left the Community, he told her, but warned her that their parents had no idea about this.

"I told those bastards that they'd better keep their mouths shut, too," he told her grimly. "Or they would have our lawyers to deal with."

So that is how Patrick came to be sitting in the convent's Glasgow kitchen as Benedicta's new, makeshift assistant, helping prepare lunch for a dozen pregnant women. He worked awkwardly yet with concentration as he chopped vegetables for homemade minestrone – Michelle's recipe, writ large.

"Mom called," she told him.

"Yeah?" he answered dully, not looking up. "How is she?"

"Fine. Well, not fine. Worried about Stacey. But not worried about Dad, for the first time in a long time."

"Yeah?"

"Yeah, he's really into the plans for the new house in Umbria. Working with the Cardinal, apparently."

"Mmmm," her brother responded unenthusiastically. He continued to chop carrots with great concentration.

Benedicta eyed her brother as she ladled the chopped vegetables into the soup.

"You think there's a problem there?" she asked him. "In Umbria?"

"Could be," he said, looking up at her. His eyes were challenging. "How should I know?"

Benedicta gathered her skirts around her and sat down opposite her brother.

"Pat, are you okay?" she asked gently.

Her brother grinned mirthlessly in response, but said nothing. His eyes were sad, and his mouth was set in a grim line.

"Did they, uh, *do* something to you?" she asked quietly.

"To me?" he echoed, with a snicker. "Nah, they wouldn't dare."

"So I don't understand, then," Benedicta said flatly. She folded her hands and waited, watching her brother closely.

"Neither do I," he looked at her frankly. "All I can tell you is that I saw things about – this..." he looked around the kitchen. "I saw things about *all* this that I don't like."

"About *this*?" Benedicta was confused. "About our convent?"

Patrick sighed and stared balefully at his sister. The Gregorian chant wafted in through the doorway.

"I don't want to disturb you," he said, finally. "You still have faith, obviously. Look at what you're doing."

Benedicta shook her head, still confused.

"I'm doing what I love," she said simply. "I thought that was why you went to the Community. So you could do what you love. So what did you mean by saying they're 'killers'? You mean that literally?"

"Did you ever feel like you were born in the wrong generation?" he asked, suddenly.

Benedicta sighed.

"I felt like that in high school," she told him. "Not so much in college. Christendom was full of Catholics like me. Why?"

"I feel like we've been born into a world at war with itself," Patrick told his sister. "Like some people's 'normal' is just intolerable to other people, and vice versa, but that ultimately none of that crap matters. What it comes down to is that everyone is racing to get as much stuff as they can, and to hell with everyone and everything else. And I include the Church in that, too."

Benedicta nodded cautiously, but said nothing.

"The Community is *not* holy," he said, quietly. "And I feel sorry for any poor sucker that goes in there thinking that it is."

"Like you did?" his sister asked.

Patrick took a deep breath.

"I had a feeling something was not right," he said finally, and let out a sigh. "Oh, everything *looked* right. All the guys in the seminary had short hair, and there was this kind of military 'feel' about the place – you know, soldiers of Christ and all that. But as I got to know most of them, I could see that they had no clue what was really going on there."

"What do you mean?" Benedicta asked. "What was going on there?"

"Nothing, to the naked eye. I mean, we had classes, and Mass and mandatory physical exercise – just like I expected. But I could tell right away that there were two kinds of guys in there. There were guys like me – more or less smart, more or less earnest, whatever. But they were not in charge. The guys that *were* in charge were *all* smart, however. And *none* of them could be described as 'earnest.'"

"How could you tell?" Benedicta asked. "You don't speak Italian, or Spanish, that well."

Patrick shrugged.

"Actually, my Italian ramped up; after a few weeks I understood a lot more than they thought I did. Anyway, the in-charge guys were always smiling, walking around carrying million-dollar leather briefcases," he told her. "At least they were always smiling when I was around. But I found out they were different with guys who didn't come from the kind of money that we do."

"Yeah?" Benedicta said.

"Yeah," he responded gloomily. "There were a couple of guys there, young guys. You know, kinda nerdy guys, real sincere, but hopeless. The kind of guy who just wants to be accepted, no matter what. And *they* were the targets."

"Targets for what?" his sister asked.

"Everything," he told her. "Mockery. Bullying. At first it was kinda subtle, but after a while I started to catch on, as my Italian got better. Though most of the guys they targeted didn't speak Italian and so had no idea what they were saying about them. All they knew was that they were out of favor – and they desperately wanted to be *in favor*."

Benedicta shook her head. "I have never seen anything like this here," she said. "This sounds awful."

Her brother stared balefully at her.

"I only figured out what was going on when it was too late."

That's when he told her the whole story about Nick, the earnest kid from the American Midwest who'd accompanied him to Umbria with the Dean and the Latin American guy from Boston. How Nick was the only son of a woman who had raised him alone, deserted by her alcoholic husband.

Nick had grown up involved with his parish, as his mother had stayed close to the church for protection against America's predatory youth culture. An indifferent student, after a few years of working in the local garden store, Nick had decided that he had a priestly vocation. The Community had snapped him up in a heartbeat, and shipped him to Rome to their seminary.

"They targeted him," Patrick said bitterly. "They preyed on his insecurities. Nothing he did was right. He was clumsy on the soccer field. Not too bright in classes. But nice, you know. A *good* guy, with a *good* heart. They mocked him, though. Tortured him, really. It was disgusting. He would have done anything for their acceptance."

Benedicta's eyes widened at the furious tone in her brother's voice. He bit off his next words.

"Well, when he was chosen to come along to Umbria, he was really excited. I didn't understand what was going on. I couldn't imagine what good the two of us could do on a real estate deal. It didn't make sense, why we'd been chosen. Only after it all happened did I understand. I was chosen for *cover*. What they really wanted was Nick."

"Oh my God," Benedicta whispered. "Oh my God."

"On the way back from Umbria, he didn't say much. I noticed he was quieter than usual. He kept looking out the window and I noticed that his hands were fidgety, on his lap. Those two bastards in the front seat kept up a smooth chatter in Spanish. I guess they figured I had picked up too much Italian."

Her brother stared dully at her.

"You can guess the rest. Nick hung himself in his room that night, back in Rome."

Benedicta inhaled sharply, and crossed herself. Her brother looked away, and swallowed.

"I can't imagine what they said to his mother. When the *carabineri* left, we were all assembled in the rectory, and the Dean told us all about how depressed Nick had been. That's when I stood up, and walked out. I just walked out – up to my room, packed my bag and headed for the front door."

"Where did you go?" Benedicta whispered. "Did they try to stop you?"

Her brother laughed mirthlessly.

"There were a couple of the Dean's lieutenants there, waiting by the front door for me with those sympathetic smiles on their ugly mugs. I didn't mess around. I got up in their faces, and shoved my finger in the face of the big one."

Benedicta smiled despite herself. Patrick could be counted on to make his point.

"I mentioned Interpol," he told her. "I said that they'd better get outta my way or they would have dad's international law firm to deal with. They backed down pretty quick."

Benedicta nodded with satisfaction.

"Well done. So you went home?"

Patrick shook his head.

"I couldn't go home. What was I going to tell dad? I had zero proof of what I knew to be true. And he's dealing with this same bishop – this guy in Spoleto – for this place for his pet project!"

"So what did you do?"

"I called Carlo."

"Mom and Dad's driver?"

"Yes," her brother smiled slightly. "He picked me up a few blocks from the seminary, which was good because I had a feeling they were going to come after me."

"Then what did you do?"

"We sat in an Irish bar all afternoon. I drank a lot of whisky, and told him the whole story. At first he seemed kinda distant, like he was suspicious or something. Not really believing me, just kinda humoring me. But when I told him what they did to Nick, it was like a light went on in his head. He just looked at me, shaking his head.

"Finally, he says, 'this is wrong. This is just wrong.' And he shivered like he was cold, or something and right then and there changed his attitude. He looked around suddenly and told me that I had better come back with him to his place, which is his mother's place. His mother made me eat some pasta, but I tell you I was pretty far gone. I remember crying in her arms. After that, I slept for about 36 hours."

"Wow," exclaimed Benedicta. "What good people! And they didn't tell mom and dad?"

"No," Patrick replied grimly. "But only on one condition."

"That you came up here to me," Benedicta guessed.

"How did you know?"

Benedicta shrugged, with an understanding smile. "Carlo needs his job. He saw you were in crisis. If you couldn't go home, the next best thing was me – and a convent!"

At this, the kitchen door opened, admitting a chattering group of nuns and mothers-to-be. Behind them loomed the tall figure of the kindly parish priest who said their Novus Ordo Mass in Latin.

"It's time to eat!" declared Benedicta, and stood up. Patrick reluctantly stood up too, and followed the crowd into the dining room.

CHAPTER 19

At that moment, Pilar and the Dean were unhappily watching the Head of the Community pacing in front of the two elegant chairs they were uneasily occupying.

"I am deeply sorry," the Head was saying. His Italian leather shoes executed a smart turn on the variegated colors of the Persian rug which adorned the terrazzo floors of his private study. "But neither of you will be leaving this building until I get the complete truth of what happened to this seminarian."

Pilar sighed to himself. All of this drama was completely unnecessary. He refused to look at the Dean, whose fault this all was, after all. If he hadn't served up the boy as being willing, the entire situation would not have gotten so out of hand.

'Rape' was such an ugly, unnecessary term. Teenaged boys were so fickle – one minute flirtatious, and the next feigning innocence. This one had been just like that, too. Pilar had actually had to wrestle him to the ground, face down, in order to gain his satisfaction.

The tears and the wracking sobs afterwards had just been plain embarrassing. So sloppy, just like all things American. The entire episode had left a bad taste in Pilar's mouth, and he'd resolved to leave Italy as soon as possible afterwards.

The Dean drove the boys back to Rome, fortunately. Unfortunately, that dunderhead in Spoleto had tried to extract an astronomical price for that old bishop's residence on the Umbrian hilltop. This required delicate negotiations in order to determine just what the bishop had in mind for all that extra cash.

When he learned that His Grace was lusting for a renovation of the diocesan palazzo, Pilar was both relieved and delighted. Greedy prelates were relatively easy to manipulate. All that was required was official signatures on some bank forms, and the money would start rolling in from America.

So it was that he'd almost completely forgotten the incident with the boy when the second black BMW suddenly arrived in Spoleto. This one was occupied by the Head's two most serious assistants; to Pilar's chagrin, within hours he and the Dean were seated in the Head's office, listening.

"Father Pilar," the Head was saying now in a conciliatory tone. "I am a man of the world, after all. I am aware that, ah, misunderstandings happen, and sometimes things get out of hand. *Claro.*"

Pilar heard this with some satisfaction. From the Head's delicate tone, at least it was clearly understood how valuable his service was to the Order. He folded his hands and waited to see what kind of deal would be offered.

"Most unfortunately, we have a wild card in this situation," the Head glanced severely at the Dean, who shrunk visibly in his chair. "It seems the other American boy has taken certain foolish notions into his head, and he has threatened to involve Interpol and his father's well-known legal team."

At this, Pilar's eyes suddenly snapped wide open.

"Preposterous! On what charges?" he reacted before he could stop himself.

"Well, Father Pilar," the Head said smoothly, his voice dangerously modulated. "of course it's always hard to guess what move the other side might make, but our lawyers tell me that the new anti-trafficking laws have been written so loosely that the Community as a whole could be implicated."

"Implicated? In what?"

"We could be described, the lawyers say, as an organization which procures and traffics in young men for sexual reasons. The suicide of this young man might be seen as just the tip of the iceberg, requiring extensive investigations of the Community's establishments, actions and, more to the point, *transactions* internationally."

Pilar stared at this last, speechless.

"I see that the possibility of such a thing hasn't crossed your mind, Father Pilar. Well, there are consequences for our actions."

"W-where is the American?" Pilar found his voice, which came out in a hoarse squeak.

"That's another problem. We're not at all sure," the Head was leaning on his desk, arms folded. "It seems that after the seminary let him get away, he simply disappeared into the streets of Rome. We've had some people watching the family apartment, but there's been no sign of him."

Pilar shook his head in misery. This was all too much to bear.

"Of course, that won't go on forever. Sooner or later, Patrick White will re-appear, and shortly thereafter a tragic accident, unfortunately so common on the unruly streets of Rome, will happen to him. That is, if we are lucky and he hasn't gone to Interpol."

"And if he has?" Pilar needed the answer to this question.

"If he has, then we are all in for a very rough time, I'm afraid. Most of all, you."

CHAPTER 20

Luigi watched the smoke from the incense climb into the dome of the church over the high altar and hover there, suspended in time. The silver, sunlit smoke billowing against the gilded Baroque dome seemed to him like the thoughts of God invading the space of man.

Then, the golden altar bells rang. The Host was lifted. All around him people knelt in deep devotion. There was utter silence. Even the babies were quiet.

How long had it been since he'd seen babies at Mass? Luigi was fascinated by the sight of the young couples with children thronging the old church. Some were Italian, but plainly others were not. Who were they?

Not tourists, though this church was steps from the Tiber in Rome's *centro storico*. No, they appeared to be young professionals and ordinary people, too. People with work, it looked like. But they had two and three children, almost unheard of in Rome.

Beside the young families, he noted with satisfaction the presence of many young, veiled women and single men, too – all dressed respectfully for *la santa missa*. And everywhere, too, he saw Italians his own age, and older.

What had the priest spoken of, during the homily? Martyrdom. The Roman martyrs, whose remains lay all around them, under the high altars of Rome's ancient churches. And the new martyrs in Iraq and Syria, where Christian families shivered helplessly in the desert camps and awaited a rescue from the West that was probably not forthcoming.

Luigi followed his wife's veiled head to the altar rail to receive communion, watching her with rapt attention. Would she kneel like the others to receive on the tongue? He was disappointed but not surprised when Valeria remained stubbornly standing, her hands cupped to receive the Host. When his wife stepped smartly aside, Luigi knelt gingerly in her place and composed himself to receive.

As the priest placed the golden paten under his chin and intoned the Latin words, Luigi struggled to control himself. Hot tears rose unbidden to his eyes.

"My Lord and my God."

The ancient affirmation of doubting Thomas arose in Luigi's mind as he received his Lord on his tongue, the tears of decades coursing down his cheeks.

As he returned to his pew, he felt the eyes of his wife and children upon him, but he lowered his gaze away from them. They did not know that he had been to confession for the first time in decades at that very church the evening before.

"Oh forgive me, Master, I have been remiss," Luigi had prayed silently in the pew afterwards, as the unstoppable tears coursed down his worn cheeks. The knowledge of his sinfulness was fully upon him. "I have allowed my children to be raised without the knowledge of You and Your great works. *Mea culpa, mea culpa, mea maxima culpa.*"

A great calm had descended upon him afterwards and he felt a newly clean heart within him at Mass. As he knelt quietly alongside his family, Luigi gave thanks to the great Mother of God, his Maddonina.

When Mass ended, he lifted his eyes and found to his surprise that Gina and Luca had approached a bank of candles before a painting of the Madonna and Child. There, they each embraced a petite blond American, the mother of two small children hovering by the candles. Behind them stood an older couple, clearly American though not dressed as tourists.

With formality, Luca introduced his father to Dyson and Michelle White. Luigi nodded gravely as he shook hands with the billionaire. To the Italians' astonishment, Michelle immediately put herself forward and embraced Luigi in the European style, kissing him on both cheeks.

When she stood back, there were bright tears in her eyes, and she was smiling.

"It is an honor to meet you, sir," she whispered in her Brooklyn-flavored Italian. "I am the daughter of Italians much like yourselves, who came to New York many years ago. I want you to know that we love your Gina as our own."

Despite her appalling accent, her sincerity was such that the tears started in Luigi's eyes again. He stared at the Americans in wonder, and then looked for Gina. To his amazement, he found his daughter, veiled and glowing with a preternatural beauty, praying on the kneeler before the Madonna. A little behind her, kneeling on the marble floor, was Carlo, the chauffeur.

Minutes later, they were all gathered on the front steps outside, waiting for Father Paul. Gina deliberately stepped away from Carlo and drew out her smartphone, her back turned to everyone; Marco had returned her call while they were at Mass.

A light snow began to fall, and Luigi put a protective arm around his wife. Valeria looked up at him.

"I'm in shock," she whispered hoarsely. "Did you see all that in there?"

"Yes," he answered. "A miracle, isn't it?"

Before she could retort, the American priest emerged from the church and the group began the short walk to the White's apartment. Luca fell easily into step beside his parents. He was smiling broadly.

"Who's this priest?" Valeria hissed. "What's his story?"

"Oh, him?" her son replied, feigning nonchalance. He grinned at his mother. "He's the Pope's exorcist."

Valeria's face was a study in shock.

"Exorcist?!" she repeated dumbly.

"Yes," Luca replied, still grinning. Just as they arrived at the entrance to the White's apartment building, he turned to his mother and winked.

"I hear the Devil hates Latin."

CHAPTER 21

They drove in a caravan to Umbria, led by Carlo driving Luigi's family in the big white Mercedes. Behind them, the Cardinal drove his rented minivan, deep in conversation with Dyson, Michelle and the two nuns. Bringing up the rear was Father Paul Corinth driving another minivan. Stacey was beside him, with Katy and Josh plugged into a Disney film in the back.

"I don't like to expose them to some of the messages I hear in these children's cartoons," Stacey was telling the priest, as the minivan dodged through the Roman traffic on the *anulare*, or city belt.

Father Paul sighed.

"I guess you know you have a fight on your hands," he observed as he deftly evaded a Fiat which, with typical Roman insouciance, was straddling two lanes. "Raising kids in the culture as it stands is a challenge."

Stacey took a deep breath and decided to take the plunge.

"Father, what do you know about online porn?" she asked, looking straight ahead.

The priest glanced over at her.

"I know that it's an epidemic," he replied carefully. "If what I hear in my confessional is any indicator, that is."

"Even guys who go to *confession*?" Stacey was shocked.

The priest nodded sadly.

"Even women who go to confession," he added. "Porn has saturated the culture."

"Oh my God," Stacey answered. She exhaled slowly. If people who were sincere Catholics confessed to this, then it truly must be everywhere.

"Do you have a bottle of holy water in your house?" the priest asked.

"N-no. Why?"

"Why do you suppose people keep holy water in their house?"

"Well, my mother's aunt used to sprinkle it on her pillow at night. My mom said she always thought it was to keep away the 'evil eye' – some old Italian superstition."

"Does your mother have it in her apartment now?"

"I-I think so. Umm, actually now that you mention it, she does. I think she uses it, too. My parents said they had the place blessed by a priest when they moved in."

"Your parents are wise," Father Paul nodded with satisfaction. "That was a good move."

"So," Stacey began slowly, "you think that holy water keeps people from becoming addicted to porn?"

"Not holy water alone," the priest cautioned. "What keeps people away from bad things is living a holy life. The Church's sacraments are the main bulwark against evil. Her sacramentals – like holy water, or scapulars, or rosaries – these help, too."

Stacey nodded, and thought about how even a year ago she would have scoffed at such 'medieval' ideas. But her experience with Phillip had changed all that and she'd become a daily communicant at the air base's Mass.

"I think my husband is possessed, Father." There, she had said it.

Father Paul glanced over at her, his face full of concern.

"What makes you say that?" he asked.

"He's not the man I married. He's not the man I had these kids with," Stacey looked away, staring unseeingly out the car window. Her voice was flat, without emotion. The last few weeks of crying and Facebook messaging with a surly, unrepentant Phillip had taken their toll. Stacey felt dead inside.

Her last shreds of pride disintegrated, she finally told the priest everything she had endured. The verbal abuse. The taunting. The constant irritability and moodiness. The unexplained disappearances for whole weekends. The fear that the children would stumble on his 'hobby.' Finally, her discovery of the sexual torture video, and her decision to take her children and flee to her parents.

He listened sympathetically, asking an occasional question.

"There's more to this, Father," she said. "My husband is slated to take over a very important job next year. He will be in charge of what used to be called the Strategic Air Command."

Father Paul's fine-lined face went a shade whiter. He cleared his throat.

"That's to do with nuclear weapons, correct?" he asked carefully.

"Yep," Stacey said, with a jauntiness she didn't feel. "They screen people pretty carefully for those jobs, of course. But they haven't been screening his porn use, clearly."

The priest shook his head.

"Or maybe, in the new post-moral America, that kind of thing doesn't matter anymore," he replied soberly.

They drove in silence for a few minutes.

"Father, you must help us," Stacey whispered, finally. "Please."

The exorcist nodded.

"We'll need to pray for an answer to this one, Stacey," he said slowly. "We surely need divine help, now."

"My sister is better at praying than I am," she asserted. "She's a nun, did you know?"

"Yes, your mother told me," the priest replied seriously.

Stacey shook her head. "I actually don't know what to tell Sophia – uh, Sister Benedicta -- to pray for. I mean, what should I ask for? That he stops this, gets off this terrible path he's on? That's about all I can think of, because I actually don't even know if I want him back, Father. I can't pray for something I don't want. And I can't ask Benedicta to pray for something I don't want."

Father Paul's face looked drawn in the dashboard light.

"He's under spiritual attack, Stacey. He's been grievously wounded, too. As have you, and your children."

He paused, letting his words sink in.

Stacey looked straight ahead, listening without comment.

"In fact, I would say that your entire family has been under a sustained spiritual attack for some years now," The priest ventured. "Possibly because of the religious vocation in your family. Definitely because of this idea of a maternity home."

128

Stacey considered the idea. The trouble *had* all seemed to start with Benedicta's entering Christendom College; shortly thereafter the lawsuit had been filed against her father. Then Patrick's getting expelled had turned him toward the Faith, inspired by his homeschooling curriculum. Then Benedicta had entered the convent, followed in short order by her parents moving to Rome and taking up this idea of a maternity home from the new Boston Cardinal.

"It's like my whole family has reacted to bad things by becoming more religious," she said slowly. "Even me, going to Mass every day in the last couple of years as Phillip has gotten nastier."

"Yes," the priest said. "It's quite remarkable, actually. Most people fall down quite easily when evil attacks them personally."

"They get depressed," Stacey agreed. "They do something self-destructive like drinking, drugs, gambling, sex, whatever."

The priest nodded.

"But here is what is remarkable," he said, carefully choosing his words, "Instead of turning towards more evil, you have each individually rejected those, er, choices of despair. Instead, you have each turned towards God. This in turn has brought you all to Rome..."

"Except Benedicta..." she reminded him.

"...yes, but it's brought you all in very close proximity to the Church and her work," he said.

Stacey nodded, as a light began to dawn on her. "That it has," she said, her brow clearing. "I mean, *look* at us. Look what we're *doing*."

"And the Devil hates this kind of thing," Father Paul observed mildly.

They drove for a few moments in silence.

"Father," Stacey asked quietly, "do you have some holy water?"

The exorcist chuckled.

"You've come to the right place!" he grinned, gesturing to the leather satchel at her feet. "There's a bottle right in there."

She opened the satchel and withdrew the clear glass bottle, gazing at it thoughtfully.

"What did you have in mind for it?" he asked.

"I think I'm going to start blessing Josh and Katy's pillows," she said quietly.

"Good idea! But I hope you don't mind if I suggest something else?"

Stacey shook her head.

"I think," the priest said, "that you should also start blessing your own pillow. And everybody else's pillow in your house, too."

In the car behind them, Dyson and the Cardinal were continuing to talk business. Michelle sat in the back seat, her arms folded, listening intently.

"So, the Bishop wants us to look at alternate properties because he has another buyer for this first place we're to look at?" Portland asked.

"That's what his priest told me," Dyson answered, his voice flat.

"And you think something's up?"

"Yep. Either he is stalling to buy time, or money. At any rate, the attitude is completely different than it was a few weeks ago, when I first spoke with the Bishop directly. Then, he couldn't have been more accommodating. Clearly, another buyer has stepped into the scene."

The Cardinal shook his head and checked his SatNav. The light was fading, though it was only mid-afternoon. Winter days were short in Italy. He'd been hoping to see this property before it got too dark.

"It's not too far," Michelle piped up from the back of the minivan. "Maybe another 30 minutes, and we'll be there. The Bishop said we should call when we're 15 minutes away and he'll meet us there."

"Michelle, what do you think about all this?" Portland asked, looking at her in his rearview mirror. He liked Michelle's street instincts.

"I think this Bishop doesn't know what he wants," she responded promptly. "I think he was expecting the job of closing down these churches out here and found out that the job has changed. Now he's trying to buy time while he figures out what to do."

"I think," Sister Mary Grace ventured calmly, "that this is all going to work out fine."

Sister Beatrice chuckled in response.

"At the convent we say that Mary Grace has a direct line to the Man upstairs," she laughed. "If she says it's a 'go' then I would go with it. No matter what."

"No matter what, huh?" Dyson echoed, looking bemused. Michelle smiled at the nuns.

"We certainly could use some divine intervention, Sisters."

"No problem," Sister Beatrice grinned. "That's our specialty."

A few minutes later, they followed the white Mercedes off the *autostrada* and under the massive 13th century fortress which the Lombards once built to dominate Spoleto. Soon, they found themselves on a windy, unpaved road which rose through the rolling hills planted with winter crops.

Carlo parked at the foot of the white road which launched, arrow-straight, up the final hillside, flanked on either side by ancient cedars. Peering through the green-black boughs in the dusky half-light, they could just make out the outlines of the palazzo at the top of the hill.

Luca let out a long, low whistle between his teeth. It was even grander than he'd imagined. Beside him, Gina stood irresolutely, unhappily watching her warm breath blow clouds in the cold air. After promising not discuss their "problem," the reunion she'd had with Marco had been ecstatic, the sex explosive.

Afterwards, though, he'd sent her a short, clipped text. Did she want him to make the appointment for her?

Thirty yards away, Father Paul and Stacey stood in the wintery chill, gazing up at the palazzo. Stacey shivered involuntarily and the priest looked at her with concern.

"Are you cold?" he asked.

"No," she replied tersely, in a low voice. "Not cold. But there's something not right about this place. Don't you feel it?"

Father Paul gazed around at the beautiful view their position commanded. Even in very early spring the Umbrian countryside was magnificent. But when he turned back to look at the palazzo, a kind of grey mist hung over his vision. He shivered in recognition.

"I feel it," Carlo said suddenly, before Corinth could answer. He was standing beside them, gazing up the hill.

Then he turned, shading his eyes with one hand and pointing down the road with the other. "And now here comes this Bishop, right on time."

CHAPTER 22

"LEAVE ME ALONE!"

Patrick sat bolt upright in his narrow bed on the nuns' guest floor, shouting and gasping desperately for breath. It took some moments for him to realize where he was, and a few minutes more for his heart to resume its normal rhythm.

This was not the first time, either. Ever since he'd arrived in Glasgow, the nightmares had come upon him in rapid succession.

In every dream, he was running. Something evil was out to get him. The fear was so palpable that Patrick often couldn't get back to sleep, so he would simply wait until the dawn came. Facebook helped him pass the time.

This morning, however, something drew him to the nuns' chapel. It was before their normal morning prayer, but for some reason the Blessed Sacrament was exposed. Candles glowed around the Monstrance, and he recognized the slight figure of his sister, prostrate in prayer before the Sacrament.

He entered quietly from the back of the chapel and knelt soundlessly in the aisle. For some moments, all was completely still, as brother and sister prayed wordlessly before their God. The Sacrament in its monstrance seemed to radiate calm as the minutes slipped away. Patrick felt the fear in his soul subside and drowsiness overcome him.

"Patrick," he heard his name pronounced. From somewhere out of the murky depths, a vision of his sister's face swam into view. Was he in another nightmare?

Patrick fought hard towards consciousness as he lay on the gurney in the emergency ambulance which drove swiftly, red lights flashing, through the early morning Glasgow traffic. Beside him, her fingers moving swiftly over her rosary beads, Benedicta's face was white, framed in her veil.

A medical technician was bent over him, working methodically, speaking in an unnaturally loud voice.

"What day is today, Patrick?" He heard the technician's Glaswegian-laced English and strained to answer coherently before he lost the fight and fell back soundlessly into the depths.

When he awoke again, he was in a hospital bed. Benedicta was asleep in a chair at the foot of the bed, but came instantly awake when he stirred.

"Oh praise God!" she whispered, her beads clicking in her hands. She fell to her knees by his bedside, grasping his hand. "Oh Patrick you scared us!"

The Scottish male nurse beside her was a brawny fellow with a shaved head, a cynic who'd seen it all.

"Looks like you're goin' to rejoin the livin' now Patrick!" he declared jovially, as he bustled about the room. "Ye had yer poor sister – the *sister* -," and here he paused for emphasis with a grin, 'yer sister was worried to death by ye!"

At that, Benedicta bent her head and wept tears of gratitude by her brother's bedside.

"You didn't tell mom and dad where I was, did you?" was all that Patrick could get out before he once more sank helplessly into a deep sleep.

He never heard his sister say, "Of course I did."

When the tests came back the next day, there was a kerfuffle around his hospital bed as the Whites, the hospital's chief of internal medicine, Benedicta and a police officer jockeyed for space. Patrick was pale and weak, but coherent.

It was a case of slow-acting poison, the doctor explained. It had taken the lab many hours of careful testing, he said, because although they suspected poisoning, they couldn't establish what the sort of poison they were dealing with. Finally, they solved the puzzle – the stuff was *crinolon*, a kind of pesticide common in the tropics but rarely used in Scotland's northern climes.

"It's imported. We have seen it used a few times by spouses -- mostly immigrants -- here," said the bluff policeman, a veteran of Glasgow's streets. "It takes a few weeks for the person to die, and since most of 'em can't speak English too well, they can't communicate with the doctors here. They die before we figure out what's wrong, but we're getting better at recognizing the symptoms. So the question to ask is if Patrick has made any enemies from the tropics?"

Dyson, Michelle and Benedicta gazed at each other in shock and consternation.

"My son has no enemies," Michelle asserted quietly, leaning tiredly on her husband. Her normally forthright demeanor was blunted, replaced by anxiety. When Benedicta had called them, Carlo had driven Dyson and Michelle at top speed to the airport in Florence. From there, a hastily chartered flight had delivered them to Glasgow, with time of the essence as their son's life hung by a thread. From the moment they had arrived at the Glasgow hospital, Michelle had adamantly refused to leave her son's side.

Dyson put his arm around his wife.

Poison.

When they arrived, Benedicta choked out the story of Patrick's escape from the Community seminary. Michelle was livid.

"That's it. I am going to see those bastards in Rome," she spat out between clenched teeth. "And I am going to tear every damned thing off their walls. They will have to get the police to stop me, but before they get there I will do some severe damage to their possessions."

Benedicta and Dyson both looked taken aback, but neither of them said a word. Dyson reached for his phone and immediately called his lawyers with a request for some deep research on the Community.

A few hours later, his *telefonini* rang. It was a call from a lawyer working late in Virginia, who had a raft of info on the Community translated from contacts in Sao Paolo.

"It seems that poisoning is in their DNA," the lawyer told him, after relating the story of the Community's founder.

In Glasgow, Dyson's heart thudded in his chest. They had almost taken his only son from him. Something deep in his being responded to this fact – something deeper than anger, revulsion, or fear. It was a growing realization, a dawning of certainty.

His family was under attack. It had begun with the spurious charges against him launched by the US government. That entire fiasco, ending with his prison sentence, had exhausted them, but it had not destroyed them. In fact, it had strengthened their faith, to the point where they were embarking on this maternity home project.

The Devil didn't like that, clearly. So he was striking them at their core – at their daughter's marriage, at their son's life.

"Yes," the lawyer was saying. "I'm so glad they caught it in time, Dyson. My wife and family, we've been praying for Patrick."

Dyson murmured his thanks distractedly.

"But sir, if you don't mind me asking at a time like this, the question is, *why*?"

Dyson was very tired, and his report about what Patrick had told Benedicta was halting and gruff. The lawyer, however, was patient.

"I understand that he suspected them of rape, and because he's a kid he shot his mouth off. I got all that," the lawyer said. "But it would have been their word against his. Why would they take the chance of trying to kill him? They had to be pretty desperate to do that."

Now Dyson stood in the Glasgow hospital room looking down at the pale, wasted figure of his son. The Community would know by now that the attempt had failed. They might even have deduced that law enforcement was on to them. If they wanted Patrick dead, they would have even more reason to try and kill him very soon, before he could do them any more damage.

"Excuse me, sergeant," Dyson said in his most controlled voice. "But can I have a word with you and the doctor, here, outside?"

At the sound of the tone of his voice, Michelle instantly raised her head. The last time she had heard that intense, focused tone from Dyson had been in the courtroom when he was convicted.

CHAPTER 23

The Community's Head was trying to control his panic attacks by utilizing the relaxation techniques he'd carefully studied over the years. An avid yoga practitioner, he was deep into a rather difficult pose when his smartphone twittered.

This in itself was quite unsettling, as literally everyone knew that this was his usual hour for meditation. Only in extreme emergencies was he to be contacted.

Sighing, he released himself from the pose, and reached for the phone. When he rang off, his face was set in deep consternation.

The operation in Glasgow had suddenly, uncannily, gone wrong. It had taken the Community only a short time to locate the boy, thanks to Facebook. It had taken a bit longer to recruit locals to do the job, but finally they were able to find a connection.

A local drug gang member's pregnant cousin was in the sisters' home. All it took was a little bit of a threat and the promise of a substantial sum of money, and the girl was easily corrupted. Then a couple more days before the *crinolon* arrived from Brazil, a tasteless, odorless tiny tablet which dissolved easily in Patrick's nightly beer.

The girl had volunteered to help in the convent kitchen. The entire scheme had worked beautifully, right up until the moment when Patrick had entered that chapel. Then, everything had gone horribly wrong.

The Head tried to think. The girl would have to be eliminated, and the Scots gang paid off. That was fairly simple, though expensive. But that left Patrick still alive, now with the Glasgow police involved. There was a chance that a judicious payment might make the evidence go missing from the hospital, but that left everything in the hands of the Glaswegians, whose bumbling had already produced this disaster.

There were also the father's international lawyers – exactly the people he'd feared most in this entire scenario. Too rich to bribe, and difficult to threaten.

No, it was clear. The only way forward that would protect the Community's interests was a perilous path. The girl was as good as dead, now, but more work lay ahead. The evidence would have to be destroyed, the police bribed and the entire White family eliminated plus whoever they could have told, and fast.

The Scots gang was too sloppy, too brutal for this work. No, the Head would have to call in professional killers for this. Discrete, thorough and horrifically expensive.

The Head shuddered at the thought of the many million euro price tag he would no doubt have to pay for this. His clients in the Americas would be unhappy, but what was the alternative? The Community had functioned like a smooth machine for them for almost two decades, with nary a hiccup. Dirty money was magically laundered to buy them the lifestyle they craved. Gorgeous young models willing to perform sexual magic, magnificent homes around the world, international boarding schools for their more tractable offspring, beautiful German cars. And as they aged, the new medical technologies made possible by the stem cells of aborted babies promised them eternal youth.

The Head sighed. After all of this was over and done with, he would have to look into retirement. It was time that he began to enjoy the fruits of his labors after all these many years.

But first, there was the matter of a little vengeance that had to be taken. Pilar and his taste for rape was the cause of all of this. He was also a real danger. The Head had no doubt that the priest could easily be persuaded to provide evidence for the Italian prosecutors, especially if they guaranteed him safe passage to a new life somewhere far away from the Community's clutches.

The Head was resolved. Pilar would be found tomorrow, an apparent suicide. Here, the Head allowed himself the luxury of a smile as he pictured Pilar sweating as he penned his own suicide note.

Of course, a media circus was inevitable, though a bit routine at this point. Another Roman Catholic priest taking his own life, distraught over the accusations of sexual abuse swirling around him. The media would cover it briefly and luridly, and then move on.

The Head picked up his smartphone and made a quick inquiry. To his fury, he learned that Father Pilar had left for Umbria early that morning. Something about a real estate deal with the Bishop there.

Momentarily blinded by an intense bout of fear and rage, the Head barked an order. His car was to be ready in fifteen minutes. He would take care of this himself.

CHAPTER 24

"Tell him we want the place, and that we're ready to pay cash," Dyson told Stacey over the Skype connection. She was in the family's Roman apartment. "Never mind who his other buyer is. We can't wait any longer to get this started."

Beside him in the Glasgow convent, Michelle nodded emphatically.

"Plus, we're flying your brother down as soon as he is ready to travel, and the renovators have to at least make part of the place inhabitable," she added. "I'm staying here with him until we can fly down together. Your father will be there tomorrow to sign whatever needs to be signed."

Stacey thought that she had never seen her parents look so fatigued, not even during the lawsuit.

"What about Benedicta?" she asked.

"Apparently, she's to stay here in Glasgow until her superior decides she can visit us on vacation," Michelle said tiredly. "But who am I to argue? I'm just glad that Pat is okay."

By her side, Dyson said nothing. Unbeknownst to Michelle, he had quietly hired the Glasgow police chief's recommended 'best' private protection firm to keep a 24-hour watch on Patrick. The police had also mounted a guard outside his own room. Michelle was staying at the convent; the firm was guarding them, too. He was flying back to Rome in the morning.

In the end, they needn't have worried. The Bishop seemed to have changed his mind and was delighted, he told Stacey. He was sure the place would be perfect for the mothers and their *bambini*.

Secretly, he'd been quite worried when he saw that some of the Americans were unhappy with the old palazzo. Though the American Cardinal and the billionaires seemed delighted with the scenic old palace, for some reason their daughter and the slender priest were apprehensive. The simple Italian family and the driver said nothing, doubtless overawed by the place, he surmised.

What was wrong with the palazzo? As the little group roamed through the ancient property on the hill, he'd found himself exchanging small talk with the mother of the pregnant girl, who seemed like a reasonable woman.

Valeria wasn't sure what the problem was, she had told the Bishop, because regrettably, her English was a bit rusty. But possibly it was too expensive?

The Bishop had nodded thoughtfully.

Did she know exactly what they had in mind in terms of renovations, he'd asked Valeria.

Again, she shook her head sadly.

They were Americans, she pointed out. This meant they would only want the newest and the best of everything. The donors were very rich.

It had not been a good day. The Bishop's feeling of unease had begun that morning when Father Pilar had called his *telefonini* suddenly to announce that he no longer wanted the palazzo. He preferred to look around more and in fact would be arriving later in the day, and would require a private office at the chancellery, if that could be arranged.

The Bishop had hurried off to see to Pilar's request then, and had been on pins and needles ever since as he waited for the Americans' decision. Stacey's call was therefore very welcome news, and he told her so.

"*Bellisimo!*" he exclaimed gladly. "I will ensure that all the contracts are drawn up! Where shall I send them? And who can the realtors talk with if there is any question?"

143

Stacey considered the question. Carlo was trustworthy, but she was unsure that he had the vocabulary in English to communicate with Dyson's lawyers. Luca was young, but he nevertheless had had a lot of experience with real estate contracts. Plus, Valeria would be there and she would double-check everything her son did.

In Spoleto, the Bishop was delighted with these arrangements. If only things would run as smoothly with the Community and Pilar, he thought to himself. He'd made sure an office was ready for Pilar when he arrived, but was a bit shocked at how much the Mexican priest's demeanor had changed since his last visit.

Gone was the urbane, unflappable Pilar and in his place was a new, bright-eyed, nervous Pilar, who dithered about whether he should stay in a hotel, and if so, where. Ultimately, a super-luxurious, discrete hotel was found, the owners delighted at the unexpected guest to pay their astronomical prices in late winter.

The Bishop wondered at the change but was too elated with his good news to worry about Pilar's manifest peculiarities at that moment. It was good enough that his second client was there, and ready to start touring buildings. He had more than enough on his plate, and could barely contain his excitement. Perhaps he could broker a great price from a local firm for the renovations to *his* palazzo as a condition for being recommended to the Americans? He rubbed his soft hands together with glee.

He would see that all the contracting ran smoothly. Once everything was arranged, it would only be a fortnight before the American donors could move in to the hilltop palazzo. About a third of the palazzo was quite habitable, though the running water, heat and electricity were delivered through 100-year old fixtures.

The plan was for the Whites to divide their time between Rome and the palazzo as it was being renovated in the coming weeks. The nuns, Luigi and Gina would move in permanently soon.

Within minutes after the Bishop rang off, Stacey's *telefonini* buzzed and Phillip's UK number appeared on her screen. Glancing in their bedrooms to assure herself that the children were fast asleep, she answered.

"Yes?" she said, in a low voice.

"Stacey, I gotta talk to you. It's important."

"Go ahead, Phillip," she answered in as neutral of a voice as she could muster. It had been more than a week since their last, furious exchange via Facebook messaging.

He wanted her back. That was the long and the short of it. He was sorry, so sorry for everything. He'd had time to think and he was really, really an incredible fool, to give up a woman like her. Yes, he knew he was an addict. Yes, he would get counseling, do anything really, if she would just take him back.

Stacey gazed out the apartment window at the lights of Rome and waited for Phillip to finish. Her stomach was churning.

He could understand it if she never wanted to see him again, but would she please consider it, for the sake of the children? This was not about him, or her. It was about their *family*. It was about their *future*.

"Phillip, it is all I can do to keep from vomiting right now," she told him quietly. "I really don't know what to think about you. I have lots of other things going on right now. But I can tell you one thing – you need more than counselling."

Phillip, taken aback, chuckled nervously.

"What do I need?" he asked. "Just say it, and I'll do it."

"I dunno," she retorted, and squirmed uncomfortably. There was no way around it. She had to tell him her honest feelings.

"You *repulse* me, Phillip. You need to be *cleansed*, somehow. You're filthy dirty. Your *soul* is filthy, Phillip. And I don't want to see you like this."

When Stacey hung up the phone without another word, Phillip couldn't actually believe it. This was not at all what he had expected. In fact, the entire night had been a near-disaster.

"Um, I hope you don't mind if I ask," the woman had said to him earlier. Phillip was studying for his MBA through an Air Force program, and had found himself drawn to his professor, a slim, street-smart Wall Street veteran fifteen years his senior. After class was over, he'd taken to hanging around to chat after the other students left.

"What?" he'd smiled indulgently at her. He liked looking at her, liked talking to her. She was a vivacious brunette with a matter-of-fact personality, sophisticated humor and a husband an ocean away. It seemed to Phillip that she was attracted to his air of command and his body, honed in long hours in the gym. No doubt he could get something going with her, in her hotel room away from prying eyes on the Air Base.

"Where's your wife?"

He'd been expecting that and explained, with a voice full of regret, that they 'weren't seeing eye-to-eye.' He waited calmly for her response.

"Phillip, I'm going to ask you something that you don't want to hear."

He kept his confident smile in place nonetheless.

"So what's wrong with your wife?" she asked, a note of irony in her voice.

"Nothing," he responded, automatically.

"Is she an alcoholic? A drug addict?"

"No."

"Depressed? Schizophrenic?"

"Uh-uh."

"Big and fat?"

"No."

"She spends all your money?"

"No."

"Um, is your house filthy and are your kids neglected?"

"No, nothing like that."

"So, what's the problem?"

"We, uh, it's gotten *boring*," he finished lamely, desperately wishing he'd never started this conversation.

"Phillip, don't be an asshole," she said kindly, disregarding the shock on his face. "Do you have any idea how many guys I know who have thought the way you're thinking right now? That they'll just 'ease out' of a marriage—and that their kids will still love them later on, when it all blows over?"

Phillip was stunned into silence. His smile faded abruptly.

"Guess what?" she continued. "It doesn't work that way. The guys I know are fifty years old now and their kids *hate* them for what they did to their mother. Kids aren't stupid. They know who loves them – and who's the asshole."

Phillip nodded, too dumbfounded to protest.

"Your kids will hate you forever if you do what you're thinking of," she told him flatly.

Phillip felt a sense of unreality.

"Don't be a jerk," she said matter-of-factly. "Why? Because in fifteen years when you're my age, you'll end up alone. No kids. No grand-kids. No family. Nothing. Like a dozen guys I know."

Phillip nodded again, and swallowed.

"And Colonel," she said quietly, "I will be thinking very carefully about whether I will file sexual harassment charges against you."

She threw on her raincoat, picked up her briefcase, and left him without another word.

Phillip stood watching her numbly. Then, much to his chagrin, he was suddenly consumed with such intense self-loathing that he found it difficult to breathe.

CHAPTER 25

Gina hated herself intensely. For, as the weeks wore on and her family became ever more deeply immersed in planning to fundamentally alter their lives in order to help her, she had become ever more addicted to deceiving them.

Gina was living a double life.

In what she thought of as her 'daylight' life, all was as before -- she was still working her job though she had told no one of her predicament. At home, she quietly took her pregnancy vitamins and tried to appear enthusiastic as she heard about the plans being made for the Sisters' new maternity home in Umbria, where she was slated to be the first resident. She also tried not to feel too guilty as she heard her parents endlessly discussing Luigi's plans to retire early.

In her secret 'night' life, Gina zealously hid the fact that she was eagerly receiving Marco's texts almost every hour. Her smartphone would buzz and there he would be, chatting like old times. He was once more the teasing, laughing, ingratiating Marco she'd fallen for. And oh, how he wanted her.

She felt a deep pang when she thought of how her family would react if they knew the truth – that hers and Marco's love affair had taken a new, more explosive turn. Now that they had to meet in secret, she was astonished at the passion that had swept over her.

She shivered as she thought of Marco's fingers creeping up her exposed throat, turning her jaw towards his hungry mouth as they shivered in a Roman doorway in the early spring chill. His eyes had smoldered as he whispered hoarsely how much his body ached for her. She belonged in his bed, he'd said.

Yes, she had replied, wiping away her tears with the back of her hand. He was right, of course. Oh yes, she knew she belonged to him. She needed him. She loved him. Yes, she told him, she would meet him tomorrow for the appointment. Yes, she knew it was for the best.

That was what she had told him yesterday. She had taken the day off today.

In her daylight life, Gina occasionally accompanied Luca when he served morning Mass at Santa Trinita. Today, she knelt wearily in the pew, resting her aching back, her head covered in a veil.

Even on this, the worst day of her life, somehow the ancient church with its votive candles flickering was comforting to her. At the golden altar, dressed in his black and white altar vestments, Luca and another young man moved in unison with the priest as they served low Mass. Gina didn't actually understand the Latin, but something about the timelessness of the Church's great prayer touched her.

What was it she had heard the priest say in the homily, about Santa Anna, the mother of the Virgin? She was apparently the Saint who had charge of unmarried women. And what about unmarried pregnant women, Gina thought, initially without any sense of irony. Then she remembered.

"Santa Anna, pray for me," she whispered, though not with much hope. After all, Gina knew that that day she was bound to betray someone. That much was certain, but who was she to ultimately betray?

Marco? He loved her and needed her. Perhaps in a few years he would be ready for a child. But not this one, not now.

The sisters? They would get their maternity home, whether or not Gina was a part of the plan.

Mrs. White? Gina considered how the American woman had almost forced herself on her. And it wouldn't be Mts. White who would be responsible for raising a child alone, in some godforsaken village someplace in Umbria.

Her family? Though Luigi and Luca would be deeply disappointed, she told herself defensively, after all it wasn't they who would have to endure the pregnancy and the delivery. As for Valeria, her mother would probably be immensely relieved to find that her life could go on as before.

Despite all of this, Gina nevertheless felt cold and bereft. She bent her head in utter misery, the tears welling up despite her frantic efforts to suppress them. The old Church seemed a place out of time and place; just being there released the flood of emotions she'd held tightly in check. Tears coursing down her cheeks, she sobbed silently, her head bent nearly to her lap.

The Mass ended, and Luca appeared beside her, genuflecting before entering the pew. Terrified that her brother would see her distress, Gina bent her head beneath her veil and whispered distractedly that she had to go to the bathroom. Then, before he could catch a glimpse of her tear-stained face, she hastened out, grasping her handbag but inadvertently leaving her smartphone on the seat.

A few minutes later when Gina's smartphone twittered, Luca reached reflexively for it, feeling irritated. Why didn't she put her phone on mute in a holy place?

Luca didn't mean to read the text, but the words glowed in the darkened Baroque church. The text was from Marco. He was waiting, he said, outside the clinic.

When Luca raised his eyes again, he found himself staring into his sister's agonized gaze. Without a word, he handed her the smartphone, stood up abruptly and stumbled out of the pew. He was out the church door in a matter of seconds.

CHAPTER 26

Realizing that he had very little time, Pilar got to work immediately. He stood in the plush hotel suite – a study in muted tones of beige, complete with leather walls – and waited impatiently for his call to go through.

The Miami-based private banker agreed to pass his message along immediately to the right people. A few moments later, the Community's largest client called Pilar personally.

He was grateful for Pilar's warning, of course. Adverse media coverage of the Community, particularly about such sensational matters, was something he didn't like to be blindsided about. When did Pilar expect this would hit the global media?

Very soon, Pilar replied and explained as delicately as possible about the boy in Scotland, and the botched work of the Scottish gangsters.

His client was understandably distressed. What more could possibly go wrong?

Pilar agreed that all of this was quite terrible, and that he himself had no idea how bad things were at headquarters here in Italy until he'd arrived.

Why was he there, the client wanted to know. A holiday? Would he be back in Boston soon?

Pilar sighed. He wished that he could say when, he assured his client. He missed America, he really did. But he'd been brought in on business, and discovered this horrific mess.

His client thanked him profusely for his support; he would now need some time in meditation, he advised Pilar solemnly, in order to understand the correct course of action.

Pilar understood, of course. This meant that the gigantic tide of money would be re-routed through secondary channels as fast as humanly possible – within hours, the spigot will have run dry.

When they hung up, Pilar breathed a sigh of relief. The Head would have a good 48 hours of frantic emails and calls to distract him, now. The broken bank connection in Boston would be way down on his list of worries, what with the global media screaming about homosexual rape, suicide, and poisoning.

Only after he came up for air would he realize that the Community's intravenous funding had been yanked. He would have no access to protection and anyway by then, his clientele would have arranged for his swift and sudden demise.

Next, Pilar dialed the private cell of the most prominent Catholic reporter in America, a man with impeccable liberal credentials who could be counted on to attack conservative Catholic Orders but to look the other way when it came to the Community's deeper secrets. He was, like most Americans, pitifully cheap to bribe.

The reporter would be grateful for the head's up on the breaking story, Pilar was sure. And once he had it on the internet, the flames ignited would be very hard to put out, indeed. The Head would be hamstrung between an angry Vatican and his unforgiving clientele.

His phone call completed, Pilar went in search of the hotel's owner. A quiet cash payment of ten thousand euros would be all that it would take to ensure that there would be no record of him ever staying there.

Then, he could relax and see what this fool of a Bishop had in stock. As the new head of the Community, Pilar would naturally continue the good work of his predecessor in acquiring a seminary far from the intrigues of Rome.

He stepped out into the hallway of the gorgeously-renovated 19th century palazzo, and shut his heavy room door with an almost-inaudible click.

Once upon a time, when he was a schoolboy with innocent faith, Pilar's nuns had taught him about the four last things: death, judgment, heaven and hell.

Like the living embodiments of these Last Four Things, there were four men waiting for Pilar around the hallway corner. They watched as he wrote his suicide note in his elegant longhand, learned from the Catholic sisters in an Order now defunct in Mexico City so many years before.

CHAPTER 27

Luigi was uncomfortable with his wife's conversation, and he showed it by shaking his head insistently as she talked on the phone with the Bishop.

Valeria ignored him. It was clear that the Bishop recognized her good sense in money matters, and as the mother of the first girl to be part of this grand venture, she wanted her say. Though Valeria loved Luigi, she had long ago recognized his limitations in dealing with the real world.

In the last week, working with Luca, Valeria had found herself the go-between the Americans and the Bishop. At first, everything ran smoothly, but in the last few days things had mysteriously slowed down. Papers were not signed; excuses suddenly appeared. Valeria began to be concerned. The date of Luigi's retirement and impending move to Umbria was fast approaching, but the Bishop seemed to be strangely unavailable. Was he pre-occupied with other things?

Luca had explained to his parents that there was some scandal in the news about one of these 'traditional' Orders, apparently one that was planning to open a seminary in the poor Bishop's diocese. Sexual abuse of children, poisoning and all manner of horrors were plastered everywhere in the media.

Valeria made a face and rolled her eyes in the time-honored fashion of the *romani* when confronted with the evils attracted to the Holy See.

"So?" she demanded. "So what does this have to do with us? We have our money ready. The renovators are already working! Gina can't stand on her feet in her job very much longer. What's going on?"

Though the Bishop seemed determined to hide, he was no match for Valeria. She was soon able to report success to Dyson White, with Luca as the interpreter. The palazzo would be ready for moving in that weekend, though renovations would of course continue for several months.

Dyson took the question to his wife.

"The air is fresher, much healthier for Patrick," Dyson argued reasonably. "He needs plenty of rest and good country air right now."

Michelle was unconvinced. Patrick was asleep in his bedroom, still fighting the after-effects of the poisoning. Although the doctors said his youth and good health were in his favor, ever since their return to Rome two weeks before, he'd been listless and apathetic. The only thing that seemed to interest him was the Mass at Trinita Dei Pellegrini, where he was an altar server with Luca.

Stacey was trying mightily to keep Katy and Josh quiet so as not to wake her brother, but with homeschooling it wasn't easy. The apartment was starting to feel cramped; nevertheless, Michelle wasn't ready to move to Umbria.

"I got a bad feeling about that place," she said, standing her ground. They were dividing plants on their terrace, as the welcome rays of spring sun shone down on them.

"What? Why didn't you say so *before*?" Dyson was exasperated.

"I didn't want to believe the feeling and then everything happened with Patrick and we had to go to Scotland and then I was taking care of him and now we're back and I gotta tell ya, I got a *bad feeling* about that place." It all came out in a rush, with Michelle shaking her head stubbornly. "And I'm not the only one. Stacey too. And Father Paul, too."

At the exorcist's name, Dyson stopped.

"What did he say?"

"He told Stacey there was something there," Michelle shivered despite the sunlight, and turned to confront her husband. "Dyson, at least talk to him first?"

Dyson, however, shook his head firmly.

"We can be protected better, there," he said. The Roman apartment, in the midst of the city's teeming life, was too hard to guard. Anyone could slip a bomb into a nearby dumpster.

"From what?" Michelle asked, her eyes narrowing, one hand on her hip.

"From whatever is trying to attack our family," he answered her evenly. The words hung between them, but before Michelle could respond, Stacey suddenly appeared in the doorway.

"It's Benedicta," she said, her face white as snow. "One of the girls in her house has been found dead. They think it's a suicide."

Benedicta wasn't so sure, however.

"Daddy," she said, struggling to keep her voice under control. "This g-girl was a bit strange ever since Patrick, er, got sick. She k-kept crying at odd times. We talked to her, but she kept insisting there was nothing wrong."

The girl's lifeless body had been found in her bed that morning, dead of an apparent overdose of sleeping pills.

"The p-police wanted to know about the pills. W-we don't have anything like that in the house," Benedicta said, her voice starting to waver. "M-maybe she had it with her all this time? She's been with us for a little over two months; she was four months pregnant. C-can I talk to mama now?"

By the time Michelle came to the phone, Benedicta was crying uncontrollably.

"M-mama, I just couldn't tell Daddy this part," she gasped, the sobs coming quickly now. "When the medics lifted up her nightgown, we could see her belly and her breasts. She was tattooed all over like a snake, Mama, it was sooo-ooo gross."

When Michelle finally got off the phone, she turned to Dyson calmly.

"Talk to Father Paul. Maybe all the palazzo needs is a --whatsit? What we did here when we moved in --a 'house blessing'? Sprinkle a ton of holy water all over the place, wave some incense around and everything will be fine."

Dyson sighed, and reached for his *telefonini*.

Father Paul, however, regretted to have to decline, explaining that he didn't have faculties in the Spoleto Diocese. As a member of the staff of the Holy See he had to be very careful about such diplomatic questions. Perhaps the Bishop could be persuaded? Gina's mother Valeria seemed to be on good terms with him – maybe she could ask?

When Luca conveyed the request to his mother, Valeria threw up her hands in exasperation.

"These Americans believe in hocus-pocus?" she asked, shaking her head in disbelief. "I'm embarrassed to put such a request to a modern Bishop. Ridiculous! He will laugh at me!"

Luigi was unsympathetic.

"He's a priest, right? We're buying the place, right? He should just do it," he said, and folded his arms resolutely.

"Yes, Mama," Luca said comfortingly. "Just ask him. He'll do it."

Luigi then said nothing, but simply picked up the Madonnina and left to work in the spring sunshine in his garden. As he walked around the building, he caught sight of Marco smoking outside his shop.

The hairdresser looked at the older man, threw his cigarette in the street and turning on his heel, re-entered his shop without a backward glance.

Luigi sighed, and scratching his head, unlatched the entrance to his garden. As he worked the redolent earth with his trowel, he prayed silently to the Madonnina gazing down at him from her wire cage.

"I renounce my will. I turn it all over to you, Maria Mama Mia, to lay at the feet of your Son. Not my will, but His be done."

CHAPTER 28

The Head was working very hard to soothe his client. They were both great followers of the work of a certain Columbian friar-turned-mystic and therefore spoke a similar language, up to a point.

The conversation was nevertheless a difficult one. Yes, the rape and all of that had happened, but Pilar was now eliminated and if the damned media circus would just stop, they could get back in business. Yes, he admitted, there had been a loose end in Scotland, but that had been cleaned up.

He managed to point out that, in any case, it had been his probity which had set a watch on Patrick's sister in Glasgow, hoping that the boy would turn up there. So far they had been successful. Now the only thing left was to decide about the White boy, and his family. For the moment, the authorities were very far from linking the poisonings in Scotland with the Community, but that wouldn't last forever.

Sooner or later that stupid American billionaire would go to Interpol or the press and the infection would spread. Inevitably, the Community would be implicated, and then the banking transactions would be investigated. The paper trail, expertly laid, would lead right back to every legitimate investment they had made for the client and his associates.

His client was silent for some moments while the Head let the implications of this scenario sink in. When he finally spoke, the client came right to the point.

"What do you need to make this go away?" he inquired casually.

He needed a great deal of money, the Head explained with regret, to ensure such a disaster did not happen. There was only one, regrettable, choice. The White family must be eliminated, completely professionally, with absolutely no chance that it would be traced to the Community. This would require surveillance of the family's every move, and the ability to strike quickly and thoroughly when they were all together.

When they ended their conversation, his client in Brazil sighed heavily. The situation in Italy was spiraling out of control. First the Dean had allowed the White boy to simply walk out of the seminary. Then, there had been the worrying call from Pilar. Now, this. It was apparent that the Head was getting old and sloppy. Clearly, none of this would have happened had he instilled the necessary discipline in his subordinates. No rape. No panic. No publicity. No trouble with the Vatican.

He was also untrustworthy and lacking in judgment. Contracting with Scottish gangsters and troubled pregnant women to do something that professional, high-paid killers could have arranged quickly and cleanly was unforgivably stupid.

The Brazilian shook his head. While he agreed that the White family would have to be eliminated, it was clear that the Head would have to go, too. This would of course be even more expensive, as it would all have to happen at the same time.

He picked up the phone again and rang the Head back.

He had decided, he told him. Of course he agreed with his analysis, and he wanted him to know that the necessary payments would be arranged for.

In Rome, the Head breathed a sigh of relief.

There was only one thing, the Brazilian said. In order to be completely sure this would be the end of it, he needed to ask the Head to be present and to direct the operation personally.

"Yes, of course," the Head said. He was so relieved, he would have agreed to anything, but he couldn't resist the temptation to add one more request to the deal.

"After this is done, I think the time will have come for my retirement," he ventured. After all, this had all been discussed previously, as part of their succession planning.

In Brazil, an ugly grin spread across the client's tanned face.

"Yes, of course," he agreed pleasantly. "That makes complete sense."

Good, the Head told him. He would await contact from the professionals. The family was in Rome, with the single exception of the girl in the Glasgow convent. However, now that the poisoner under her charge had been found dead, the accidental death of the foreign Roman Catholic nun in Scotland would inevitably attract publicity. Even the slow-witted Glasgow police would be bound to make the connection.

Clearly she had to be brought to Rome, the client agreed. Perhaps a special request from the Boston Cardinal would soften the heart of her Mother Superior to permit a family vacation – away from gloomy Glasgow? The Community had always had such excellent relations with the Boston chancellery.

The Head hesitated. Pilar had managed to botch that relationship, too.

"Yes...?" The client waited.

Of course he would contact the Cardinal immediately, the Head lied. Once the girl was in Rome, a simple traffic accident on the *autostrada*, unfortunately very common with tourists inexperienced in the ways of Italian drivers, would eliminate all of their problems.

"Good plan," the client praised him. But perhaps it should wait for the expert touch of the consultants? This was, after all, their forte.

After he hung up the phone, the Brazilian was philosophical. Everything was, in the larger scheme of things, falling into place.

The Head and the Community had been fast becoming redundant, after all.

The Brazilian's daughter had been educated far from the nitty—gritty of her father's business, and at the insistence of his ex-girlfriend, her mother, had been at the very best American boarding schools. Though an indifferent student, she was as beautiful as her mother, an ex-model, had once been and thus made an excellent photo model. She could most often be seen in extreme close-up, a knit cap pulled down over her luxurious hair, luscious lips and upraised arms campaigning for the homosexual rights movement at her American university.

There were international foundations, she'd told her father, who were deeply in need of financing for this very important work. They were not-for-profit organizations, she assured him. Although his daughter was naïve enough to think this a guaranty of their fiscal probity or liquidity, the Brazilian knew better and made discrete but necessary inquiries. Only last week his bankers had assured him that the organizations they'd selected were completely reliable; hence, it would only be a matter of days before the first investment transactions would begin.

His daughter would be delighted with his beneficence and forward-thinking, he reflected with pleasure. And the not-for-profits didn't ask too many embarrassing questions; nor did they get themselves involved with rape and murder like these undisciplined clerics. All in all, it was looking like a most satisfactory option.

Meanwhile, in Rome the Head had just hung up when he looked up to see his very attractive executive assistant waiting anxiously in the doorway.

"It's the Bishop of Spoleto," he announced, with an apologetic grimace.

"Here?" The Head was annoyed.

"I told him you were very busy, but he's quite upset," he replied primly. "I didn't want a scene."

In point of fact, the Bishop had arrived in a state of deep pique and appeared fully capable of making a scene. The discovery of Pilar's suicide the day of his arrival in Spoleto had shaken him badly. The subsequent firestorm of publicity had further undermined his confidence in any prospective deal.

Furthermore, the Bishop had made some inquiries, and had unearthed a raft of uncertainty about the Community. Who were they, really? They had an enormous property in Boston. Were they connected with the Cardinal and if so, how? Determined to get to the bottom of this, he'd reluctantly given his verbal assent –but no written contracts -- to the Americans and driven to Rome personally. He *would* see the Head, and he *would* get some answers.

Unfortunately for him, the Bishop's brief visit with the Head did exactly nothing to allay his fears. The Community's address in a beautifully restored palazzo on the Via Giulia in Rome's *centro storico* was so expensively outfitted that it quite took his breath away. Further, the Head's smooth, mannered conversation left him feeling extremely uneasy.

Yes of course they had always worked closely with the Archdiocese of Boston, and had very cordial relations with this Cardinal. No, they were not aware of any association the Cardinal might have with these American billionaires, and certainly they knew nothing of their real estate interests in Umbria.

A project to house pregnant Italian women? How quixotic. Seemed an odd thing for Americans to be involved in. Was the Bishop aware of the increase in child trafficking happening these days? Oh yes, it seemed that healthy white babies fetched a premium price on the world markets. In any case, the Community was re-thinking its plan for a new seminary now, due to Father Pilar's tragic death. He hoped the Bishop understood.

Twenty minutes later, the Bishop found himself ambling down the Via Giulia in a daze of consternation. None of this made any sense to him. Two days before he had two eager buyers; today one was dead and the other cast under a shadow. Worse, he was feeling somehow guilty for his involvement in any of this. Though logically it made no sense, he couldn't rid himself of this deep unease. What had he done wrong? Moreover, what should he do next?

At that moment, he turned a corner and found himself gazing at the tall, Baroque front of an ancient church, its door open. Obeying a sudden urge to step inside, he noted a cassocked figure stepping into an old-style mahogany confessional. A discrete light clicked on, signaling that the priest within was hearing confessions.

The Bishop was not a regular recipient of what he called the 'Sacrament of Reconciliation.' In this, he was not alone, as most of the laity and almost all of the clergy in his diocese had long since abandoned the Sacrament as unnecessary and old-fashioned. He performed his Easter duty at a nearby abbey, and left it at that.

But today his guilt drove him into that strange confessional, and to his enormous surprise he found himself confessing everything on his conscience to an American priest with excellent Italian. In a torrent of uncertainty, anger and guilt, he unburdened himself completely and then heaved a sigh of relief.

"So, what is it you are guilty of, Your Excellency?" the priest said quietly, after a moment.

"Guilty of?" the Bishop echoed, uncomprehending.

"Yes, where do you think your culpability lies in all of this?"

The Bishop considered for a long moment. All he wanted was to save parishes, and to renovate the bishop's residence. That was his job, wasn't it?

"Why is it that you think Our Lord has entrusted you with the care of souls in your Diocese?" the priest asked, seemingly reading his mind.

A thought, unbidden, came to the Bishop.

"M-my job is to save souls," the Bishop whispered back, slowly. "My job is to support my priests and to help them save souls."

"So, have you been doing that?"

The Bishop was silent. He didn't need an updated bishop's palace to save souls. But he couldn't save souls with closed parishes, could he?

"I think the Devil has been tempting you, but Our Lord took pity on you and has removed a great source of temptation," the priest said.

"Now I only have one buyer," the Bishop whispered.

"Our Lord has given you a clear path, Your Excellency," the priest replied. "You have one buyer, and you have need for those funds, don't you?"

"Y-yes," the Bishop said, sighing. "I need those funds to keep parishes open."

"Yes," the priest said. "So the Holy Sacrifice of the Mass can continue to be offered in your Diocese."

The Bishop frowned at the old-fashioned terminology, but said nothing. He exhaled a long breath, however. His way seemed clear before him.

"Finally, all of this is of course very upsetting but it seems to me you don't have all the information you need, Your Grace," the priest said politely. "Perhaps you should talk with Boston's Cardinal?"

"Thank you, Father," the Bishop said gratefully. "I will do that."

"You are most welcome," the priest said warmly. "Now bow your head and ask for God's grace."

When the Bishop emerged from the confessional a few moments later, he was somewhat disconcerted to see a small congregation arriving for a Mass. He took a seat in the very last row, behind a veiled young woman with golden skin.

From somewhere, a sweet-voiced bell rang, and the celebrant entered, attended by two male altar servers in traditional dress.

The Bishop saw to his great surprise that one of them was the billionaire's son he had last seen in Spoleto.

Inside the confessional, Father Paul Corinth prayed deeply and assiduously for guidance. Around the Bishop -- though thankfully not within him -- he'd sensed the grey haze of evil. If only he could find the strength inside himself to combat this. But he was weak, and he knew it. A minute later, he stood up and prepared to hear Mass.

After Mass, the Bishop was lost in prayer for a few minutes, but looked up just in time to see the other altar server approaching the veiled young woman in front of him. An electronic twittering disturbed his prayers a few minutes later and he looked up again. This time he saw the young woman's stricken face reflected in the smartphone's screen light as the young man stumbled on his hasty way out of the pew, and out the heavy church door.

CHAPTER 29

On Santa Trinita's worn front steps, the Bishop stepped out into the Roman late afternoon, which smelt faintly of the Tiber in early spring. He felt more than a little dazed, given the day's events. After his unexpected confession, hearing the ancient Mass had unsettled and, inexplicably, calmed him. What exactly was going on, he wondered.

Before he had the chance to muse further on this strange state of affairs, he felt a tap on his shoulder. He turned to find himself face to face with the veiled woman, who appeared to be very much in distress. Strangely, there was something quite familiar about her.

Gina didn't actually know what compelled her to approach the kind-faced, gray-haired priest, but when she emerged from the church to find Luca nowhere in sight, something gave way inside her.

"F-Father?" she whispered in a choked voice. "C-can you help me?"

Her eyes were brimming with tears as she searched desperately inside her handbag for a Kleenex. As she rummaged, her smartphone fell to the pavement with a clatter.

"*Signorina?*" the Bishop responded in a concerned, fatherly tone. He bent to retrieve the smartphone. As he straightened, the phone buzzed and a text appeared.

"Where are you, *cara mia?*" it said.

This last text threw Gina into a paroxysm of tears. She sat down hard on the church steps, burying her face in her hands and began to sob helplessly, her breath coming in big, ragged gasps.

The Bishop sighed, looked around and crouched down next to her.

"Why don't you come inside the Church?" he suggested gently.

In her distress, the young woman didn't appear to hear him.

"We can sit inside and figure out what your trouble is," he tried again, attempting to hand her the smartphone.

In response to his offer, Gina cried even harder. She knew what her trouble was, and she knew this priest was not going to help her do what she needed to do. And now her family knew that she was betraying their trust.

The smartphone buzzed and another text appeared. Gina accepted the device, glanced at the text and began to wail afresh. This attracted the attention of some passing tourists, who paused to gawk at the spectacle of a beautiful young woman furiously crying in the uncertain care of a bewildered-looking prelate.

Noting this and suddenly remembering that Roman churches are often locked when not in use, the Bishop stood up quickly to check the church door. As he pushed open the door, he caught sight of the holy water font.

An idea occurred to him.

"*Signorina*," he ventured, his voice quietly soothing as he returned to tap her shoulder. "You need the Lord's help. But first we must drive whatever is bothering you away. Can you hear me, *Signorina*?"

Something in his voice penetrated Gina's distress and she looked up at him.

The Bishop was smiling.

"Can I give you a blessing?" he asked her.

Gina nodded, though she couldn't say why. On the street below, the tourists seemed fascinated.

"Good," he responded, and ignoring the stares of the tourists, raised his right hand, moistened with holy water. "I am therefore blessing you in the name of the Father, and of the Son and of the Holy Spirit."

A minute later, Gina had recovered herself enough to agree to return to the church with the Bishop. Once inside, the Bishop requested that they be allowed to stay for a while inside the closed building. The parish secretary was gracious, and they settled into a back pew for a whispered conversation.

A few minutes later, the Baroque gloom was pierced by the electronic burble of Gina's smartphone. The screen lit up with a Facebook photo of a well-groomed Marco mugging for the camera.

Gina sighed and eyed the Bishop, who extended his hand for the phone. Surprised, she handed it to him. He put it to his ear.

"Pronto. This is the Bishop," he said shortly and then listened. "Yes, she's here with me."

He listened again.

"No, sorry, she can't come to the phone at the moment," he said evenly. "Shall I ask her to call you when she's free?"

A few seconds later Marco rang off abruptly and the Bishop shrugged. He put the phone on mute and turned to Gina.

"I think he's a little upset," he said noncommittally.

"You're the Bishop of Spoleto?" Gina gasped through her tears. "Why, I was just in Umbria and I met you a few weeks ago!"

It was a few moments before the Bishop realized that this was the pregnant girl whose mother he had been negotiating with. Fifteen minutes later, the Bishop had heard the whole story, after which he had just one question.

"So what is the choice you are making?"

Gina considered this.

"I am choosing my life with Marco," she said softly.

He nodded solemnly.

"And what choice must you make to have this life that you want?"

"N-not to have a b-baby."

"And you say Marco has children?"

"Y-yes."

"Tell me, would you tell Marco he would have to kill his children in order to be with you?"

This was too much. Gina began to cry again, and the Bishop handed her a Kleenex.

"I'm sorry, Gina, to be so blunt. But as I understand it, these are exactly the terms that Marco is presenting you with."

Gina nodded, then shook her head and began sobbing anew.

"Y-you're right," she finally managed to say. "I-I know you are right, but..."

"Yes?"

"B-but you don't know Marco. He is not an evil person."

The Bishop sighed.

"Gina, we don't have to 'be' evil to *commit* evil," he said. "We can just be doing what we think is right, what we think is best – especially for us. For our careers. For our peace of mind. For our pocketbooks."

Gina nodded slowly. She looked drained, exhausted.

"Gina, I have a feeling that *you* don't really know Marco," he ventured, and before she could protest, he held up his hand for silence.

"Oh, you know what he has told you about his life. But have you ever spoken to his family? To his wife? How about to the people who work in his salon?"

Gina eyed him apprehensively.

"You want to marry him, right?"

Gina nodded cautiously.

"Well, do you realize that he is already married in the eyes of the Church?" the bishop asked quietly.

"What do you mean?" Gina reacted quickly. "He's got a divorce. He's *divorced*."

The Bishop sighed. Young Italians were so badly catechized that they confused the State with the Church. After a few quick questions to ascertain the status of Marco's marriage, he explained the Church's position to her.

"Marco was married in church. His marriage has not been annulled. This means that in the eyes of the Church, he is still married."

"You're saying that I have been sleeping with a married man. I have been helping him commit adultery?" Gina was incredulous.

"Well, you may not be the first one to have, er, helped him commit adultery," the Bishop explained as kindly as he could. "But the sin is that of fornication. That is, having sex outside of marriage."

Gina sighed heavily.

"So this means that if I have this baby, it will be illegitimate? Can it be baptized?"

The Bishop smiled.

"In the eyes of the Church, no child is 'illegitimate' and of course your baby can be baptized. As for the State, their main concern will be the financial support of the child. But because of the new maternity home, this won't be your problem in the beginning. That is, if you have the baby," he finished portentously.

Gina nodded, thinking hard. So there would be no church wedding. She knew that Marco wouldn't want to bother with an annulment, just to satisfy her.

"Gina," the Bishop's voice was gentle. "There's a lot you don't know. You don't know why Marco left his wife. You don't know how many women he has had since then. You don't know what his financial situation is. How can you marry someone you know so little about?"

Gina sighed. "I suppose you're right. I guess I really should get to know him – I mean, before I marry him."

"So, answer me this – if you don't know enough to marry him, how can you say that you will sacrifice your child for a man you don't really even know?"

Gina nodded slowly, considering this.

"Gina, you want Marco. Marco says he wants you, but only if you abort your child. You would never say such a thing to him, right?"

Gina shook her head.

"You think you want to marry him but you admit that you don't really know him, right?"

Gina nodded.

"Tell me, what do you really know about him? About his character?"

Gina nodded again and sighed.

"I-I know," she began, "that he won't get an annulment. I also know that he doesn't want this baby."

"So what do you think will happen if you have this baby?"

Gina sighed heavily and looked away, unseeing.

"I will lose Marco," she whispered slowly. She knew this for certain.

The Bishop gazed at Gina intently.

"The question you need to answer is *what sort of man are you losing* if you have your baby? And if you don't have your baby, *what sort of man are you trading your baby's life for?*"

Gina nodded sadly and regarded the Bishop.

"The sort of man," she whispered faintly, "who doesn't want what he doesn't want."

"You don't know much about him, but you do know this one thing," the Bishop said.

"Yes," Gina replied slowly as her voice gathered strength. "He is the kind of man who doesn't want me if I have his baby."

The Bishop nodded.

"I don't understand myself," Gina said suddenly, distressed.

The Bishop waited.

"I don't understand why I do these things," she continued, miserably. "One minute I feel one way, and the next minute I feel completely differently. I was so sure that I would have the baby, and then, and then, I missed Marco so much..." Her voice trailed off.

"And you are worried that you will change your mind again?"

Gina sighed dejectedly. "It's an awful thing," she whispered. "I can't actually *trust* myself."

The Bishop sighed.

"And how does this mistrust make you feel?"

"Frightened," Gina admitted slowly. "It's so scary not knowing how I will feel or what I will do. It makes me so angry at myself. Then I feel depressed, and empty. And that just makes me want Marco again, to make the bad feeling go away." A tear began rolling down her cheek, and she sighed heavily.

"This," the Bishop told her, "is completely normal. In fact, it is so normal that it is what we call 'the human condition.'"

Gina looked at him, confused.

"St Paul said it best," he explained. "'*For the good that I would, I do not, but the evil which I would not, I do.*' Sound familiar?"

"R-right," she responded tentatively, looking away. "I know I *want* to do the right thing, but then I do the *wrong* thing."

"What you are experiencing is the effect of sin on our human nature, and it is common to all of us," the Bishop explained seriously. "It's the reason why we need the Church, and her Sacraments. We learn, over time, that on our own we have no power to resist temptation. All of our power to do that, and to do good, comes from God."

"Everyone? You mean that *you* feel this way?" Gina asked him, suddenly, her dark eyes fixed on his countenance.

The Bishop chuckled.

"Where do you think I was, just before this Mass?" he asked her, his eyes twinkling.

Gina shrugged.

"I was in that confessional right there," he indicated. She turned her head to follow his gaze and then turned back to scrutinize his face.

"I was confessing my sins," he told her gently. "I haven't done that in far too long, because like you I thought I was in control. We all slip into this frame of mind, even priests. But then of course I realized I wasn't, and how much I depend on the sacraments. They are like a medicine for our souls – a medication which brings God's grace to us, to strengthen us against temptation.

Gina considered this.

"So you say that all this *agita* that I have, will go away with the sacraments?" she asked, in wonder.

"I am saying that the closer you are to Jesus, in prayer and His sacraments, the more temptations will fade and the surer you will be of yourself, Gina," he said comfortingly.

 A few minutes later Gina and the Bishop emerged from Santa Trinita. Gina was holding a bottle of holy water in her hand as she climbed into the Bishop's car. The Fiat nosed into traffic, bound for Luigi and Valeria's apartment.

On the way, Gina blocked Marco's number.

CHAPTER 30

Colonel Phillip Toffler arrived at the entrance to the White's Roman townhouse with a tremendous bouquet of red roses.

The old Italian concierge, accustomed to the sins and vagaries of men, took one look at the American military man, nodded sagely and lifted the receiver to call upstairs.

His heart in his throat, Phillip disdained the ancient lift, obeyed the adrenaline rushing through his body and bounded up several flights of marble steps. When he arrived on the fifth floor, he found himself face-to-face with his father-in-law.

Dyson held the elegant apartment door open.

"Hello, Phillip," Dyson said cordially, and gestured for him to come in. "Isn't this a surprise?"

"Is Stacey here?" Phillip said eagerly, stepping inside the door and following Dyson obediently into the apartment.

"You just missed her," Dyson said calmly. "She's driven up to Umbria with Michelle, Patrick and the kids."

"Oh," Phillip answered, crestfallen. He gazed around the empty apartment as Dyson stood, arms folded, watching him closely.

"I hope you didn't think those flowers would have much effect on Stacey," Dyson said.

"S-sir?" Phillip was taken aback.

"I said," Dyson repeated carefully, "that I hope you didn't get your hopes up about Stacey."

Phillip felt the quick anger rising inside of him. Who did this old man think he was?

Dyson read this, and adroitly sidestepped the moment by offering his son-in-law a beer.

"W-well, if Stacey isn't here..." Phillip replied, hesitating.

"You have time for a beer," Dyson told him equably. "You've come a long way. Plus, I have a lot to fill you in on."

He popped the cap on the Peroni bottle and handed it to Phillip.

"Have a seat," he said easily. "This may take a while."

Out of the corner of his eye, Phillip saw movement. To his shock, he turned and saw two priests stepping in from the terrace.

Dyson introduced Phillip to Cardinal Portland and Father Corinth. The men all shook hands gravely. The Cardinal accepted a Peroni; the exorcist contented himself with blood orange juice.

"Father Corinth is one of the ten best exorcists in the world," Dyson informed Phillip bluntly.

Phillip's eyebrows rose in surprise, but he said nothing.

"I'm telling you this because we've run into a problem," Dyson said. "And because you are a member of this family and your wife and children are involved, you have a right to know."

At this, Phillip started anxiously.

"They're okay, right?"

Dyson folded his arms and looked steadily at his son-in-law. The effect on Phillip was un-nerving; he shifted uneasily in his seat.

"Phillip, a year ago I might have said that your personal problems would be none of my business."

Phillip reddened, deeply embarrassed. He struggled to maintain control of his facial muscles. Dyson wasn't finished, however.

"But what you've been messing with is illegal, and it's evil. Even if you have no regard for your career, which I doubt, I don't want my daughter or my grand-kids besmirched with your nasty little secret."

Phillip's face was a study in conflicting emotions. He wondered briefly if a fast break for the door was feasible, but then gave up the idea. He would never get Stacey back if he didn't hack through this little drama his father-in-law had arranged.

Or had he? Phillip was enough a military man to think hard about this odd meeting. There was no way Dyson could have known that Phillip had requested emergency leave. Why were these high-ranking prelates in Dyson's apartment?

But Phillip quickly forgot about any questions he might have under the pressure of what turned out to be a thorough, if somewhat brutal, interrogation session conducted by Dyson, with the Cardinal and Father Paul as witnesses.

Was he paying for porn? How many times a day? Chat sessions? Skype sex? How much had he spent? Prostitutes? How often? How old were they?

He'd resisted, of course, pacing angrily around the White's living room. No, no, no, he'd insisted at first, to every question. But the other three men had been calm but immovable. When he looked pleadingly into the eyes of the exorcist, he saw a kind of pity there, but also determination. They were going to get to the bottom of this, today.

Finally, he threw himself in a chair, his eyes reddened with emotion. A lot of the shock had come from hearing himself recount in a monotone what he'd done. He'd spent thousands of dollars that Stacey had no idea about - all on a credit card she didn't know existed. He'd had virtual sex with women from all over the world via Skype before he'd followed his craving for the real thing and found himself in assignations in his car, parked behind massive lorries on the side of rural motorways in England.

How old were the girls? He had tried not to think about it then but now, he guessed they were teenagers. Young teenagers. Possibly no more than fifteen years old. Most were immigrants, though not all. There wasn't any need to speak, really, so it didn't matter. They got down to business quickly, as time was money.

At the time these experiences had temporarily inflated his ego, making him feel lord of all he surveyed. When Stacey or the children had irritated him, he'd let his contempt for them, mere mortals, show. After all, they were there because he'd willed them to be there; they would come or go as *he* wished.

Now, utterly deflated, his swollen pride shrunken to a pinprick, Phillip sat with eyes cast downward as he spoke. When he finally stopped, he didn't look up. The room was silent as his father-in-law regarded him grimly.

The Cardinal stood apart; head bowed, he appeared to be praying.

Father Paul was the first to speak. Did he wish to make a full and formal confession? Of these and any other sins he may have committed?

Yes? This would require a rather long stop in the confessional at Trinita Dei Pellegrini, this evening.

They were all leaving for Umbria, together, first thing in the morning.

CHAPTER 31

It was a nearly four hour journey, but Gina found it interminable. Ever since she'd blocked Marco's phone, time had slowed to a crawl. Fifteen minutes felt like a whole day, and every footstep in the hall outside her family's apartment made her cringe, thinking it must be him, there to confront her.

Luca had been the only one home when the Bishop delivered her to their door. He had declined to stay, begging off because of the traffic and the length of the journey to Spoleto. When the Bishop had taken his leave, Gina turned resolutely to face her brother.

"It's over this time, Luca," she said quietly.

Luca shrugged.

"I mean it," she said, pleadingly.

Luca rolled his eyes and crossed his arms. "Who can believe you?" he said.

Gina sighed. She felt tired, but filled with a fragile peace. "You'll see," she told him with finality, and made for her room, where she picked up her First Communion rosary, and began to pray. Luca ambled into the kitchen disconsolately, where he found the Madonnina perched on the window sill.

"Help us," he whispered softly. The little statue stared at him with unseeing eyes.

Two weeks later, when Luigi, Gina and Luca finally arrived at the palazzo in Umbria, they found that the now-absent workmen had stirred up an angry hive of *vespi* under the eaves of the front entrance.

Unfortunately, this was the only door to which they had a key.

Without a word, Luigi shrugged cheerfully and retreated to the barn, emerging a few minutes later with a short ladder and a can of gasoline. Luca followed him uncertainly; Gina watched suspiciously from the car.

She had not been bothered by Marco since blocking his number, and a few days afterward had received a holy card in the mail from the Bishop of Spoleto. It featured a delicate medieval illumination of Santa Anna, the patroness of unmarried women. The Bishop had recommended that she pray a 54 day novena to the Saint, invoking her intercession on her behalf – and on behalf of the entire project. She tucked the holy card into her purse, and slipped out the apartment door, bound for Trinita Dei Pellegrini and the confessional where she poured out her worry and her temptations before receiving absolution and a deep sense of peace.

Today, as she watched her father clamber up the ladder and with a quick flick of his wrist, nonchalantly douse the hive with gasoline, the first words of the novena formed on her lips.

"*Beata Santa Anna*," she whispered, as to his children's utter shock, Luigi lit a match and threw it in the hive.

The subsequent explosion of spectacular orange flame sent Luigi flying off the stepladder. Shouting, Luca sprang into action, vaulting to catch his father. Father and son fell, sprawling, onto the gravel.

Meanwhile, maddened wasps fleeing the flames shot out in every direction.

Undaunted, Gina threw herself wildly in the direction of her father and brother. Luigi and Luca scrambled to their feet and raced for the protection of the car, only to find Gina collapsed on the ground, her ankle painfully twisted under her.

In a flash, they picked her up and, paying no heed to her remonstrations, raced for the safety of the car. They were all still sitting there, shaken but unharmed, a half hour later when the white Mercedes drove up beside them. Carlo was at the wheel, with Patrick alongside him. Michelle, Stacey and the children were in the back.

The scene they surveyed of the palazzo's facade was a bleak one. The mellow stonework was blackened, the stepladder was overturned and they could smell gasoline. But before the others could pile out, Carlo put up a cautious hand.

"Stay in the car, *per favore*," he said quietly. Patrick subsided impatiently as Carlo opened the car door to investigate. Stacey exchanged an alarmed glance with her mother and put a protective arm over Josh and Katy, shushing their questions.

Carlo's mind was focused on Gina. Despite her coolness to him, if she was hurt, Carlo wanted to be the first one there.

An hour later, he had everything under control. Gina was propped up in a newly-made bed, her swollen ankle somewhat mitigated by ibuprofen. Carlo and Luigi were clearing the debris of dead wasps, and Patrick and Luca were endeavoring to light the palazzo's several wood-burning stoves against the chill of the early spring evening.

Luca stuck his head inside the bedroom door and smiled at his sister. In the time since their exchange after Mass at Santa Trinita, a sudden change had come over Gina. First, he'd noticed her new, lower-heeled shoes. Next, her long frizzy swathes of brassy hair had disappeared, dyed back to her natural, rich brown shade and shaped into a shoulder-length bob. Then, she'd taken to wearing her makeup in a more muted look, which he thought actually flattered her immensely. Finally, just a couple of days before, she'd quit her job.

Now, despite her injury, the young woman who looked up at him from the bed seemed somehow stronger, more resilient. She exuded an unmistakable glow.

"Carlo checked on you yet?" Luca teased her.

"Shut up Luca," she answered mechanically, and stuck her tongue out at him.

"You know, I could send him up here if you want," Luca hinted broadly, dodging and winking as his sister threw a pillow at him.

"Shut UP, Luca!" Gina laughed, despite herself.

Carlo had picked her up out of the car when he'd arrived, and held her all the time in his arms until, once they'd gained entrance into the palazzo, he could lay her safely on the kitchen sofa inside. Then he'd busied himself, making sure he found her a comfortable bed upstairs. He'd carried her gravely up the stairs and once she was safely ensconced, sat by her bedside for a brief moment, shifting uncomfortably in the plain wooden chair.

"You all right?" he'd asked, and she noticed, despite herself, how his eyes were a warm brown; trustworthy eyes, she thought.

"I'm okay," she'd said, looking at him carefully. "*Grazie.*"

Now, she was trying to fend off the ever-watchful Luca.

"You want me to call him?" Luca teased her, grinning broadly. "*Ascolte*, he's right here..."

In response, Gina giggled at her little brother-- a carefree sound, Luca thought. Like she was twelve years old again.

In the kitchen Stacey was stocking groceries and Michelle was beginning dinner preparations. Both were keeping a weather eye out for the children exploring every nook and cranny of the two floors of the 18th century house on the hill. Outside, the long spring dusk was gathering.

"You know, I'll bet Luigi has done that a bunch of times before," Stacey was saying to her mother. "That move with the gasoline must be the standard Italian peasant method of getting rid of wasps' nests."

"Yeah, but still stupid," Michelle grumbled as she chopped garlic. Despite her husband's patient arguments, she still hadn't shaken the 'bad feeling' she'd had about the palazzo. She'd only agreed to come because the Bishop had agreed to bless the houses and the grounds.

"I wonder where he found the gasoline?" Stacey mused. Her own feelings of foreboding about the place had hardly been stilled, though she hadn't discussed them with anyone since their visit weeks before.

"Probably out in the barn, or whatever that is," Michelle answered her, indicating an outbuilding they could see through the back window. "They probably all have extra gasoline around, these Italians."

"Where's Valeria?"

"No idea," Michelle shrugged. "I guess she decided to stay in Rome for the weekend."

"You said the Bishop said he would come tomorrow to bless the place personally?" Stacey asked.

"That's what Valeria told Luca," Michelle replied, her voice betraying her impatience. "And this guy has been waffling all over the place, so who knows? But for sure the nuns will be here soon, because they're the ones who are most eager to get this off the ground. Though of course we can't *call* anyone to find out what's what."

In classic Italian fashion, the promised mobile phone service and internet access had not materialized.

"Look," Stacey admonished her mother practically. "We have electricity. The water heater is on, and the gas stove is working. Speaking of which, I'm going to make sure the kids are washed before dinner."

She turned to leave, only to encounter Luigi standing somewhat sheepishly in the kitchen doorway. Carlo was smiling behind him, holding Gina cradled in his arms. The hairdresser looked tired but pleased as she leaned her head against Carlo's shoulder.

"*Venga*," Michelle beckoned to them with a smile. She handed Luigi a glass of chianti and said in Italian. "Tell everyone to get ready for supper. We're having linguine with truffles, a local specialty."

That night after dinner, Carlo, Luigi and Luca made the rounds of the ground floor windows and doors, checking that all was secure. Patrick, still easily tired, had fallen promptly to sleep in one large bedroom, alongside his exhausted niece and nephew.

"I just feel better knowing Patrick is in there with them," Stacey told her mother and Gina as they prepared for bed down the hall. The three women were in a tall-ceilinged room with a balcony overlooking a stupendous view of the valley below.

Gina nodded drowsily from her narrow bed a few feet from the glow of the wood-burning stove, her ankle propped up on pillows. Despite her mishap, she was surprised to find how content she was. In fact, for the first time in days, time had resumed its normal flow for her. She was idly thinking of Carlo, and his kindness when she fell asleep, lulled by the whispered voices of Michelle and Stacey, finishing the Rosary.

"St Michael the Archangel
Defend us in the day of battle..."

Downstairs, Carlo, Luigi and Luca were in agreement. The palazzo had definitely been used by the Mafia, and fairly recently at that. The windows were fortified with the very best locks and in the basement, Luca had happened upon a cache of almost-empty heavy-duty black plastic bags. Coming up the cellar stairs, he reached into one and withdrew a fistful of dried herbs.

"Marijuana," Carlo sniffed the leaves and peered into the bag. About a half kilo, he estimated. There were about ten empty bags still bearing traces of the stuff.

"You think they used this place for storage?" Luca asked, wide-eyed.

Carlo shrugged and exchanged glances with Luigi.

"This place is too fancy for a storage unit," Luigi said softly, looking around.

Carlo nodded in agreement.

"Looks more like a place for parties," he ventured.

"Should we call the police?" Luca asked.

"Tomorrow, we'll let Dyson and the priests decide," Carlo answered him. In the meantime, he decided grimly, he was going to sleep on the sofa downstairs, just in case.

A half hour later, he fell into an uneasy sleep. He'd said the prayer to St. Michael silently and drifted off, one hand on his Saint Joseph medal on a chain around his neck, the other grasping a baseball bat that Patrick had slipped into the car.

Upstairs, Luigi whispered his prayers to the Madonnina now ensconced on his dresser. In the other bed, Luca crossed himself in the darkness and was instantly asleep.

CHAPTER 32

Sister Mary Benedicta strode through Fiumicino Airport, one hand trailing her rolling suitcase, the other clutching her briefcase. The nonchalance of the Romans at her appearance at first struck her as odd; airports were normally prime territory for nuns in habits to be accosted by strangers.

Most Americans were thrilled at their appearance ("I had sisters just like you in grammar school!"); a few people gave her wild-eyed stares of fright, particularly in atheist Scotland or in America's Bible Belt cities. One man had even attempted to make his confession to Benedicta.

But in the heart of the Catholic Church was the first time she had encountered complete indifference from passersby. Not even the sight of three American nuns in full habits noisily embracing and laughing interested them in the least.

"They've seen it all, the *romani*," laughed Mary Grace as she piloted the nuns' used Fiat Panda past the gigantic statue of Leonardo Da Vinci that stood guard over the airport entrance. The sun was shining brightly on the early spring green fields, and Benedicta felt her spirits soar for the first time in weeks.

"Oh, it's so beautiful here!" she cried. The other sisters agreed, laughing. They were delighted that Mother Superior had broken her normal rule about sisters traveling in pairs to permit Benedicta to fly solo to Rome.

The other nuns were desperately needed in Scotland, as the publicity about the death of the pregnant gang member had had the opposite effect to what they'd expected. Instead of a mass exodus, the sisters' house in Scotland had suddenly been inundated with enquiries from Scotswomen. Some were pregnant. Some were discerning an interest in the sisterhood. All of them required expert fielding.

The increase in traffic and responsibility was such, Mother Superior explained, that a more experienced sister was needed to run the Glasgow house. Plus, Benedicta had had a terrible shock – a "one-two" punch was the way Mother put it. Therefore, she'd thought better of her earlier decision, and was sending Benedicta into the capable care of Mary Grace and Beatrice, who were just about to embark on the launching of the Umbrian house. This, after Benedicta had had some weeks together with her family in the Italian spring sunshine.

Even if Benedicta had wanted to argue, she couldn't. She was simply too tired. And so it was that she'd agreed with alacrity to Mary Grace's plan to surprise her parents with the great news on their arrival at the old palazzo.

"We'll be there in about two hours," Mary Grace said, deftly shifting gears as she merged onto the *autostrada*.

"It's no luxury ride, but this little Fiat is built like a tank," Sister Beatrice informed Benedicta.

"Yeah?" Benedicta said. The little car certainly seemed sturdy to her admittedly inexperienced eye.

"Yep, Fiat has had fifty years of making tough little cars that can survive Italy's roads," Beatrice grinned. "That's why they're doing so well in the Indian and Chinese markets."

"Sister Beatrice has been reading the financial press again," Sister Mary Grace explained drily, as she pointed the Fiat towards Umbria. "Go ahead, ask her about the sovereign debt in Greece."

Mary Grace and Beatrice, however, spent most of the ride listening, as Benedicta had plenty to tell them about the convent mission they had managed for years.

"Mostly," Benedicta finished with a heavy sigh. "I feel so terrible for the women who live with us. They came to us for comfort, for *protection*. And then this, this *poisoning* starts. It's a wonder that they have all stayed with us."

189

"Most of them don't have anywhere to go, except back to the council housing," Mary Grace observed, practically. "To be honest, I'm surprised you have had so much, er, positive response."

Benedicta sighed. "It *is* strange. The police so far haven't discussed any of it, so the media coverage has only been on the pregnant girl. Apparently she was connected with a drug gang member. No one in the house knew her before. I got this from people at the parish. There's been no press coverage about Patrick, thank God."

"Don't take this the wrong way," Beatrice spoke up, grimly. "But I think it's a good thing Mother Prior got you out of there pronto. I can just see the headlines: 'Convicted American Billionaire's Son Poisoned in Glasgow Convent.'"

"Yep," agreed Benedicta, half-humorously. "I can see the sub-head ―'While Visiting His Sister, the Nun.'"

The other nuns smiled, despite themselves.

"For sure," Mary Grace nodded, as she drove the tiny Fiat off the autostrada exit. "And that would just be the start. The media would have field day with this."

"Yeah," Benedicta agreed, slowly. "But the strangest thing is that the Scottish people don't seem to be too, um, 'spooked' by what's happened. In fact, it's brought dozens of them to the convent Mass. Most are just curious, of course. But we're starting to see some of them coming to daily Mass, believe it or not."

"Catholics?" Mary Grace asked.

"Some," replied Benedicta. "And some not, oddly. Many of them are young, raised without any religion, at all."

"Like our whole generation," Beatrice sighed. "Supposed to be free to 'choose for ourselves' when we got older."

"Yeah, well," Mary Grace chuckled, thinking of her mother. "A convent is definitely a surprise choice, right?"

Now the nuns found themselves driving through an early spring landscape of rolling hills, like a Renaissance painting come to life. Everywhere, dazzling yellow-greens set off lavish sprays of white blossoms in flowering pear orchards. Over it all, the sun shone in an azure sky.

"It's *so* beautiful!" Benedicta exclaimed again in delight.

"God is an Italian artist," Mary Grace remarked, smiling. "Let's sing a *Te Deum* to Him, shall we?"

The professional killer watching the Fiat's lone progress on the country highway was momentarily nonplussed to hear the sounds of the Church's great hymn of thanksgiving wafting out of their open windows as the nuns sailed by. His black BMW was parked on the side of the road, stationed on the approach to Spoleto.

He was careful to keep their Fiat at a discreet distance as he followed.

Ahead of him, the nuns prayed a fifteen decade rosary of thanksgiving and supplication, followed by a *Salve Regina* as they came within sight of Spoleto.

CHAPTER 33

"Pop, what are you doing?"

Luca was standing in the grand entrance of the palazzo, arms folded as he watched his father. The spring morning sun was pouring gloriously through the open doorway; just outside, Luigi was intent on sprinkling holy water around the door frame.

Luigi had risen early, as had Carlo. Almost before the sun was up, the two men were silently roaming the house, in tandem. Carlo held a small silver ice bucket of water, following Luigi solemnly from room to room. Every few seconds, Luigi would stop and dip a metal wand into the beaker, withdraw it and fling drops of water around the room. They worked methodically, carefully covering every square inch of the massive palazzo. Bend, dip, withdraw, fling. Intone a prayer, move a few steps and repeat.

"*Benedicta nos,*" Luca heard his father intone. Behind him, Carlo responded in Latin, crossing himself.

Without quite knowing why, Luca crossed himself, too. He shivered then, improbably, in the full spring sun of Umbria. He was aware of something, an air of foreboding, something disturbed.

Perhaps some movement in the periphery of his vision? Luca scanned the wide lawn around the palazzo, behind the figures of his father and Carlo, now intent on sprinkling the gravel driveway in the front of the house.

Was there someone out there, in the trees?

Luca shook himself, deciding it was his over-worked imagination.

"What're they doing?" came a voice from behind him. It was Patrick, nursing a cup of strong black coffee. He looked pale and wary.

"Holy water," Luca replied briefly.

"Looks like they're cleaning out every last little devil that may be hiding around the place," Patrick said, half-joking. "But I thought the Bishop was coming to do that, later today?"

"He is," Luca said shortly. "But maybe they want to be sure, eh?"

"Looks like they're preparing for a siege," Patrick responded.

Luca glanced thoughtfully at Patrick, remembering how it had only been a scant few weeks before that he'd first encountered him in his stylish clothes at the White's apartment. Now, Patrick looked years older, and decades sadder.

"More coffee in the kitchen?" Luca inquired.

Patrick nodded silently, and turning, followed the Italian down the echoing hallway to the back of the house. Outside, Luigi and Carlo moved on to the outbuildings behind the palazzo, stopping at each ground floor window in the palazzo to bless and sprinkle.

The two men standing behind the massive trunks of the trees were careful to remain hidden until everyone was out of sight. Then they, too, quietly retreated back down the drive, successfully completing a key element in the plan. The drone would have precisely accurate information upon which to operate, and the team would have perfect surveillance.

Ensconced in a Spoleto hotel, the Head waited. He was uncomfortable; it was true -- unfamiliar with the modus operandi of his new consultants. At first, the secrecy seemed a bit too cloak-and-dagger to him, though of course he realized quickly that he really had no choice in the matter. He knew he had just a few minutes with the one human being he would ever meet from these 'consultants.' This conversation, unnervingly, would only take place over Skype.

In his hotel room, the image on the screen flickered and wavered, and all at once was there. The Head was somewhat taken aback. The mask on his correspondent's face was complete; the voice disguised by the latest equipment. He could well have taped the interaction, but it would have done him no good.

There was no way he could tell the gender, the age, or indeed anything about the human being he was speaking with about killing at least a half a dozen other human beings.

But despite the bizarre appearance, his correspondent was all business, conducted at a level of refined courtesy. Was everything to his satisfaction at the hotel? Had he slept well?

The Head replied in the affirmative, albeit with a touch of impatience. He understood that he was being given top-drawer service for the top-echelon price they were being paid. But frankly, he wanted this all done with as soon as possible. His Brazilian client had promised that a private jet would be waiting for him at Perugia that very evening. Tonight would be his last night in Italy. Tomorrow his new life began, with a new identity, in Sao Paolo.

But first, this evening, he was given to understand, he was to drive himself to the gate house at the foot of the long drive bordered by an alley of trees which led to the palazzo perched on the brow of the hill. Once there, he would be contacted in person by one of their 'colleagues'.

His role was to be purely supervisory, of course. In fact, to his great relief he learned that it was preferable that he remain in the car to act as a lookout. The job shouldn't take long at all, he was told. They had the element of surprise, and the targets were unarmed. Once everything was complete, he would be instructed to drive up the road, where he would inspect their work to ensure that everything was in order. At that point, he would be free to leave.

Yes, the Head thought to himself. This ordeal would require calm and focus. It was important that he meditate in advance. He retrieved his yoga mat and breathing consciously, slowly and deeply, put himself in a preparatory 'down dog' pose.

CHAPTER 34

Father Paul Corinth was driving the Cardinal's wagon towards Umbria. In the back seat, Dyson gazed wordlessly out the window at the featureless *autostrada* landscape. Phillip Toffler slumped beside him, utterly drained from his experience in the confessional with Father Paul.

He'd been led matter-of-factly through an agonizingly thorough examination of conscience. Had he done *this*? How many times? Had he done *that*? How many times?

More than once he'd had to resist the overwhelming urge to bolt – out of that baroque confessional, out of that ancient church, into the freedom of the streets of Rome. When the urge was upon him, his anxiety skyrocketed, his breath grew short.

On the other side of the grille, Father Paul had recognized the symptoms of a small demon under stress.

"Phillip," he'd said quietly, "you must have courage."

Phillip had been feeling anything but courageous as he battled with his emotions, his knees on the hard wooden kneeler. He was no longer in denial.

It was definitely the nadir of Phillip's life, whispering his many sins to this priest. But he fought the urge to run. He finished his confession sobbing silently, crumpled on his knees, begging the Lord for forgiveness.

And finally, when the words of absolution came in the darkness, he felt a terrible weight lift off his shoulders. As he knelt in the pew to pronounce his penance, Phillip breathed easily for the first time in years. He considered his newly-clean soul, and the Glock strapped to his ankle. Hopping an Air Force flight into Ciampino had obviated the need to travel through civilian body scanners.

On the other side of the confessional screen, as was his custom after hearing a confession, Father Paul had drawn in a deep breath. As he breathed out the memory of the sins that had been his lot to hear and forgive, he nevertheless couldn't shake the feeling that this episode was far from over. He suddenly felt the urgent need for cleansing and strengthening grace, himself.

He walked to the rear of the church where Dyson and the Cardinal were waiting.

"Your Excellency," he said formally and humbly. "Will you hear my confession, now?"

The Cardinal's eyebrow had shot up in surprise, but he assented without hesitation. And after Father Paul left the wooden confessional, Dyson took his place.

Afterwards, they were a bit delayed, due to a call the Cardinal had taken from his executive assistant, Carol, in Boston. Father Paul used the time to review his thoughts.

The day before, he'd felt profound pity for the hapless Phillip under Dyson's withering cross-examination, but could readily see that the demon haunting the Air Force officer had been only slightly put off by his host's public humiliation. It was only in the confessional that morning that the demon had been put to flight, though Corinth also doubted that was permanent. Colonel Phillip Toffler still had quite a personal struggle ahead of him, that much was clear.

Now, as he drove, he glanced at the leonine profile of the large man beside him. Cardinal Portland was praying, clicking through the worn wooden beads of the old rosary his father had left behind when he died. The Cardinal's father had been a daily communicant since his conversion to Catholicism after he'd returned from wartime service. He'd been in the infantry in the Philippines, and was deeply affected by the faith of the people there. In deference to his Protestant mother, Portland had been raised a nominal Presbyterian, but had converted to his father's adopted Faith in college.

Today, the Cardinal would be a formidable foe, Corinth thought, more than a match for your average demon. Paul felt his own inadequacy in sharp contrast. Since settling in Rome again, his own strong points -- intelligence and insightfulness --had come to seem paltry in comparison with the Cardinal's blunt strength. His meeting with the new Pope had gone well, and he was preparing his teaching agenda for the following semester. He had no idea who would be under his tutelage; all he knew was that the Holy See was making quiet inquiries in dioceses around the world.

Left to his own devices, Corinth had used the time to tour the lesser-known churches of Rome on his own. As he walked the city sidewalks, he'd felt an odd loneliness descend upon him. Moreover, from somewhere in his consciousness, a kind of niggling doubt arose. Whatever the Pope might have in mind for him, was he actually prepared? More to the point, was he *strong enough*?

In response, Corinth doubled-down on his prayer routine, and as the days and weeks passed, somehow found himself more and more drawn into the Cardinal's plan for a maternity home. Also, upon meeting them at that unplanned *pranzo* in their apartment with Carlo, he'd found that he trusted Dyson and Michelle White. They were down-to-earth people, the kind who could weather great storms with resolve and faith. He had been deeply impressed by Dyson's lucid analysis of the desperate situation of Italy's younger generation. So, when he'd met Gina and her family that day, he'd gladly agreed to accompany them all on the tour of the palazzo.

It had only taken a couple of weeks more in Rome for him to see that what had at first seemed like a pet project for a billionaire's passing charitable impulses was in fact an important stake in the future. He knew the Sisters in Boston; they would be perfect to staff this foundation.

He'd therefore agreed to meet the Cardinal at the White's apartment the day before to discuss the fine points of the palazzo real estate deal. It was while they were there, enjoying the view from the apartment's terrace, that they'd received news of Pilar's suicide.

Naturally, the Italian media was full of speculation about the Community.

The Cardinal, too, was thinking about Pilar and the Community. That the Mexican priest had been a sexual predator, the Cardinal had no doubt.

"What do you think Pilar was doing in Italy – and in Spoleto, of all places?" he suddenly asked the men in the car, breaking the ruminative silence.

"I think," Dyson responded. "No, actually I am *sure* that he was the mysterious rival bidder for the palazzo."

"Maybe," Father Paul said slowly, "but for what use? What would the Community want with a palazzo in the middle of nowhere?"

The Cardinal said reflexively that he didn't want to speculate, but after the call from Carol he was certain that it had something to do with the broken bank connection in Boston. After her branch audit revealed the cash being accepted and millions being transferred through the Archdiocese's accounts to fund offshore accounts, the new manager had contacted the bank's fraud unit. They, in turn, had gone to the FBI, who today had arrived, unannounced, at Carol's door.

For his part, Corinth had not formulated his thoughts yet, and was hesitant to say that he had a bad feeling about the Community, and an even worse feeling about that palazzo. On the day of their walk-through weeks before, all of his senses had been engaged, and not in a good way.

First there had been the invisible grey mist that he knew signaled the lingering presence of evil – visible to him from a distance. Once in the palazzo itself, he'd had the sense of bone-chilling cold, with occasional sharp pains glancing his eyes. By the time their tour was finished, Corinth was convinced: something evil -- past, present or future – was associated with that place.

Immediately after arriving back at his flat in Rome, however, he'd come down with a bad flu. A few days later, on the mend with antibiotics, he had to admit that he wasn't so sure about the source of his uneasy feelings on the Umbrian hilltop. It had probably just been the effects of the flu, he told himself sternly. But still, there was this lingering doubt, this sense of weakness within himself.

By the time the four men neared the Umbrian border, Corinth had himself half-convinced that the palazzo was in all likelihood a perfectly fine place.

Meanwhile, the Cardinal, deep in contemplation beside him, was thinking about his father. He remembered the conversation they'd had – could it have been 50 years before? The vision of his father rose, unbidden, before him and he heard, once again, the old man's voice.

"The Filipino priest had just given us the information we needed," the elder Portland had told him that time when he was home from university, "when the lookouts outside the church gave us the high sign that the Japs were on their way in. I managed to hide under a pew in the choir loft, just lay there, scared to death."

The Cardinal looked out the car window, remembering how his father's eyes had watered.

"They tortured him, and we couldn't do nothing," the words had come out, tersely. "We had the info we needed, we couldn't be discovered."

The Cardinal let out a sigh. He thought about how all his life, his father had been a daily communicant, and how very happy he'd been when his son, too, had become a Catholic. He gazed unseeingly out the window at the gathering dusk in the Italian countryside and sent a private petition to his dad, dead these many years.

"Pray for us, Pop," he prayed silently, with an intensity he had rarely felt in his whole, long life.

CHAPTER 35

As the long spring evening approached, Luigi strolled among the mature olive trees off the white road leading to the palazzo's gatehouse. The years in Rome had fallen away easily in the last twenty-four hours as he once more breathed the country air, so like that of his youth in the Abruzzi forty years before.

Though he was tired from the day's exertions, Luigi was satisfied and at peace. The entire palazzo and all of the outbuildings had been painstakingly cleansed of whatever evil it had been within his limited powers to address. Carlo had followed him mutely, carrying the little silver ice bucket filled with blessed water, wordlessly watching Luigi's every move with an air of respectful reverence.

At the end of their exertions, when they had finished blessing the barn, Luigi had turned to Carlo.

"Leave the holy water on the ledge. Take the salt and throw the rest around in here," he instructed, and Carlo carefully did as he was told, sprinkling the barn floor with the blessed crystals. As the older man watched him, Carlo thought suddenly that he'd never felt quite so happy in his entire life.

Patrick had kept silent about Carlo's role in spiriting him away to Scotland, thereby saving his beloved job with the White's. And lovely, golden Gina seemed to silently acquiesce to the uncertain court he was paying her. Up until the night before, he'd always maintained a respectful physical distance, his eyes alone communicating his feelings for her.

"That's good," Luigi told him, afterwards. "Now, you better get inside and look after the women."

Carlo wasn't sure, but it seemed to him that the taciturn Luigi's eye cast a conspiratorial gleam his way as he passed the Madonnina perched on the barn shelf. Half in response, Carlo suddenly stopped, crossed himself and touched the statue's base. When he turned to look at Luigi, the older man nodded gravely, hands folded reverently before him. Quietly elated, Carlo took himself off to the house.

Now, Luigi leaned on his walking stick, his rough hand carefully examining the silvery leaves and budding fruit on the branch nearest him. He'd learned the care and feeding of olive trees long ago as a boy. He reflected that it had been a twig like this that the dove had brought back to Noah, signaling the appearance of dry land again after the Great Flood.

Neither the driver nor the passenger of the black BMW that swept past him on the white road ever saw him, so much a part of the landscape did Luigi seem. They were intent on their assignment, adrenaline pumping, bloodstreams loaded with Ritalin for concentration. They were the advance guard, there to take up their positions behind the outbuildings and await further orders.

Luigi watched the BMW speed past the entrance to the gatehouse and disappear from sight around a wooded curve. A few minutes later he saw the two men outfitted in the latest hiking gear with large pack frames on their backs steal softly, most-un-hiker-like, back up the road. The clean-shaven one looked Italian, but the other had the look of the desert, bearded and tanned. The two conferred for a moment and then each went their separate ways, melting into the tree line that framed the expansive open fields around the palazzo.

Luigi took cover behind a thick, gnarled ancient olive trunk and considered what he had seen. Mafia returning? For what? And why such secrecy? What did they want in that house?

Luigi and Carlo had combed the place from top to bottom that day and had found nothing of value or interest. The leftover marijuana was not enough to justify a house invasion – if that's what they were up to.

A few seconds later, a battered Fiat drove up and he hailed it, climbing in quickly with the sisters, who were delighted to give him a lift up the hill to their new home.

"Wow!" Sister Benedicta let out a whoop as the palazzo came into view beyond the elegant alley of trees. "Wowee!"

The other nuns laughed in delight as the Fiat rumbled up the gravel road, and despite his worry, Luigi contemplated their shining faces with satisfaction. What evil could possibly come to a place with such good nuns in it? There was probably some explanation for the hikers' odd behavior. In any case, they were nowhere to be seen over the broad lawns that encircled the palazzo as they drove up.

Nevertheless, when they arrived at the top of the hill, he jumped out of the Fiat and used sign language to indicate that he had some work to do in the barn. The sisters were too busy exclaiming over the beauty of the place to pay him much attention, and soon the front door opened and out poured the others.

Luigi used this as an excuse to steal out of sight around the building. Mostly, he was thinking of the Madonnina; for some reason, he needed to be sure she was secure.

As he glanced over at the enthusiastic greetings being exchanged, however, Luigi noticed an ivory dust cloud – the telltale sign of another car on the white road below. From his vantage point, it looked exactly like the BMW that had disgorged the mysterious hikers not a half hour before.

He sighed and turned on his heel. He must consult the Madonnina.

Down below in the second car, the driver was following his SatNav to the location it had been instructed to take him to. The Head was to park at the foot of the long drive to the palazzo, behind the empty gatehouse on the gravel driveway. There he would be well-hidden until he received the call to come and inspect the consultants' handiwork.

The Head parked the big German car and noticed that his breathing was shallow and ragged. This wouldn't do at all, he told himself sternly, and began in-place breathing exercises to control his stress.

High above him, a light camera drone hovered, all but invisible in the darkening evening sky.

Meanwhile, after the Cardinal's Ford Focus turned off the autostrada onto the country highway, another black BMW swung out of a side road at a safe distance behind them.

The team leader's phone twittered discretely and he answered it in clipped tones. While he'd been waiting for the Cardinal's car, he'd been monitoring events on his laptop. The drone camera was working perfectly; it had obeyed his every direction.

Nevertheless, he wasn't happy.

The plan had been to execute the kills in small groups, easily controlled by two gunmen. The first group in the palazzo was to have been dead by the time the second group – the nuns – arrived. Two of the three nuns would then have been promptly taken outside and dispatched, leaving only Benedicta as live bait to draw her father and her brother-in-law inside.

Unfortunately, there were also a middle-aged priest accompanying Dyson and Phillip, but the plan could easily accommodate additions to the kill list. In fact, more dead bodies meant a higher invoice that could be submitted to Brazil.

This, though unexpected, was not a problem.

There *was* something odd afoot, however. For some reason, just before they turned onto the white road leading to the gatehouse, the nuns had been temporarily lost from the sight of the gunman assigned to follow them. They had rounded a bend in the road ahead of him and when he arrived at the same spot, their Fiat was nowhere in sight.

For more than twenty minutes, the panicked driver searched frantically, checking every side road he passed, but to no avail. It was the drone high over the palazzo that spotted the nuns' Fiat coming up the white road, and though it was momentarily hidden behind an olive grove at the foot of the hill, it was never lost to sight again.

The hapless gunman would be twenty minutes delayed in arriving at the palazzo. By that time the Cardinal's Ford would have arrived, followed by his deadly escort.

The team leader cursed and thought hard. The kill would have to take place all at once -- a plan he greatly disliked because the potential for chaos posed unacceptable risks. He had just two gunmen on site -- 'hikers' hidden on the periphery. The third was hopelessly late and the fourth was on time. The fifth, assigned to monitor the Head at the foot of the hill, couldn't be spared.

A massacre of everyone in that house, all at once, with two gunmen stationed outside to intercept any fleeing victims was too risky. Desperate people do desperate things, and the chaos would be hard to control. No, it would be better to take them outside one at a time, under some pretense.

The team leader strapped on his detonator jacket, and stepped out into the spring evening air as the Tuscan sun sank in the west. He had a brilliant idea – perfect for murdering Catholics.

CHAPTER 36

Stepping from the train platform at Spoleto, Valeria was feeling irritable. The journey from Rome had been dogged with numerous unexplained delays, par for the course with Trenitalia. If this is what she had to look forward to on future weekends visiting Luigi and Gina, she was not going to be happy. She was over two hours late, and it was already almost dark.

A few minutes later, she was a bit overawed to find herself ensconced in the passenger seat of the Bishop's car in Friday night traffic. Once free of the provincial traffic snarl, he pointed it towards the country road that would take them to the palazzo.

She had been unable to contact Luigi or her kids, Valeria explained apologetically.

The Bishop nodded understandingly. He couldn't contact Mrs. White either, he told her. Probably to do with a delay in the telecommunications being set up. But he had promised Mr. White that he would be there to bless the house that very evening, and he would be as good as his word.

"Ah, si," Valeria said, somewhat doubtfully. She glanced sidelong at the Bishop's placid profile.

Sensing her hesitation, the Bishop smiled broadly.

"Probably been a long time since you've been to a house blessing, si?" he asked good-naturedly.

Valeria's eyes widened in disbelief.

"I should say so!" she exclaimed with a gesture indicating the futility of arguing common sense with foreigners.

The Bishop chuckled.

"Ah, but a little holy water never killed anyone, right?" he smiled.

Valeria shook her head.

"These are modern times!" she ventured, eyes rolling for emphasis. "I can't believe these rich Americans actually want the palazzo blessed. I think it's a bit strange, is all."

The Bishop shrugged, still smiling.

"And the Mass in Latin that they all love so much!" she exclaimed with a derisive smile. "With all the incense and stuff I haven't seen since I was a girl! Now they even got my Luigi, and Gina and even Luca, going. What is this about?"

The Bishop sighed. A week before, he would have agreed with Valeria. Even now, he didn't exactly disagree.

But that was before Pilar's suicide, and the unsavory interview he'd had with the Head. And even though he had not gotten entangled with them, he was wise enough to acknowledge that fact with relief. He knew now that it had been a close call.

He'd also had time to think after that fateful confession in Santa Trinita Dei Pellegrini, followed by his first experience of low Mass in Latin. He'd watched the priest carefully, thinking how so very different the preparations must be to celebrate such a Mass. No need to worry about the choreography of untrained altar servers, or whether the Eucharistic Ministers were speaking to each other, or indeed what to say in a homily.

No, this Mass was completely different. The priest and his altar server seemed to move as one, strangely anonymous in their ornate vestments. Their personalities, in fact, seemed beside the point. Furthermore, everything –gestures, words, movements – seemed to convey that these two men were in fact indifferent to the existence of the congregation.

At first, he'd reacted with instinctive disapproval to this, but as the Mass wore on, he began to take notice of an altogether different atmosphere in the church. It was as if all of them – priest, server and laity – were focused on something happening at the altar. Something that stood outside of the here and now, apart from this time and this place.

To his amazement, the Bishop found himself gazing, spellbound, as the Holy Sacrifice of the Mass took place on the altar before him. He felt it as a gift, in fact, and soon found himself kneeling at the altar rail with everyone else, waiting to receive Communion on the tongue.

It was a profoundly humbling experience, and one he hadn't quite understood yet. All he knew was that when he stood up after that Mass had ended, he was in a completely different frame of mind.

His confusion and his fear were gone. In their place was calm and focus. This was what had enabled him to counsel the distraught Gina, who miraculously had been delivered into his care.

And from that day forward, he knew. He was the Bishop of Spoleto. His mission was to save souls, support his priests and administer the sacraments. He would return to Spoleto and do exactly that.

Now in his car, he and the girl's mother, Valeria were approaching the area around the palazzo; he wondered if she had had any inkling that her daughter had very nearly aborted the child she was carrying. It was a dark night, and his headlights illuminated the limestone dust on the white road. From their distance, the palazzo was the only house visible, a shining white structure on a faraway hill.

CHAPTER 37

It was Luca who heard the knock as he passed the front door on his way to the kitchen where the household was gathered to welcome the newly-arrived nuns. Expecting Dyson and the American prelates, he was somewhat taken aback to find two stylish Italian hikers smiling sheepishly in the palazzo's doorway. They looked to be about his age, with expensive gear. One, more taciturn than the other, was fashionably bearded and deeply tanned.

"Sorry, very sorry," said the clean-shaven hiker, indicating his IPhone. "I have no signal on this, and we are lost."

"Of course," Luca said politely. "What are you looking for?"

"Localita Petrognano?" the other hiker answered. "It's around here someplace, do you know it?"

Before Luca could answer, Michelle appeared in the doorway, wiping her hands on a kitchen towel. "What is it?"

The hikers shrugged apologetically.

"They're lost." Luca explained in English about the lack of mobile phone service.

"Yeah, we know all about that," said Stacey, who had joined them at the door.

"Well, do they want to look at our map?" Michelle asked, noting their stylish appearance with approval. "I have one in the kitchen."

Soon, they were in the midst of the chattering group assembled around the farmhouse kitchen table. Within minutes, the kitchen was the scene of a cheerful discourse in broken English and Italian as everyone offered their advice as they pored over the unfamiliar map. On the corner sofa, Stacey's children merely glanced at the hikers with brief interest before returning to their Disney film.

"Do you mind if I use your bathroom?" The tanned hiker asked politely in accented Italian; he was promptly directed to one in the back of the house. The lively discussion carried on in the kitchen.

"Hello?" Dyson's voice suddenly intruded from the front hall. He appeared in the doorway, followed in short order by the Cardinal, Father Paul and lastly, a chastened Phillip Toffler.

"DADDY!!!" Katy and Josh screamed and were across the kitchen in seconds, throwing themselves into their father's arms with abandon. Phil crouched down and embraced them fiercely, then looked up at Stacey. He was greatly embarrassed to find that there were sudden tears starting in his eyes.

For her part, Stacey said nothing. She looked away, her face a mask.

Luckily, the merry noise around them covered up their awkward reunion. Laughter and greetings were exchanged all around; Michelle especially was loudly declaiming her delight, embracing Sister Benedicta gleefully. The other nuns were laughing and shaking hands heartily with the Cardinal and Father Paul.

The joyous hubbub was such that no one noticed the front door opening again, or heard the soft tread of boots on the marble floors.

In a heartbeat, the team leader was suddenly in their midst -- a stocky, 40-ish Italian wearing what looked to Phillip was a detonator vest. His face was covered by a black balaclava. In his arms was an automatic machine gun, a Kalashnikov, favored by terrorists for its lightweight efficiency as a killing machine.

It all happened so fast. In seconds, the bearded hiker had emerged from the back of the house, similarly armed. He silently

211

handed a Kalashnikov to the pale hiker, who took up a position standing in the middle of the kitchen.

"Wh-what is this?" Michelle demanded. She clung to Dyson, who stood very still, stunned. Stacey pushed the children quickly behind Philip. As the realization of what was happening took hold, Gina began to whimper. Carlo quietly took her in his arms. The nuns moved together as a single unit, instinctively feeling for the rosary beads slung onto their belts.

For their part, the Cardinal and Father Paul stood perfectly still, watching the gunmen carefully. It was Patrick who moved quickly – too quickly – for the door.

But to no avail.

"HALT!" The team leader shouted at the boy in a loud, stentorian voice. Patrick stopped in his tracks and put his hands up. Michelle screamed her son's name. Katy and Josh promptly burst into frightened tears.

"SILENCE!!" The team leader roared. Both Phillip and Stacey crouched down in an attempt to hush the children. Gina buried her face in Carlo's shoulder, biting hard on her index finger to keep from screaming.

"What do you want?" The Cardinal spoke up finally. His voice was steady as he stepped up and stood immediately before the team leader.

"Now," the team leader spoke in a matter-of-fact way, ignoring the prelate and addressing his words to the entire group. "No one will be hurt if you each listen carefully to instructions, and do as you are told."

"What instructions?" The Cardinal was not cowed. "Who are you? What are you doing here? I..."

"...SILENCE!" The team leader cut him off.

The Cardinal stood his ground, but did not speak again. He folded his arms gravely, and waited.

"You," The team leader intoned menacingly, pointing to the Cardinal with his Kalashnikov. "You will be the first to do as I say. You will follow my colleague outside, where he will prepare you for your sacred office..."

"...what are you talking about?" The Cardinal waited, unmoved, for a response.

"I am talking about your ability to forgive sins, of course," the team leader sneered. "We are civilized people. We will permit you to hear the confessions of everyone present..."

"...and why am I to do that?" The Cardinal enquired, one eyebrow raised.

"SHUT THE FUCK UP!" The team leader screamed at him. The entire room drew in a sharp, shocked breath. Katy and Josh started to wail again, this time impervious to their parents' attempts to shush them.

"Do as I say," hissed the team leader through clenched teeth, and then pointed to his detonator vest with a grin, "or you will not have the chance to ask any more stupid questions. I will hear not one more word from any of you. Take him!" he barked, pointing the muzzle of the Kalashnikov at the Cardinal.

The bearded hiker stepped forward and grabbing the Cardinal roughly by the arm, propelled him across the room and out the back door, past the outstretched hands of a stricken Father Paul. There was a terrified silence in the rest of the room, broken occasionally by the sobs of the children. The other hiker kept his gun trained on the occupants.

"Now, you will prepare yourselves for your final confession," the team leader said, with a tight smile. "Outside, with a Prince of the Church..."

His words were drowned out by the sound of a thunderous explosion coming from the front of the house. Astonished, the entire group gaped as a tower of fire erupted, filling the kitchen windows with a solid wall of searing flame.

CHAPTER 38

In a flash the team leader had bolted for the front door, staring in disbelief as four meter high roaring flames engulfed the gleaming new BMW 7 series he'd parked there not five minutes before.

This was all the distraction that Phillip Toffler needed.

Fifteen years of combat training kicked in, and he moved with the compact speed that comes from long practice. In one movement, he shoved his children into their mother's arms with a grunt.

Then he sprang into action. Yanking his concealed Glock from under his pants leg, Phillip abruptly opened fire at short range on the pale hiker guarding the back door.

Terrified, Stacey instinctively pressed Katy and Josh to the floor, throwing herself on top of them. The nuns, praying aloud as one, stepped in front of Gina and Carlo.

Dyson took a screaming Michelle into his arms and dove for cover. "Get down, man!" he yelled at Father Paul, who stood as still as a statue in the midst of the chaos, seemingly too shocked to move.

Even as the hiker slumped to the floor, dead, Phillip was running past him, headed out the back door. Patrick was close on his heels.

For Father Paul, time seemed suddenly to slow from the moment the team leader appeared in the kitchen. As events unfolded around him, he felt as if he was standing apart from reality. Nevertheless, he was deeply conscious of his ragged breathing, and he could smell his own weakness, shock and fear. But his training kicked in, too, and he silently began the Prayer to Saint Michael, the warrior archangel, desperately appealing for strength.

Beside Father Paul, Luca stood perfectly still, heart beating loudly, mesmerized by the wall of flame outside. As the pungent reek of gasoline fumes flooded the house, he was certain that the car torching was Luigi's work.

Out back, the explosion of flame had momentarily distracted the bearded hiker, who had the Cardinal in his iron grip as they crouched in the barn doorway. Seconds later, Phillip appeared at the edge of the palazzo's back door, wielding the Kalashnikov he had taken from the dead gunman inside. Beside him, Patrick gripped his brother-in-law's Glock awkwardly. They were both breathing heavily, and despite the cold spring night, sweating heavily. They peered wildly about in the twilight, trying to locate the Cardinal.

From the shelter of the barn door, the bearded hiker carefully raised the muzzle of his machine gun and took aim, softly uttering a curse.

Momentarily loosed from his captor's grip, the Cardinal had milliseconds to act. As the hiker took deadly aim, he suddenly leapt up, lunging for the machine gun with all his might. The ensuing struggle provided a perfect opening for Phillip, who took expert aim at the hiker's exposed back.

Inside, in the midst of the screaming chaos, Sister Beatrice was trying to concentrate. Outwardly intoning the rosary with her fellow sisters, she was nevertheless thinking quickly. Whoever and whatever these men were, she was certain that they weren't terrorists on a suicide mission. That 'bomb jacket' the team leader was wearing would have been detonated by now, she told herself. No, there was something else going on.

In front of the palazzo, the team leader had recovered sufficiently to bark instructions at the gunman who had been following the nuns. Neither of them saw the dark figure of Luigi as he melted silently into the dusky shadows, just outside the range of the light from the flames rising from the torched BMW.

The Italian moved slowly and carefully to avoid making a sound. He was on his way to the rear of the house.

"Is he dead?" Patrick said to Phillip, his voice a strangled whisper. They were bent over the Cardinal, who was crumpled in the barn doorway. A few feet away, the bearded hiker was most certainly dead; Phillip's bullets had caught him full in the back.

"Nah, he's still breathing," Phillip replied curtly, as he gingerly examined the unconscious Cardinal, who had taken at least one bullet in the belly. A second later they were both profoundly shaken when Luigi suddenly appeared beside them, gasoline can in hand.

"Stop!!" Patrick cried, catching Phillip's arm as he instinctively took point blank aim at the Italian. "Stop! That's Gina's dad!"

Terrified, Luigi's eyes bulged, but he stood perfectly still. As Phillip slowly lowered the muzzle of the gun, the Italian exhaled and crossed himself. The *Madonnina* was watching out for him.

Meanwhile, Phillip and Patrick both surveyed Luigi's can of gasoline. Phillip broke out into a rueful grin.

"Crafty old bugger," he snorted briefly.

A brief volley of whispered Italian ensued.

"He says you need to go up the fire escape," Patrick translated quickly, "and wait until you hear breaking glass."

"Yeah?" Phillip replied sardonically. "And what's he going to do meanwhile? Torch another car?"

Another hurried exchange of whispered Italian.

"He says he doesn't know who these guys are, but possibly Mafia. Whatever they are, he says we got to take the Cardinal inside the barn. You need to wait for him inside."

"Can't leave the Cardinal alone..." Phillip said stubbornly.

More Italian, this time more vehemently pronounced.

"He wants me to stay with the Cardinal," Patrick whispered, finally, looking unhappy.

"Now *that* I agree with," Phillip replied and nodded emphatically at Luigi, who smiled briefly. Then he pointed to the second floor of the palazzo with an urgent nod.

Phillip looked doubtfully at Patrick.

"You gonna be okay, kid?"

"I'll be fine," Patrick said, squaring his shoulders and glancing meaningfully at the Glock.

"Right," Phillip grunted, "let me show you how to work that thing."

Minutes later, hoping that Patrick knew the basics, Phillip took his leave. He was up the fire escape and through an expertly-broken window in seconds.

Luigi and Patrick gingerly carried Portland, who was bleeding heavily from his stomach wound, into the barn. They laid him carefully on some clean hay, his head cradled in Patrick's lap.

"L-Luigi, do you know what's going on here?" As the reality of the situation began to sink in, Patrick's youthful bravado started to wear thin. "What'll I do if he wakes up?" he whispered in broken Italian. He looked young and desperate.

As he prepared to leave, Luigi gazed at the young American and the fallen Cardinal. He thought he'd never felt such fear in his life.

Madonnina, he prayed silently and grimly, *come to my aid. Madonna del soccorso.*

"You pray," Luigi told the boy grimly, and patted him on the shoulder. "And then you shoot anyone who comes near."

CHAPTER 39

"W-who are they?" Sister Benedicta managed to gasp out. She was gray with shock, and clung to Beatrice and Mary Grace for support in the shifting chaos that reigned in the palazzo kitchen. Nearby, Dyson was attempting to calm Michelle, Stacey and the children. Luca and Fr Paul Corinth appeared to be frozen statues. The nuns and Carlo were all huddled protectively around a gasping, weeping Gina.

"I dunno, but it looks like the boss is back," Sister Beatrice whispered grimly. "And he's got reinforcements."

The entire panicked group looked up to see the team leader return, striding arrogantly into the kitchen. He was followed deferentially by a gunman, the sisters' stalker, newly arrived.

The team leader was in a cold rage.

He swiftly surveyed the kitchen and its cowering occupants while his men fanned out, guns at the ready. To his deep shock, he beheld the clean-shaven hiker lying dead against the wall, his weapon gone.

"Who the *fuck* did this?" he said, his voice an unnaturally low whisper. With a cold, curt nod, he ordered one gunman out the back door to investigate.

Then, he whirled on his terrified captives, his eyes sweeping over the kitchen.

"WHO DID THIS?!" he shrieked suddenly. His high-pitched scream echoed loudly through the nearly-empty rooms, shocking everyone. The children began to whimper. "You gonna TALK, or WHAT?"

"YOU shut up!" It was Katy, her defiant childish voice piping above the terrified silence of the others. "YOU go away!"

The team leader's eyes swiftly came to rest on the girl. Before anyone could move, he lunged the few feet between them and snatched her roughly from her mother's grasp.

"NO!!!" Like a tigress, Stacey leapt forward, heedless of the danger. The gunman casually blocked her; a well-aimed kick with a steel-toed boot caught her full in the small of her back. She went sprawling onto the hard kitchen floor. The others gaped, unable to comprehend what was happening to her, or to them.

Only Father Paul Corinth, seeing everything in slow motion, detected the slight movement outside the rear-facing kitchen window, in his peripheral vision. It was Luigi. With an effort, he kept his eyes glued on team leader, and continued his intensive internal prayer.

"Mommy!!!" Katy cried, but to no avail. In a flash, the team leader had the child painfully pinioned against him, his gun held to her chestnut hair. He looked up with a sneer at the horror-stricken captives.

"Okay, so NOW is somebody gonna talk?"

Before anyone could speak, a violent crash of breaking glass smashed into the room. A hail of glinting window shards exploded behind the second gunman, who slumped to the palazzo's kitchen floor. A few feet away from him, dead center in a blossom of broken glass, lay the well-aimed Madonnina.

Simultaneously, every captive in the room dove for cover, except Sister Beatrice. With a silent prayer, the doughty nun seized her opportunity. Grabbing a burning log from the wood stove beside her with a single, deft stroke, Beatrice thrust it at their tormentor. The glowing embers caught the team leader full in the face, though just short of the nun's goal -- his unprotected eyes.

The team leader's balaclava, however, shielded him. Enraged, he released Katy and struck back blindly but viciously at the nun, catching her in the head with the butt end of his Kalashnikov. Katy nimbly darted away, but Sister Beatrice went down moaning.

Sister Mary Grace instinctively raced to help her. Abruptly, she felt a rough restraining hand on her shoulder.

"OUT!!" a man's voice roared in her ear. With a start, she realized it was Father Paul. "GET OUT OF HERE NOW!"

With this, Corinth snatched Katy's hand, and thrust it into Sister Mary Grace's grasp. Seconds later, she found them both pushed bodily towards the front door.

Instantly, all around her, people were crawling and lunging, screaming in terror, as they made desperately for freedom.

"MOVE! MOVE! MOVE!" Corinth's voice roared, urging them on. His undeniable voice boomed, driving everyone before it. They heeded the order unthinkingly, frantic to escape the palazzo. Seconds later all of them except Fr Corinth emerged, tumbling and crying, blinking in the glaring driveway lights.

But to no avail. There, standing in silhouette, was yet another armed gunman brandishing his machine gun. The BMW was a black, smoking hulk beside him.

"DOWN!" the gunman shouted at them. To make his deadly point, he let loose a volley of shots into the air. Everyone dropped to their knees on the sharp gravel.

"ON YOUR FACES!" he roared. The captives, seeing no alternative, reluctantly complied.

Luca was the first to drop down, wildly searching the darkness for a sign of his father. He knew it was Luigi who had aimed that *Madonnina* so expertly. But where *was* he?

Beside him, Gina was crying uncontrollably; Carlo gently helped her lay down and then half-lay beside her. His heart was beating wildly, his body half-covering hers as they lay face down on the gravel. He heard her murmuring softly, beseeching the help of Saint Anne.

Crouched next to them, Dyson craned his neck briefly, searching in the glare for his son and son-in-law, but to no avail. He had an idea.

"Carlo, tell him if it's money they want, they can have it," Dyson said quietly to his chauffeur. "Tell him – I don't think he speaks English."

"No, they don't want money," Carlo looked up and whispered back. "I don't know who they are, but they don't say nothing about money."

"ASK him," Dyson ordered nevertheless, peering through the glare anxiously.

"SILENZIO!" the gunman bawled at them, waving his Kalashnikov threateningly.

Defeated, Dyson slowly and grimly lay down on the driveway, his arm firmly around Michelle, who lay gasping beside their dazed daughter. Stacey in turn was holding the weeping Josh and Katy. Still stunned from the blow, she was praying with all her might.

"Pray for Daddy," she whispered fiercely to her children. "Pray for Uncle Pat!"

There were only two nuns lying beside her; Sister Beatrice had not made it out of the palazzo. Mary Grace was attempting to calm Benedicta, struggling in the throes of a panic attack.

"B-Beatrice is probably dead, or dying. And he's g-gonna shoot us all in the back," Benedicta whimpered. As she lay in the driveway, the gravel biting into her face, she was beyond tears. Her entire body was convulsed in fear.

"It will be okay," her superior responded. She regarded Benedicta with calm equanimity as she lay beside her on the driveway.

Benedicta could only stare at her strangely. Was Mary Grace in shock?

"S-sister..." she started to say, but Mary Grace cut her off.

"...*Saint Michael the Archangel, defend us in the day of battle*," she intoned, by way of answering.

Just then, the entire scene was bizarrely swept by the headlights of an oncoming car, as another luxury BMW swung majestically into the driveway, scattering a spray of gravel over them. The Beamer halted.

Any forlorn hopes the captives might have entertained for rescue, however, were cruelly dashed when two pairs of men's feet emerged from the car and strode briskly past them - one in boots and the other more elegantly shod in highly polished Italian leather shoes. Both halted briefly at the gunman, exchanged a few words in Italian, and then continued into the house.

"...*seeking the ruin of souls*," Sister Mary Grace continued, staring meaningfully at the shivering Benedicta. Slowly, haltingly, the other nun joined in her whispered prayer.

CHAPTER 40

Once past the gunman, the Head stepped gingerly through the open doorway. His finely-honed instincts for self-preservation were aroused. After that uncanny scene out in the driveway, he didn't know what to expect. Worse, his armed escort, now walking behind him, was strangely incommunicado.

The summons from the team leader had come, as expected, as they waited at the bottom of the hill. What was not at all expected was that the victims would be still alive, lying outside, guarded by that taciturn gunman, nervous as a cat.

Though he noted with approval that Dyson White and most of his family were outside on the gravel driveway, there were people missing, too. Where was that American Cardinal, and the White boy – the seminarian that had gotten away?

The Head wanted answers.

As they moved into the hallway, too, he seemed to hear a kind of muffled sound, a whispering chant. It was coming from the driveway behind them. He glanced at his escort, who shrugged indifferently and gestured abruptly for the Head to move forward.

Stung, the Head took instant umbrage. It was not properly respectful, the kind of gesture one would use with a million-euro client.

And then, with a sudden, piercing clarity, he knew.

He was not the client.

He had no time to react, however, because they had emerged onto a singularly distressing scene. The first thing he took in was the dead gunman – pale and clean-shaven, leaking blood against the back wall. There was another, too, sprawled in a spray of glass shards, an old statue a few feet from his skull. Next, he saw what he took to be a dead nun, crumpled in a heap of black and white by an open wood stove. A still-burning faggot lay near her outstretched hand.

The only living people in the room were the team leader and a tall, gray-haired priest who brandished a crucifix before him.

Outside, on the gravel driveway, the voices of the captives began to rise, first in mutters and then in ragged unison. Michelle was the first to take up the prayer from the nuns. Soon, Dyson joined her, followed by Carlo, Gina and Luca.

"St Michael the Archangel, defend us in the day of battle," they prayed as one, following the lead of the nuns. *"Be thou our defender...."*

The gunman guarding them was neither religious nor superstitious, but this strange cadenced prayer was un-nerving him.

"BASTA!" he shouted, trying to give his voice that same roar of command that they had all so readily obeyed not ten minutes before. "FACES DOWN!!"

But it seemed to him that there was something eerily dreamlike happening. He felt like he was mired in a nightmare -- the kind where he couldn't make anything happen, no matter how hard he tried. He shook himself, and cast an uneasy eye around. He wished that he would just get the execution order already, be done with this *merda* and collect his considerable pay. When his *telefonini* rang, he grabbed it impatiently, without looking at the number.

This was just the move that Phillip Toffler -- taking careful, silent aim at him from the palazzo window above -- had been waiting for. His military-issued battlefield smartphone had efficiently picked up the number of the mobile phone he'd photographed.

The sudden burst of gunfire from above that felled the distracted guard, however, was the very last straw for his would-be victims. All of them, except the nuns, abruptly ceased praying

226

and began to scream hysterically, convinced they were being massacred.

But Phillip, intent on finishing off the team leader, ignored them. He turned from the window and raced for the stairs, headed down to the first floor and the kitchen. He was praying silently for Divine assistance when a spray of machine gun fire caught him.

The last thought that raced through his stunned mind was a plea to God to save his family. A wave of blackness came over him. Phillip pitched, insensible, headlong down the stairs and knew no more.

The team leader turned away from shooting Phillip with a quick grunt of satisfaction. The American military man had been his main problem. The two priests inside were well guarded, and would be easy to dispose of with an efficient staccato burst of Kalashnikov fire.

First, however, he needed to ensure the execution outside had gone as planned. The screaming had gone on longer than necessary, and he was wary.

CHAPTER 41

Just a few minutes before, the Bishop of Spoleto's dusty blue Fiat van could be seen carefully negotiating its way to the top of the hill crowned by the palazzo.

"Looks like a party going on up there," Valeria remarked as they began the final ascent up the tree-lined white road. The lights brilliantly lit the old palace and its environs, and they could see a number of cars parked outside.

"I didn't realize they knew that many people in the area," the Bishop remarked mildly.

As they neared the drive, Valeria lowered her window and sniffed the air, wrinkling her nose.

"Do you smell that?" she demanded of the Bishop. "Smells terrible – like a chemical fire."

A strong whiff of gasoline-scented smoke wafted through the car, and they glanced at each other in confusion.

"You don't suppose the Americans set the place on fire, do you?" Valeria asked, beginning to be alarmed.

The Bishop shrugged. It was within the realm of possibility. The place was old, and heated with wood stoves. But that didn't explain the chemical, gasoline smell.

"Seems strange," he said, cautiously picking his way up the gravel driveway.

As their car swung into the palazzo's garishly-lit front yard, Dyson was the first to see their headlights. They spurred him into action.

"RUN!!" he erupted. A moment before, he and Carlo had been the first to raise their heads above the screaming group of victims cowering in the driveway. To their utter amazement, they saw that their gunman was down, felled by a burst of machine gun fire.

"RUN for the trees!" Dyson thundered, rising with Michelle clinging to his arm. "NOW! It's our only chance! RUN!!"

Beside him, Carlo obediently lifted an unresisting Gina and started for the darkness. The nuns quickly scooped up both overwrought children and followed suit. Dyson and Michelle, supporting a stricken Stacey between them, brought up the rear.

Moving swiftly, Luca darted over, yanked the Kalashnikov out of the dead gunman's hands and followed the group, guarding their rear flank warily.

"MOVE, MOVE, MOVE!" Dyson bellowed at them, but in vain. Stunned and slowed by their shock and injuries, they were all soon caught in the full glare of the headlights. The van cut off any chance of escape, halting directly in front of them.

Luca whirled around and began to take aim with the Kalashnikov. Behind him, Gina suddenly began to scream his name, a high, keening sound.

With a jolt, Luca registered that the small woman who vaulted out of the car and hastened towards them through the headlights' glare was -- his mother. Too shocked to move, he lowered the machine gun and stood with the others, staring dully. The figure of Valeria seemed to be an apparition from a world of normalcy that they had, suddenly and inexplicably, left behind.

"WHAT is going on here?!" his mother demanded loudly, as Gina detached herself from Carlo and threw herself, sobbing, into her mother's arms. "Luca, *what* is that thing in your hands?"

Behind them, the Bishop of Spoleto stood quietly, taking in the over-lit driveway, the dead gunman and the ragtag state of the people who stood – obviously terrified, panting, sweaty and scratched – before them.

Before anyone could answer, a piercing whistle from behind them broke through the confusion. Out of the gloom beyond the tree line, they heard a voice, speaking softly in Italian.

"Valeria, *cara mia*, you have arrived at a very dangerous time." It was Luigi, barely visible in the darkness, speaking softly but distinctly in Italian.

"L-Luigi?!" His wife responded, her voice rising imperiously, though tinged with panic. She detached herself from her children and hurried towards him. "W-What is going on here? W-why do you all look like this? Whose car is that?"

"*VALERIA!*" Luigi's softly commanding voice interrupted her.

She stopped, frozen in her tracks.

"There's no time to explain now," he continued quietly from the shadows, though with great urgency in his voice, "but we are all in grave *pericolo*..."

"*Mi dispiace*," the Bishop interrupted him politely but firmly, speaking in Italian. He had followed Valeria. "But I must ask, where is the Cardinal?"

Luigi regarded him with stoic complacency.

"Is he quite alright?" the Bishop pressed on. "I am sorry, but you all seem so fearful, and something is clearly very wrong here."

He pointed to the gunman splayed across the gravel driveway.

"Is that man dead? Who is he?"

"*Eccelencia*," Luigi inclined his head politely. "I am sorry too, but we may have no time to explain. We hardly know ourselves..."

As if to illustrate this, they were all suddenly aware of a low, menacing rumble.

"Rain?" Michelle was the first to react, searching the cloudless sky. The air had a metallic taste. "Is that thunder?"

Suddenly, the lights of the palazzo flickered and died. Then, as they stood together, caught in the glare of the Bishop's headlights, something odd happened.

With a deep, low rumble, the earth swayed under their feet.

CHAPTER 42

Above the screams of the others, Luca's incredulous voice could be heard. He was coming to grips with a completely new view of his humble father.

"P-Pop, y-you set off a bomb?"

But Luigi shook his head and remained hunched over, silent and wary, as the tremor began to abate.

"No, *certo!*" Carlo barked at Luca. "*This* is not man-made."

As the tremor slowly subsided around them, the air nevertheless seemed to be rapidly growing thicker and more oppressive.

"*C-cosa?!* W-what is happening here?" Valeria gasped, turning to Luigi.

Luigi merely shrugged in response, his eyes fixed on the dark palazzo. Then he stepped close to his wife and put an arm around her, drawing her close.

"It's coming from in there," he remarked grimly. "Now all we got to do is wait. And pray to the Madonna. Because she is the strongest weapon we have."

Then he crossed himself.

The Americans did not understand; under the stress, Michelle found that her limited command of the language was evaporating.

"W-What's he saying? W-What's going on?" she demanded of Carlo. The Italian was sweating profusely in the cold night air.

"Luigi thinks there's something happening in there," Carlo began in English, indicating the house.

"Like what?" Dyson wanted to know.

A rapid exchange of Italian ensued.

"He says," Carlo translated slowly, "he says the place is evil. No. It *has* something evil in it. What do you call it? 'Possessed?'"

"Possessed? Like with demons?" Michelle breathed.

"So what does that have to do with these terrorists?" Dyson asked. "Or are they Mafia? Anyway why do they want to kill us?"

Another volley of Italian, this time with the Bishop contributing. The Americans couldn't tell what was being said, though one thing was clear: Valeria was scoffing, shaking her head vigorously at whatever the men were saying. Gina was silent, clinging to Carlo.

Finally, Michelle lost patience.

"Yeah, well, whatever this is," Michelle's pragmatic Brooklynese kicked in, "we are getting out of here, and pronto. Tell that Bishop to get in his car; we're all cramming in there and getting the hell outta..."

"...no," Dyson interrupted her. "That's too good of a target for them. Those guns have enough range..."

"...okay but where *are* they?" Michelle was adamant. "We can't just sit here and wait to die...the kids can't take much more of this..."

"...we don't *know* how many there are," Luca interjected emphatically. "They could have more guys waiting down the..."

He was interrupted by another wave of sustained rumbling, as the earth shook under them. This tremor seemed louder than the first.

"...what *is* that?" Michelle cried over the noise.

"...shock waves," Dyson answered her. He looked exhausted, still cradling Stacey against his chest. His daughter leaned on her father heavily; she hadn't spoken since they'd emerged from the palazzo, though she still held both whimpering children's hands in her silent grip.

Beside them, Sister Mary Grace drew out her rosary beads and once again began the prayer to St Michael. Sister Benedicta obediently followed suit.

"*Sancte Michaelae...*" the nuns prayed, as the unearthly rumbling rose around them once again.

"Earthquakes take out electricity?" Michelle shouted to her husband.

"Earthquakes do all kinds of strange things!" Dyson shouted back, as the tremor grew stronger.

"ADDESSO!! NOW!!" Suddenly Luigi was beckoning them urgently away from the tree line. He dragged a protesting Valeria out into the open lawn.

"I don't think we should go out there!" Michelle called back to him.

Before anyone could answer, they were all transfixed by the stupendous sight of a fiery blue bolt of lightning slicing through the night sky. With a gigantic crash, it struck the palazzo full on.

Everyone was frozen in their tracks, except Michelle.

"NOW!" she shouted over the din, starting for the car and gesturing wildly for the others to follow her. "*Andiamo!*"

But no one heeded her. Instead, the nuns darted over to Luigi and Valeria, dropped to their knees in the grass and began to pray aloud, rosaries gripped in their hands. Luca, too, strode resolutely over to stand guard beside his parents, the Kalashnikov cradled in his arms.

In the gravel drive where he'd stopped, the Bishop of Spoleto also knelt. As the wind started to whip around them, Dyson left Stacey and the children beside the Bishop, and ran to retrieve his wife.

"Dyson, we have to *leave!*" Michelle cried piteously. In response, he silently wrapped his arms around her. Michelle's face was running with tears and sweat and bits of gravel clung to her hair and clothes.

In the noise and confusion, no one noticed that Katy had broken loose from her mother's grip and was running towards the old palazzo. She was calling for her daddy.

CHAPTER 43

When the Head arrived in the palazzo's kitchen, he stopped short and surveyed Fr Paul Corinth's outstretched hands and the crucifix they held with a mixture of wariness and amusement.

"Father," he smiled, bowing slightly, his voice dripping with amused contempt, "I am very sorry to disturb you, but what exactly is it that you think you are doing?"

"*Exorcizo te, omnis spiritus immunde, in nomine Dei Patris omnipotentis,*" the priest replied, looking steadily and unsmilingly back at him. "*et in nomine Jesu Christi Filii ejus, Domini et Judicis nostril...*"

"...oh please Father..." despite the extreme circumstances, the Head couldn't restrain himself. He smiled in a superior way. "Reciting curses in a dead language -- you don't think for one instance that anyone takes you seriously?"

"...*et in virtute Spiritus (X) Sancti,*" the priest continued, his expression one of great absorption. "*ut descedas ab hoc plasmate Dei, quod...*"

At that, the earth beneath their feet began to quake violently. Immediately, the electricity flickered and died, and they were plunged into blackness.

"W-what is this?" The Head demanded peremptorily. His annoyance, he quickly strategized, would seize command of the situation. "Where's the fuse box? What's going on?"

"*Dominus noster ad templum sanctum suum vocare dignatus est,*"under the cover of darkness, the Head could hear Corinth's voice droning on steadily in the hated Latin. He could also hear shuffling and soft footsteps somewhere quite near him. It was a sound that made his skin crawl.

"Get a light, you idiot! MOVE!" he barked at the gunman. He thought he caught the whiff of the man's aftershave near him.

Then the unmistakable stench of his putrid breath caught the Head full in the face.

The Head recoiled, his fastidious senses reeling. Then to his horror, a gigantic clap of thunder and a blinding lightning blitz revealed the scene before him in a flash of bizarre blue light.

The burly Italian was pointing his pistol directly at the Head's face. He was at point blank range, not two feet away.

Instantly, the Head dropped to the floor. In a cold panic, disoriented, and on his hands and knees, he attempted to slither out the way he had come. Unfortunately, in the pitch darkness his eyes couldn't make out anything at all. And for some reason, all he could hear was a loud hum, like the sound of a hundred angry wasps.

In the front hall, the terrific crash of the lightning's impact sent the team leader reeling as he slipped off the stairs. He collapsed in an ungainly heap on the floor, shouting orders that went unheard.

By the time he regained his feet and snapped on his flashlight, he discovered to his shock that Father Paul Corinth was now leaning heavily against the massive front door. The team leader's way outside was barred. In the priest's hands, a gilt-and-wooden crucifix glimmered in the pearl-white light from the flash.

"*Ut fiat templum Dei vivi, et Spiritus Sanctus habitet in eo,*" the priest pronounced.

An abrupt crash sounded, which caused the team leader to jump. It was a painting which fell from the wall nearby.

"*Per eumdem Christum Dominum nostrum, qui venturus est judicare vivos et mortuos, et saeculum per ignem.*"

The team leader turned his flashlight away from the intense concentration on the priest's face just in time to see the Head rise from his knees behind him. Immediately in back of the Head, the gunman emerged from the kitchen, his gun drawn.

In the semi-darkness, the team leader shook his head. He seemed to be having an auditory hallucination. A sound like hundreds of swarming bees was emanating from the second floor. The team leader squinted, peering upwards distractedly. A battle-hardened veteran, he was struggling to maintain control of himself.

Suddenly, a black shadow flew through the air at the periphery of the flashlight's reach, followed by another, loud, crash.

CHAPTER 44

The Head ducked instinctively and looked up to see a wooden chair tilting at a crazy angle at the top of the stairs. Propelled by some unseen force, the chair toppled down the steps.

Next to him, the gunman cursed sharply, and taking a sweeping aim at the darkness upstairs, let loose a volley of gun fire. Beside him, the Head could smell the man's fear.

"EXORCIZO te, immundíssime spíritus, omnis incúrsio adversárii," Father Paul spoke loudly and clearly, gazing fixedly at the crucifix in his outstretched hands.

"Omne phantasma, omnis légio, in nómine Dómini nostri Jesu+Christi eradicáre, et effugáre ab hoc plásmate Dei +. Ipse tibi ímperat, qui te de supérnis cœaelórum in inferióra terrœ demérgi prœcépit. Ipse tibi ímperat, qui mari, ventis et tempestátibus imperávit. BMW ergo, et time, sátana, inimice fidei, hostis géneris humáni, mortis addúctor, vitœ raptor, justítiœ declinátor, malórum radix, fomes vitiórum, sedúctor hóminum, próditur géntium, incitátor invídiœ, origo avaritiœ, causa discórdiœ, excitátor dolórum: quid stas, et resistis, cum scias, Christum Dóminum vias tuas pérdere?"

"SHUT THE FUCK UP!" the team leader screamed at him. But Corinth, undeterred, continued to hold the crucifix, murmuring in Latin, his eyes focused in front of him.

With a grunt, the gunman swiveled and took aim, pointing the Kalashnikov's muzzle directly at Corinth. He was not six feet away from the priest, who continued to intone the Latin.

A sudden gasp and an exclamation from the others, however, distracted him, and he looked in the direction of their gaze.

To their astonishment, the three found themselves watching, dumbfounded, as the chair at the foot of the stairs righted itself, once again as if in the grip of an invisible hand. Then, it slowly lifted into thin air.

Suddenly, with great certitude, the Head knew the chair was aimed at him. With a harsh cry, he plunged to the marble floor. A split second later, the chair crashed off the wall behind him.

"Illum métue, qui in Isaac immolátus est, in Joseph venúndatus, in agno occísus, in hómine crucifixus, deinde inférni triumphátor fuit. Sequentes crucis fiat in fronte obsessi," Father Corinth went on calmly, seemingly unaffected by the proceedings around him.

"Recéde ergo in nómine Patris," he crossed himself.

"Et Fílii," he crossed himself again.

"Et Spíritus," he crossed himself a third time, and then continued, *"Sancti: da locum Spirítui Sancto, per hoc signum sanctæ,"* a fourth time. *"Crucis Jesu Christi Dómini nostri: Qui cum Patre et eódem Spíritu Sancto vivit et regnat Deus, per ómnia sæcula sæculórum."*

The din of humming wasps grew louder. Completely unnerved at this point, the Head, the team leader and the gunman began to clutch at their ears.

"ADJÚRO TE," the priest continued, slowly and deliberately. *"Serpens antíque, per júdicem vivórum et mortuórum, per factórem tuum, per factórem mundi, per eum, qui habet potestátem mitténdi te in gehénnam, ut ab hoc fámulo Dei N., qui (ab hac fámula Dei N., quæ) ad Ecclésiæ sinum recúrrit, cum metu, et exército furóris tui festínus discédas. Adjúro te íterum,"*

The others stared, wild-eyed, around them as the buzzing of the wasps reached an excruciating crescendo.

Corinth calmly crossed himself once again, and continued.

"Non mea infirmitáte, sed virtúte Spíritus Sancti, ut éxeas ab hoc fámulo Dei N., quem (ab hac fámula Dei N., quam) omnípotens Deus ad imáginem suam fecit. Cede ígitur, cede non mihi, sed minístro Christi. Illius enim te urges potéstas, qui te Cruci suæ subjugávit. Illíus bráchium contremísce, qui,

devíctis gemítibus inférni, ánimas ad lucem perdúxit. Sit tibi terror corpus hóminis," the priest declared, extracting a flask from his cassock with one hand, all the while continuing to recite the Office of Exorcism.

The others watched spellbound as he held the flask aloft.

"*Imperat tibi natus ex Vírgine. Imperat tibi Jesus Nazarénus, qui te, cum discípulos ejus contémneres, elísum atque prostrátum exíre præcépit ab hómine: quo præsénte, cum te ab hómine separásset, nec porcórum gregem íngredi præsumébas. Recéde ergo nunc adjurátus in nómine ejus ab hómine, quem ipse plasmávit. Durum est tibi velle resístere. Durum est tibi contra stímulum calcitráre. Quia quanto tárdius exis, tanto magis tibi supplícium crescit, quia non hómines contémnis, sed illum, qui dominátur vivórum et mortuórum: Qui ventúrus est judicáre vivos et mórtuos, et sæculum per ignem,*" Father Corinth said firmly, and began to make the Sign of the Cross over them, holy water in hand.

"What is THAT?"

The Head, still on his knees, heard the terrified cry of the gunman above him. He looked up just in time to see what the man was gaping at.

What he saw, he could not believe. In the wavering beam of the team leader's flashlight, they stared as a river of dark red blood rolled down from the second floor, flowing down all sides of the staircase at once.

The cold terror that gripped him then was like nothing the Head had ever known. Immobilized by fear, he could not take his eyes off the horror unfolding before his eyes. He heard nothing but swarming insects. He smelt nothing but blood.

In his agitation, the Head's early priestly training suddenly came to mind. "There were locusts and the Nile turned to blood," he remembered idly.

Then, from unfathomable profundities in the earth came a deep rumbling noise.

And as Father Paul Corinth let the holy water fly over them, the palazzo floor rippled beneath them like molten lava.

CHAPTER 45

While the others struggled to maintain their balance on the tilting floor as it undulated in a great wave under them, the Head remained crouched on all fours, close to the ground. He was thus the only one who noticed that the handle of the palazzo's front door had slowly begun to turn.

As the tremor subsided, the team leader and his gunman remained transfixed by the uncanny sight of gore oozing down the stairway's wall. Huge, blood-red drips stained the stucco. The clamor from the swarming insects made it almost impossible to hear anything but Father Corinth stubbornly intoning the exorcism prayers.

"Deus cæli, Deus terræ, deus Angelórum, Deus Archangelórum, deus Prophetárum, Deus Apostolórum, Deus Mártyrum, Deus Vírginium, Deus, qui potestátem habes donáre vitam post mortem, réquiem post labórem..."

"SHOOT HIM!" The team leader's hysterical voice broke, but his gunman, now sweating profusely and shaking his head in confusion, ignored the order. Instead, he lowered the Kalashnikov's muzzle and backed away from the group, shaking in terror.

From his position on the floor, the Head tried to calm himself, rapidly calculating his chances of escape. Any sudden movement on his part would be sure to bring down the Kalashnikov's deadly fire on him, and at that close range he knew he hadn't a chance.

"Quia non est álius Deus præter te, nec esse póterit verus, nisi tu, Creátor cæli et terrae, qui verus Rex es, et cujus regni non erit finis; humíliter majestáti glóriæ tuæ súpplico, ut hunc fámulum tuum (hanc fámulam tuam) de immúndis spíritibus liberáre dignéris. Per Christum Dóminum nostrum..." Corinth said, and threw more holy water on the gunman.

Behind him, the door began to inch open. Through it, the Head could see the figure of a child, silhouetted against the car headlights shining on the palazzo's facade.

The team leader was the first to fire. He caught his gunman full in front, but as the man went down, he expertly returned the fire.

The Head did not wait around to assess the outcome of the furious exchange. Leaping with all his might, he yanked violently at the colossal door. Katy fell face forward, and was immediately swept up in his powerful grip. Then, holding the little girl in front of him as a human shield, the Head darted madly for the BMW.

As the dark figure emerged, running, from the palazzo, Luca raised the muzzle of the Kalashnikov and prepared to take aim.

CHAPTER 46

"KATY!!" Stacey's high scream pierced the night.

"NO! LUCA!" Luigi's voice barked a staccato command, and his son froze with his finger on the trigger. All around them, people were screaming.

Racing across the drive, the Head plunged into his car, clutching Katy, her body a shield between him and the thunderstruck onlookers.

"NO!!!" Stacey's piercing cry was heart-rending. "KATY!!!"

Gunning the BMW's powerful motor, the Head was away in a flash, spraying the little group with a cloud of dust and gravel. With a strangled whimper, Stacey collapsed into her mother's arms.

Standing beside Michelle, Dyson grimly demanded the car keys from Carlo, who protested vigorously.

"Let me drive!" he cried, pleading. "Sir, you're in no shape to do this alone!"

"She's my grand-daughter," Dyson growled fiercely. He was brooking no dissent. "You stay here with Gina and take care of all of them. They need you. Gimme the keys – NOW!"

Defeated, Carlo reluctantly handed the keys over and took Josh into his arms. Seconds later, Dyson was in the white Mercedes and down the white road, leaving a deep silence, broken only by Stacey's sobs, behind him.

"*Sancte Michaelae,*" The bishop whispered.

"*Ora pro nobis,*" The nuns responded.

"*Sancta Lucia,*" he prayed.

"*Ora pro nobis*," the nuns responded.

When the front door opened again, Luca warily raised the Kalashnikov's muzzle once more. But to his and everyone's complete shock, it was the only tall, slender figure of Father Paul Corinth which emerged from the palazzo, alone and unharmed. He beckoned to them.

Carlo was the first there, with Luigi at his heels.

"They're dead and gone," the priest told them haltingly, in Italian. He looked utterly drained, and swayed slightly on his feet.

"Don Paolo, you need to sit down," Carlo urged, but Corinth waved him off.

"No time," the priest said wearily. "*Dove il Cardinale?*"

"*Venga*," Luigi understood instantly. "In the back. Follow me."

Thirty seconds later, the men rounded the corner of the palazzo.

"STOP OR I'LL SHOOT!" It was Patrick, shouting bravely. They could see the muzzle of the Glock pointing at them from the edge of the barn door.

Once he was reassured as to their identity, it was only thirty seconds more before the priest was kneeling over the fallen Cardinal. Portland was conscious, but barely alive.

"It's me, Excellency," Corinth whispered tenderly. "I'm here to take you into the arms of Holy Mother Church."

As Luigi reached for the glass jar of holy water they'd left there, Carlo experienced a wave of shock. Could it only have been *today* that they had blessed the house?

Beneath them, Patrick knelt in the fragrant straw, gently holding the Cardinal's head.

"He's a good man, this one," the Cardinal answered weakly, looking up at Patrick. "You will follow him, won't you?"

Patrick nodded, unable to speak.

"Promise me that?" Portland whispered.

Tears were running freely down Patrick's face as he nodded again.

"I promise you, Excellency," he said softly. At this, Father Paul began to recite the Church's ancient prayer of extreme unction, in Latin. Nearby, the Bishop of Spoleto knelt, praying silently in Italian.

"*...Paradisi portas aperiat, et ad guadia sempiterna perducat.*"

As the final words died away, Cardinal Portland gasped, gripping Patrick's hand. As he witnessed the American priest pronounce the final words of absolution, farewell and benediction, hot tears started in the Bishop's eyes.

Lit by the very last of the dying evening light, they remained just as they were, a fixed tableau in the barn. The only sound was the Cardinal's labored last breaths. They waited, whispering Ave Marias, huddled around the Cardinal as his spirit slipped away into eternity.

And then there was only silence in the deepening Umbrian dusk.

"'Well done, good and faithful servant,'" the Bishop said huskily in Italian to Corinth as they emerged from the barn a few minutes later.

The priest stopped and returned his gaze steadily.

"'This day you will be with Me, in paradise,'" he replied quietly. Then he turned and headed into the palazzo.

In his wake, the Bishop nodded, made the Sign of the Cross, and turned back. He would stay with the Cardinal's body. In the gloom beside the dead Cardinal, he found Patrick wiping his tears. The Bishop placed a fatherly hand on the American boy's shoulder.

"*Coraggio*," he told him and then in halting English. "You - must - have - courage."

"I can't believe it," Patrick murmured distractedly. "He was just here, *alive*. He was talking to me."

"And what did he say?"

"H-he said," Patrick stammered, trying to control his tears. "H-he told me that life is always worth living. H-he said I must live my life with purpose...

"Yes?"

"H-He told to stay close to the Church, not just for shelter but to help me m-make my way in the world."

The Bishop nodded gravely. "Yes, the Sacraments keep us on a steady path, the right path. Especially Confession."

"I-I asked him for his blessing," Patrick choked then, fresh tears starting in his eyes. "So then he blessed me. He gave me his benediction."

"And what did you say to him?"

There was a few seconds of silence while Patrick grappled with his emotions. Finally, he spoke.

"I told him," Patrick whispered hoarsely, "that I want to be a priest."

The Bishop nodded somberly.

With that, Patrick rose, wiping his eyes with his sleeve. Then, following in Corinth's footsteps, he pointed his feet towards the palazzo.

The electricity had been restored and the old palace was glowing with light.

CHAPTER 47

When Patrick entered the kitchen, he found Father Paul already there. Nearby, Benedicta was carefully tending a conscious-but-very-sore Beatrice on the sofa. Turning, Patrick stared at the dead gunmen on the floor.

"Patrick," his sister said immediately, indicating his right hand. "Stop waving that thing around."

Her brother glanced down at the Glock, seemingly conscious of it for the first time.

"It's Phillip's gun," he explained, idiotically.

"Yeah, well," she retorted grimly, "put it someplace safe,"

"'Safe?'" Patrick wondered aloud. "Where is 'safe'?"

Benedicta looked at him, eyes narrowed, and realized that her brother was in shock.

"Well, these guys are no longer a problem," she said slowly and kindly. "Phillip got this one, as you'll recall," she said, pointing to the pale gunman by the door. "And I have no idea who clobbered this other guy with the Madonna statue..."

Despite himself, Patrick let out a long, low whistle. "WELL-played, Luigi!"

Benedicta allowed herself a small smile. "He did the torched Beamer, too, right?"

Patrick nodded.

"Luigi is my hero," he began to grin. "We saw him with the gas can outside."

"Yeah? Excellent," his sister replied and pointed to the gun in his hand, her manner no-nonsense. "Now put that thing in a drawer or something."

By the front door, Mary Grace was calmly taking Phillip Toffler's vital signs as he lay unconscious on the stair landing. A quick exam told her what she needed to know – the spray of bullets had pierced his legs, but his vital organs were untouched. It had been the fall down the steps that had knocked him unconscious.

"He's alive," she turned to Luca, still guarding them by the front door. "But he needs a doctor, and fast."

"Beatrice too," she heard Benedicta stage-whisper as she hovered briefly in the doorway to the kitchen.

"I heard that!" Beatrice called weakly. Patrick grinned. The sisters exchanged glances and smiled.

Back in the kitchen, Father Paul bent his tall frame to have a closer look at Beatrice on the sofa.

"Hey, what happened after that terrorist knocked me out?" the nun asked, looking up at the priest.

Corinth shrugged and smiled slightly.

"Fireworks," Patrick answered for him, his eyes on the exorcist. "You missed the fireworks."

Corinth didn't react.

"Yeah, but that detonator vest he was wearing wasn't real, was it?" Beatrice ventured, a triumphant note in her voice.

"No, Sister," Corinth told her soberly. "That was fake."

Beatrice flashed them all a grin. "I *knew* it!" she pronounced, triumphantly.

"But everything else was real," Corinth finished soberly. He caught Patrick's eye, and shook his head slightly. Patrick understood. They would say nothing about the Cardinal until the injured people were taken away.

"Sister will be fine, I think," Corinth said heartily.

Beatrice eyed him with suspicion.

"I sure will," she announced. "I just want to know what these terrorists wanted with us!"

"My mother," called Luca just then, from the front window, "is on the phone right now. If anyone can get the *ambulancia* here fast, it's her."

Mary Grace favored him with a brief smile. She was covering Phillip with a blanket when the massive front door suddenly opened.

Everyone gasped reflexively. To their immense relief, it was Stacey and Josh, supported by Michelle. The three stepped inside and stared down at the unconscious Phillip.

"I-Is he dead?" Stacey whispered, instinctively covering her son's eyes. Her eyes were sunken in dark shadows.

"He's going to be just fine," Mary Grace said firmly, as Stacey slowly lowered herself onto the landing beside her husband. "He's had a bad bump on the head, and he needs medical attention soon, but he's definitely not dead."

Stacey exhaled a long, slow breath and took Phillip's hand into her own. She held it to her cheek.

Just then, Valeria stepped smartly through the doorway, with Luigi obediently following in her wake.

"Medical help is coming up the hill," she announced triumphantly in Italian, as Luca translated. Outside and behind her, the others could see red lights blinking in the distance.

Then Valeria noticed Luca with the Kalashnikov in his arms.

"Oh, *Madonna!*" she gasped. "What are you *thinking?* Put that thing *down!*"

Luca exchanged a covert glance with Luigi, who nodded slightly.

"Put it in the chapel," Luigi advised and his son did as he asked, laying the weapon below the makeshift altar there. Despite the circumstances, Luca had never felt prouder of his father. For some reason, he reflected, this new-found pride and love made him feel stronger, more capable in the world. He was no longer the son of a street cleaner, doing a despised job for meager pay. Now, he was the son of a freedom fighter.

When the emergency medical technicians entered the house a few moments later, a composed Sister Mary Grace met them with Luca beside her, acting as interpreter. After a quick look at the dead gunmen and several hasty calls on their *telefonini*, the medics turned their attention to the living.

A few minutes later, Beatrice was rolled out with Benedicta in attendance on her wheelchair. Beatrice gave them the thumbs up sign on her way out the door.

"Go easy on the Italians," Sister Mary Grace advised her sisters wryly. "Remember, they're not used to American nuns."

Within minutes, Phillip was strapped to a gurney, IV tube in place.

"Stacey, you need to go with him," Sister Mary Grace urged her. "They need to have a look at you, too."

Stacey, too numb to reply, only nodded.

"We'll hold down the fort here," Sister Mary Grace told them. "Patrick and your mom will wait with Josh."

"But Daddy and Katy..." Stacey protested weakly.

"They'll be okay," Mary Grace assured her, her ready smile radiating confidence.

Beside her, Michelle chimed in, as she found her voice again. "Honey, we'll be sure to let you know if we hear any news. You need to go with Phillip, now. He needs you."

Just then, Father Paul wandered into the room. Stacey looked up at the tall, graying priest; the fine lines on his face were etched even deeper than when they'd met last. His glance looked ancient. She watched as Corinth stood, carefully surveying the scene in the front hall without uttering a word. He seemed to be listening for something.

"Father Paul," she whispered up at him. "Is everything all right? I mean, are you all right?"

The priest regarded her stricken face soberly. The muscles in his face visibly relaxed.

"Yes," he said quietly, and put a reassuring hand on her shoulder. "I'm fine. Everything is all right now. You need medical attention, and you should go with Phillip."

"*Per favore*," Valeria interjected quietly. She addressed her son. "The young lady, she needs a wheelchair, too, yes? Tell these medics what to do."

A few seconds later, as Stacey was gently lowered into a wheelchair, Phillip stirred beside her on the gurney. She took his hand again and they exchanged a wordless glance. Tears sprang to her eyes.

"Babe, I'm so sorry," Phillip whispered, with an effort, but she quickly put her finger to her lips.

"Don't talk now," she answered with an attempt at bravado. "It's all right. It's gonna be all right. We're not worried."

He was smiling weakly as the medics wheeled them both outside. Minutes later, they were all in the ambulance, which departed, red lights silently flashing.

"Father," Michelle turned to Corinth as the ambulance faded from view. She was beginning to recover her equilibrium, and had her arm staunchly around her son's shoulders. "Patrick told us what happened to the Cardinal," she said wearily. "Thank God you were there."

The priest shook his head.

"Thank God Patrick was there to stay with him," he replied. "Thank God for the good bishop, who is out there with him, now."

"Ah," said Michelle briskly, "We need to care of the bishop, now. Take him these blankets," she commanded, pressing a stack into his hands.

The priest nodded obediently.

"And while you're out there, give him a belt of this," Michelle continued, handing him a tall glass bottle with a slender neck. It was filled with a clear liquid.

"It's *grappa*," she advised stoutly. "Italian moonshine. It'll help."

The priest looked at her quizzically, but said nothing.

"Something tells me you could use something medicinal, too," Michelle advised. She assessed him frankly, head cocked. "You look like you've been through a battle."

"Yes, Father," Sister Mary Grace chimed in. "Indeed you do."

The exorcist smiled gratefully at both women, and accepted the bottle. With a last glance around, he shook his head ruefully, and ambled off.

He was satisfied. The horrifying, otherworldly sound of insects was stilled. Though the two chairs lay overturned, there was no trace of the cascade of blood on the stairs. Moreover, the gray haze he had sensed in and around the palazzo had lifted entirely; the house was normal, again.

CHAPTER 48

"Where's dad?" Patrick suddenly looked around and asked his mother. He felt like he was waking from a dream.

"Your father is getting Katy," she answered him evenly, hoping she sounded far more confident than she felt.

"W-what do you mean?" he wasn't fooled. "W-where's Katy?"

"Patrick," Michelle stepped in front of her son, and grasped him by the shoulders. She looked deeply into his eyes. "Your father is in charge of this. He's chasing that creepy guy, that..."

"One of these guys has her?!" Patrick's eyes widened in terror as the adrenaline began pumping again.

"Your father can handle this," Michelle said.

"Look, I don't think so," Patrick said flatly. "This guy is a pro, Mom."

"Pro, what?" Michele retorted. "Your father knows all about bad guys, Patrick..."

"Gimme the keys," he interrupted her, hand extended. His face was grim. Behind Patrick, Luca stepped into her view, looking resolute. "Look, we are armed, here. Dad is not...."

"But the guy isn't armed..." she protested.

"...we don't know that, Mom," he cut her off, open hand still extended insistently.

She gave her son a long, searching look and shook her head.

"Patrick, you boys are not trained to use those things," Michelle said slowly, her arms folded. "Your father can handle himself..."

Suddenly, flashing blue lights outside announced the arrival of the *carabineri*. Michelle exhaled sharply. She turned to the others, who had been watching them closely.

 "Carlo, you take Gina and her mother upstairs and make them comfortable," she commanded. "Then come down here and help us talk to the cops. And Luigi, *non tocare!*"

In response, Luigi suddenly straightened, hands in the air, smiling broadly. He'd been crouched over his Maddonina, which was lying in shards of glass.

"Carlo, tell him that's criminal evidence, or whatever they call it," she commanded, and turned her attention to her Josh.

"Patrick's gonna take you upstairs now and watch a movie," she said to her grandson. "I'll bring you something to eat in a little while."

 "But I want to see the *police!*" Josh cried, pointing to the burly *carabineri* as they were making their polite entrance into the palazzo.

"Well, they don't speak English," Michelle told him quickly. Patrick bent to pick up his unwilling nephew.

"WAIT!" Josh screamed in protest as he was lifted up in the air. "Wait, wait, wait!"

He was pointing to the open front door, behind the carabineri.

"It's KATY!"

CHAPTER 49

All eyes upon her, Katy stepped primly through the front door of the palazzo and regarded her stunned audience with equanimity.

"Where's Daddy and Mommy?" she demanded, looking from one to the other. Her eyes settled on her grandmother.

"Nonna? Where are they?"

Michelle opened her mouth to speak, but Dyson beat her to it. Laughing out loud, he stepped in the door behind Katy and scooped his grand-daughter up into his arms.

"Dyson!" Michelle cried, her face lighting up as the others gasped and a round of applause started. She threw herself into his embrace.

But they had no time to speak, as just at that moment the ambulance workers wheeled into view outside. On their gurney lay the covered body of Cardinal Portland. Behind them, walking slowly with hands folded and heads bowed, were Father Paul Corinth and the Bishop of Spoleto.

The ambulance workers looked a bit nonplussed as the Whites, Carlo, Sister Mary Grace and Luigi's family immediately rushed outside and knelt on the ground, crossing themselves. Even Josh and Katy followed suit unquestioningly.

The *carabineri*, interrupted in their official duties, maintained a respectful distance. Everyone looked at the Bishop, who took a deep breath before speaking.

"*Ripose en pace*," he said softly, and, eyes lowered and hand extended in benediction, blessed the body on the gurney.

"*Era cardinale*," one ambulance worker explained in a hushed whisper to his co-workers. *He was a Cardinal.*

The medics all nodded, shifting a bit uncomfortably in the silence. Everyone waited, anticipating that they would be dismissed.

Instead, the Bishop straightened up and scanned the group.

"A cardinal wears red because it shows his willingness to die for the Faith," his voice whispered tentatively in Italian. The medics and the *carabineri* stood stock still, their attention riveted on the prelate.

"Today this American, Alexander Cardinal Portland of Boston, has given his life for his fellow man -- and for the Faith," the Bishop said with quiet authority. "Do you know what we call such a man, in our tradition?"

No one made a sound. The red lights of the ambulances and the blue lights of the police cars flashed intermittently over a scene gone eerily quiet.

"We call such a man a *martyr*," the Bishop continued, his voice rising. "A man who spills his blood for our holy Faith is a *martyr*."

At the unaccustomed word, a ripple went through onlookers, but no one dared respond aloud.

"And the place where a *martyr* spills his blood," the Bishop continued, "we call this hallowed ground."

Kneeling beside Luigi in the silence, Valeria found to her annoyance that tears were starting in her eyes.

"What is this?" she nervously whispered to her husband. "What 'martyrdom'? This cardinal died at the hands of the Mafia, or terrorists, or whatever they were..."

"... he sacrificed his life for *me*," came a fierce whisper in American-accented Italian, from behind her. There, kneeling on the gravel, tears streaming down his face, was Patrick.

"He shoved that muzzle away, and took the bullets himself," he continued, making an heroic effort to be understood in Italian. "And they took him outside to kill him because, because, he was ..."

Unable to continue, Patrick bowed his head, his face crumpled in grief. Michelle wrapped her arms around him and offered a silent prayer of thanksgiving to the God who had spared her son.

"...because he was a priest," Father Paul Corinth answered for him with quiet finality, in Italian.

Horrified and confused, Valeria turned back towards her husband. Luigi met his wife's eyes with a piercing look. She exhaled finally, and was silent.

"We are standing on hallowed ground," the Bishop continued, his voice carrying clear and strong through the night. He looked around at the stunned Italians, his face alight.

"Two thousand years ago when our ancestors were brutally fed to the beasts in the pagan coliseums, those martyrs also shed their blood for the Faith."

Dyson knelt, arms around his grandchildren, silently nodding. Beside them, Carlo and Gina held each other, tears streaming down their tired faces.

"And afterwards, when their poor, battered remains were gathered up and given to their Christian friends, they were carried away with great reverence and buried. Over the graves of these martyrs our ancestors erected the altars upon which they celebrated the sacred mysteries."

Luca folded his arms in wonder and took in the scene in front of him. The exhausted survivors were weeping openly. Even the hardened medics and *carabineri* were surreptitiously wiping their eyes.

"We celebrate the Mass at these same altars today, two thousand years later, for the same reason," the Bishop continued, his countenance glowing. "That ground beneath our altars is sacred – hallowed -- by the relics of saints and martyrs."

Luca looked at the nuns. Sister Benedicta and Sister Mary Grace were smiling brightly through the tears that shone on their faces.

"Cardinal Portland's blood has sanctified this ground," the Bishop continued, pointing to the earth before him. "There is no place on earth closer to heaven than this hallowed ground on which we stand."

All around Luca, people were nodding their heads – even the Americans seemed to understand the Bishop.

"St Paul said that we see through a veil, but darkly," the Bishop concluded, his gaze sweeping over them. "*Allora*, tonight the veil between us and the hereafter was parted for a moment. And Alexander Cardinal Portland stepped through the gap in that veil."

Then he raised his right hand in blessing over them.

"*Nel nome del padre e del figlio e dello Spirito Santo,*" he intoned, making the sign of the cross in the air.

As Luca watched in wonder, every person there – including the medics and the *carabineri* – crossed themselves in unison with the Bishop's blessing.

Minutes later, as the medics reverently wheeled the Cardinal's body away, Sister Benedicta turned, bestowing a radiant smile on her brother.

"Patrick," she whispered through her tears. "Take me to where the Cardinal died."

Without a word, her brother turned and led the way to the now-empty outbuilding. He flicked on the overhead light and in its cold glare, brother and sister both stood looking down at the blood-stained hay where Patrick had cradled the Cardinal's body.

"The blood of the martyrs is the seed of the Church," Benedicta whispered.

Patrick nodded, too overcome to speak.

"The Cardinal *has* sanctified this ground," she said, urgency in her voice. "First he made this foundation possible, and now he has shed his blood for it."

Patrick exhaled, took a deep breath and gazed at his sister, his mind suddenly quite clear.

"Really," Benedicta said slowly, "this is now hallowed ground."

Then, the young nun knelt, and kissed the bloody ground.

CHAPTER 50

As he guided the BMW onto the autostrada, the Head breathed deeply, fighting to regain his equilibrium. Terror still possessed him; he gripped the wheel tightly, though after a longish while he began to relax. The traffic was light. The night was clear.

From time to time, he glanced in his rearview mirror nervously. To his immense relief, nothing seemed amiss. He was not being followed.

As the powerful car raced through the night, he thought hard. What had happened? Obviously, everything had gone horribly wrong, for reasons he was at a loss to understand. His consultants -- trained professionals who were paid millions not to make mistakes—had completely botched the job.

Whatever had been going on inside that palazzo, the Head was too pragmatic of a man to speculate on. An atheist, he'd never given much thought to the supernatural. If there was no God, then of course his counterpart, Satan, was an early Hebrew myth as well. He certainly had no time for deluded American exorcists or their 'demons'.

The Head had actually come to these conclusions while in seminary. Trained in the Liberation Theology of the prominent Jesuits of his youth, he knew that Christianity was a bundle of myths. This was self-evident, but at the time he'd been convinced that the Church was a great platform for the overriding passion of his youth, social justice.

The Head had had no personal experience of social *injustice*, of course, coming as he did from a well-connected Mexico City family. His forebears had been instrumental in the purging of Mexico of the pestilential Cristeros, that gang of miserable upstarts in the 1920's. Since then, preferred positions in safe government jobs had been pretty much assured for his family, most of whom though espousing vaguely socialist leanings had precious little interest in the plight of the poor.

No, his feelings of sympathy for the underdog came mainly from his own experiences at boarding school, where his laziness and ineptitude at sports had earned him the contempt of his peers. He was a fat, ungainly teenager, and no amount of cajoling from his sports teachers inspired him to exert himself physically. Over time, he'd come to hate his rich, football-obsessed classmates and their haughty, privileged girlfriends.

Though his own background was one of similar privilege, when he encountered his first Marxist professor at university, he knew he had found his calling. He loved the feeling of solidarity, of hating the rich; he loved being united with the oppressed and the poor.

When he'd announced to his father that he'd opted for the priesthood, his father had nodded but had asked no questions. His proffered speech, delivered in his father's elegantly understated study in the leafy Polanco neighborhood, about the need to enlist the Church on behalf of the poor, had fallen on deaf ears. The old man had listened, without comment.

He would never forget his father's final words to him when he left for the seminary.

"You think you are in for a good time," his father had said, waving his hand in dismissal. "I know you. I know what you are after. You think the Church will offer you glory. But the Church offers no man glory. It is the biggest mafia in the world."

In the years following, of course, he'd outgrown his youthful interest in Liberation Theology, though he was always able to 'talk the talk' in the presence of leftist prelates. As he lost his baby fat through careful diet and yoga immersion, his good looks and pliable sexuality served him especially well as he worked his way through the treacherous ranks of ambition. He'd grown quite savvy, learning to keep his own counsel while letting other men disclose far too much. He became adept at scenting weakness, and proficient at exploiting fear. His yoga practice helped him a great deal in all of this, calming his anxieties and helping him stay focused on his goals.

He had smoothly side-stepped the papal inquiry into the Community, quietly offering up evidence on a few trusting friends and colleagues and thereby deftly turning the spotlight from himself. His diplomatic manner was such that he seemed the natural choice to lead the Community after the dust had cleared. And all had gone so well until Pilar and his stupidity.

The Head roused himself from his reverie long enough to note that he was about halfway to the airport, and his waiting jet. His phone remained quiet. No one was following him. His thoughts turned back with dark misgivings.

One of the gunmen had pointed a gun at him in the kitchen. Was he mad? Confused by the darkness, the lightning, that idiot priest's Latin chanting? When he'd bolted from the palazzo with the girl as his hostage – a singularly prescient move on his part – he'd been unprepared for the situation outside. Not only were all the 'victims' still alive, but in his mad dash he'd noted that they had somehow killed the gunman.

How could this be possible? He would have to have a serious word with his client when he arrived in Sao Paulo. He'd seen nothing but grave ineptitude on the part of these so-called 'professionals.' Up against unarmed nobodies, and there's dead bodies everywhere – theirs, and almost his!

Such amateurish tricks, too. Red paint pouring down stairs. Chairs manipulated by unseen wires. A sound machine pumping out the din of a locust swarm. And what were those 'earth tremors'? Clearly controlled explosions, badly timed. The entire thing had been a disaster, and he'd only been saved by his wits.

The Head considered his next move as he pulled into a nearly-empty Repsol station on the side of the autostrada. He parked the car in a dark corner, and headed for the toilets.

As he rounded the building's corner, he was stopped in his tracks. As if in a dream, he beheld a small child standing before him on the dirty concrete floor. She was wearing a simple red frock. In disbelief, he realized it was the girl he'd dragged from the house to use as a human shield.

Katy regarded him equably.

Frozen in his tracks, the Head glanced warily around. Though there were motorists fueling up in the middle distance, for the moment they were quite alone.

Thinking quickly, the Head reasoned that he must have been followed. This meant that a return to his car was probably too dangerous. What he needed was a crowd of people to disappear in. He decided to play for time.

"W-What are you doing here? Is e-everything all right?" he asked her.

"That's very kind of you to ask," Katy responded equably. "But I am worried about *you*, Father."

"W-Why?" he asked, unnerved. Was he dreaming?

"Your immortal soul," she replied evenly.

"M-my immortal soul?" he repeated automatically, and glanced nervously around them.

"Do you know what the most important thing in life is?" she persisted, seriously.

"N-no," he answered. Feeling the alarm rising, his eyes began searching frantically for an escape.

Just then a large group of young Italian men appeared, emerging from the toilets. They were in high spirits after a football game. As they passed between him and Katy, laughing loudly and joking, the Head grabbed his chance.

He smiled good-naturedly and fell into step with them. As the group ambled around a nearby corner, however, the Head couldn't resist a look back.

Katy was gone.

In her place was an elderly Italian in bright blue coveralls, the mark of a working man. He was lighting a cigarette with a Bic lighter, which he then pocketed, before looking briefly up with narrowed eyes. His gaze locked onto the Head's.

The Head felt a cold shiver run down his spine. He shook his head. The stress must be doing things to his mind, he thought. When he looked again, the old man was gone.

Relieved, he headed back to the empty toilets and the quiet parking lot.

It was only as he felt the BMW accelerate smoothly onto the dark autostrada that he realized the elderly Italian bore an uncanny resemblance to his own father, dead these many years.

CHAPTER 51

At the palazzo, Dyson finished explaining to everyone how he'd found Katy at the bottom of the hill, minutes after the Head drove away. Then, Luca, the Bishop and Valeria had to carefully explain to the *carabineri* who everyone was, presenting them with US passports and Italian *documenti* as proof.

Once this was clarified, the senior officer graciously contacted the hospital and was immediately connected with the surgeon who had just removed the bullets from Phillip's legs. The operation had gone well, the surgeon said cautiously, though Phillip would require some healing time and rehabilitation. He also had a concussion from his fall, but was now awake.

His wife, in the next bed, had been diagnosed with a bad bruise and exhaustion. They were both overjoyed to hear that Katy was unharmed.

"Mom, the doctor says we need to hang up now," Stacey whispered into the phone, after she finished her tearful conversation with Katy.

"Honey, of course," Michelle responded at once, fighting back her own tears. "I just thank God you are okay. And is Phillip okay?"

"Phillip is fine, Mom," Stacey answered, with audible catch in her voice. "He's our hero."

"You tell him we love him," Michelle told her daughter firmly.

"Th-Thanks, Mom," Stacey said, so quietly Michelle could barely hear her. "That will mean a lot to him."

Michelle's overloaded short term memory began to fade after the homicide unit had staked out the barn and removed the weapons. By the time all the officials left – except for the *carabineri* stationed outside the house as a precaution – she was running on a combination of exhaustion sustained by adrenaline, augmented by slurps of red wine.

Thus, she was grateful for Valeria's stepping in to take over the running of the kitchen, the nerve center of a jangled household. It left her space to escort the utterly-exhausted Josh and Katy upstairs. Soothed by a few pages of the *Velveteen Rabbit* read by Dyson, they were almost instantly asleep.

Hand in hand, Dyson and Michelle tiptoed out of the children's room and down the palazzo's dark upper hallway, past the nuns' room. All was quiet.

Next, they stopped at Gina's open door. Inside, Carlo was lying flat on his back, snoring softly on the floor next to her bed. Gina herself was fast asleep, curled up under the covers on the single bed above him, one slender arm draped down, hand clasped in Carlo's big hands.

Just an hour before, he had carried Gina reverently to her bed.

"You mind, d'you mind if I give you a hug?" he'd asked, humbly.

Gina had felt the smile spread slowly across her face. As exhausted as she was, she was also blissfully sure that she had chosen the right path. She would have her baby in this beautiful place. And maybe, just maybe, she and Carlo would make a marriage.

"*Si,*" she'd given her assent.

Carlo had stood up, and slowly bending over, extended his arms. She folded her own arms across her chest and waited. Carlo's squarely-built bulk enveloped her, and she breathed in the scent of him as his strong arms warmed her. It had been dizzying and comforting all at the same time.

When he'd released her, she'd looked up at him and smiled beatifically.

"*Bella*," he'd whispered, and leaning forward, he'd kissed her, chastely and deliberately, on her forehead. Then he lay down on the floor, and they were both asleep in seconds.

Emerging into the warmly-lit kitchen downstairs, Michelle and Dyson found the table laid for supper. Luca was pouring wine for everyone. Luigi stood beside them, quietly smiling and trading jibes with Valeria, who was boiling pasta. Beside her, the Bishop obediently chopped green and white finocchio on a wooden board. They all looked up as the Whites entered the kitchen. Everyone grew quiet.

Dyson cleared his throat. "The *carabineri* want to see all of us tomorrow. They will be interviewing Stacy and Phillip at the hospital."

Everyone eyed each other.

"Why would the Mafia want to kill us?" Michelle said, breaking the silence.

Luigi shook his head.

"*No, no mafia*," he said, wagging a finger for emphasis. "*Questo non e mafia.*"

"Then if not the mafia, who?" asked Dyson. "They didn't want any money."

"*No, no soldi*," Luigi agreed. The Bishop, sitting next to him, nodded his agreement vigorously.

"*Terroristi. Semplicemente*," Valeria shrugged.

"No, I don't think so," Dyson said. "Terrorists want money and fame. These guys wanted neither. They just wanted to kill all of us, and get out. Like it was a job."

"A job they botched," said Luca with a grin, glancing at his father. Luigi shook his head in self-deprecation and looked thoughtful.

"*Il prete,*" he said quietly.

"You mean the last two guys?" Michelle asked. "One of them was a priest?"

"*Si!*" Luigi said. "*Senza vestidi sacerdotale. Pero un prete, definativemente.*"

"Not wearing a collar..." Patrick began.

"...but definitely a priest," Luca finished.

"*Lui non e italiano,*" Luigi offered.

"Not an Italian priest," Michelle translated.

"What did he look like?" Patrick wanted to know.

"Tall, dark and handsome," Michelle said bitterly. "I saw him so quickly, from the back, that's all I got."

"I too believe he was a priest. He spoke English with a Spanish accent," Father Paul volunteered, and explained about their brief encounter in the kitchen before the lightning struck. "But he wasn't from Spain. Someplace in the new world, by his looks. I had the impression that he was brought in at the last moment, and wasn't happy with what he saw."

"Talked like a boss?" Patrick asked.

Father Paul nodded thoughtfully. "Certainly like someone used to being obeyed."

"Wait a second," Michelle said. A memory was coming back to her. "I saw his shoes. When he walked by me, outside on the gravel."

"His shoes?" Patrick echoed.

"Yep," Michelle nodded. "Gucci or similar. Beautiful shoes. A thousand euro, minimum. The kind your father won't let me buy him."

"Your mother has been shopping here in Rome for the past few months," Dyson allowed himself a small grin. "She knows her Italian luxury products."

Father Corinth, who has been simultaneously translating for the Italians, suddenly put a finger in the air. The Bishop had something to say.

"He believes," the priest said slowly, "and he says he has no proof for this, only a hunch, but nevertheless he believes that this was a priest from the Community."

At that, Patrick slammed his hand down with a loud bang. The sound made everyone jump.

"Patrick!" Michelle's hands flew to her throat. Beside her, Dyson reddened.

"Sorry, Mom," Patrick said, excitedly. "But I gotta say I think he's right. I didn't see the guy, but it all fits together – tall, dark, Latin American, wearing fancy shoes, driving a Beamer. Sounds like a Community priest to me! Father," he said, turning to Corinth, "how old was this guy?"

"Hard to say," the priest knit his brow pensively. "He looked to be in excellent shape, from what little I could see. But he wasn't young. I would guess in his fifties."

"So, probably a senior guy," Dyson ventured.

"Yes," Corinth replied, and then grinned. "One thing I can tell you, though. He didn't like Latin."

When Luca finished translating all of this for his parents and the Bishop, he winked broadly at his mother.

"I told you the Devil hates Latin," he smiled. Valeria rolled her eyes at her son, but said nothing.

"*Si! Si!*" Suddenly, the Bishop was nodding excitedly. He began to speak rapid-fire Italian, waving his hands for emphasis, with Corinth translating for the Americans. "He says that when the guy ran out with Katy, it was so dark outside and everything happened so quickly that he didn't get a good look at his face, but he thinks it may have been the Community's prior general. He met him in Rome, on the Via Julia, recently, he says."

"Of course it was the Community," Dyson spat out bitterly, and folding his arms, looked hard at the Bishop. "So it was the Community bidding against us?"

Corinth began to translate, but the Bishop had understood. He hung his head, and nodded.

"And what happened?" Dyson was relentless.

"Buh." The Bishop reacted with the classic Italian shrug of resignation and disgust. Then he spoke, tiredly.

"He says the Community priest who he had dealings with is dead, from suicide," Corinth translated.

"Father Pilar?!?" Patrick practically exploded. "That rat bastard?!?"

At this outburst all the Italians looked taken aback. After a second, the Bishop nodded cautiously before continuing in Italian. Once his story was finished, the room subsided into a thoughtful silence.

"So, it was the Community trying to kill me, and all of us," Patrick said flatly.

Dyson nodded, but before he could speak, his wife jumped in.

"Wait a second, this rich Community is trying to kill all of us because -- of Patrick?" Michelle looked perplexed. "Because he ran away and threatened them? And then survived the poisoning?"

"*No, no!*" Luigi began to speak again, shaking his head vigorously.

"Pop says that can't be it," Luca translated. "The risk wasn't big enough. Not enough reason to hire expensive professionals like this to kill all these people. He says there's something else. Something big. That there was no reason to kill us all except to silence us."

"Silence *us*? But what do we *know*?" Michelle responded tiredly. Everyone looked at each other blankly. The clock on the kitchen wall struck one.

Luigi spoke then, nodding calmly.

"Pop says that sometimes we have to wait," Luca translated. "He says the answer will come."

"Well, Luca, if your dad believes that," Dyson said slowly, "I for one will give it some thought. Your father knows what he's doing. If it wasn't for him, I doubt we'd all be standing here now. We owe him our lives."

When Luca finished translating, Valeria's eyes filled with tears and she drew closer to Luigi, who nodded humbly, but said nothing. He looked down at the kitchen floor.

"And, we need to pray." It was Father Corinth. His voice sounded hollow with exhaustion. "Tomorrow, I will offer a Mass of thanksgiving here."

"Oh, Father, thank you! I can't think of anything more fitting," said a calm woman's voice from the kitchen doorway. It was Sister Mary Grace, with Carlo standing behind her. Both looked sleep-rumpled and bleary-eyed.

"Sister, we thought you were asleep!" Michelle cried. "What are you doing up?"

The nun smiled.

"Force of habit, you might say," she explained. "Running a home for pregnant women and new babies trains you to get up and check out the place during the night. I walked down the hall and found Carlo here sound asleep on the floor of the ladies' bedroom. I thought it might be better if he slept somewhere else."

Everyone laughed, including Carlo, who scratched his head sheepishly.

"So, tomorrow, Mass at nine in the morning?" Michelle asked.

And so it was agreed, as everyone made their way to bed. But not before Dyson and Luca paid a visit to the carabineri stationed outside the palazzo. Satisfied that they were adequately protected for the night, before he retired, Dyson nevertheless left a message for his Virginia lawyer to arrange for surveillance and protection for the palazzo and its occupants. He was taking no chances.

CHAPTER 52

The rest of the Head's trip to Perugia Airport was blessedly uneventful. The *autostrada* was clear at night, though when he arrived at his hotel, he felt a twinge of regret as he parked the gleaming BMW. The bungling Italian *carabineri* would trace him, but the trail would end there. He checked in, asked the concierge for a recommendation for a late night supper, and stepped into a waiting cab.

On the way to the airport, his smartphone twittered. In the taxi's dark interior, the screen lit up. The Head's eyes bulged as he scanned the blaring headline from a Boston newspaper, 'Catholic Priests Laundering Millions for Drug Cartels'.

The Head felt his gorge rise, and when the next minute his smartphone rang, he struggled mightily to control himself. It was his Sao Paulo client.

"Yes, yes, I have seen it," he muttered, in Spanish.

The source was Pilar, of course. He'd threatened the Head with exactly this, just before he 'committed suicide'. But the Head hadn't been overly concerned, as the Community had other priests in their nearly-empty Boston corporate offices. They would simply explain to the Boston media that the late Father Pilar, who had tragically shot himself in Italy days earlier, had been demonstrating symptoms of extreme stress. Then, off the record, they would explain about the Rome scandal, and provide a helpful translation from the Italian of the media reports there. Though this was certainly a tragedy, there should be zero tolerance for the sexual abuse of a child, they would assert indignantly. Obviously Fr Pilar had problems; clearly, his rambling phone call to a reporter shouldn't be the basis of a news story.

The Head had left all of this in the capable hands of Father Pilar's assistant, a man he'd exchanged pillow talk with on more than one occasion. What had gone wrong?

"The story is not based just on one call from Father Pilar," his client asserted in a neutral tone. "It actually seems the Cardinal, Portland, has corroborated this as well."

"Portland?" The Head's vision had begun to blur. Hadn't he been at the palazzo? Wasn't he dead?

"Yes, it seems the good Cardinal actually went directly to the FBI, and he wore a wire when he paid an unexpected visit to your friend, Pilar's assistant -- a Father Cromwell, I believe? Yes, well, this was immediately before he departed for Rome."

The Head made no reply, and tried to concentrate on his breathing to lower his heart rate.

"Though I see from the updated story on my newsfeed that the Cardinal is now deceased," his client continued. "He was dead on arrival to the hospital at Spoleto just a few hours ago, the story says."

"Y-yes," the Head whispered.

"May he rest in peace. Overall, a very nice piece of reporting, I must say," his client observed.

The Head tried to think of what to say, but the events of the evening had finally overwhelmed him. He remained silent, staring dully out of the taxi window at the metallic glare of the airport lights drawing near. What would become of him now?

It would take the Vatican a few hours to react publicly. They would order an immediate investigation and strict compliance with secular authorities.

"They have raided your property in Boston, apparently," his client ventured.

Another link appeared on his phone, this time a video. The Head watched in horror as TV cameras focused on Community priests being escorted in handcuffs into waiting Boston police cars. Of course, most of them had no inkling of the source of its funding, and so would be useless to investigators, he knew. But his heart started to beat wildly when he saw Cromwell, looking very pale indeed as a Boston cop put a protective hand over the priest's head as he climbed into the back of the police cruiser, its red lights flashing.

A perp walk? Was there a warrant out for *his* arrest? Could they find him here in Italy?

"It's a good thing you're coming to Sao Paolo," his client said comfortably.

"Y-yes," the Head replied, trying to calm himself.

"And don't worry about anything, my friend. We have taken the necessary precautions. There will be no need to produce your identification before boarding the jet."

"N-no?" The Head exhaled.

"Not at all. Though of course you will have to pass through security. We will have someone greet you at the check-in desk and direct you to the proper gate."

The Head felt dizzy with relief, but a few minutes later somehow managed to find his way to the right desk. And his client was as good as his word. Less than an hour later, having been very cordially conducted by an official to a gate in a little-used corridor, the Head soon found himself ensconced in his own private plane.

The handsome, all-male crew was equally solicitous of his comfort. To his delight, he was presented with an extra-large, extra dry martini when he returned from performing the necessary ablutions in the plane's luxurious bathroom.

As the elegant little jet rose through the blue-black skies and circled out over the Mediterranean Sea, the Head exhaled and leaned back into his fawn-colored leather seat. His client had thought of everything, it seemed. The gin was working its magic.

Even before he could ask, another martini appeared, which he downed with uncharacteristic gusto. He gratefully accepted a third martini, too, though tried to sip this one. By the time he'd finished a half hour later, he was feeling no pain at all.

When the Head decided he'd better visit the men's room again, he found that his limbs wouldn't obey him. He looked up at the smiling flight attendants, who for some reason didn't seem to hear when he summoned them. Flustered, he willed himself to stand.

Just then the reality of his plight dawned on him. He made one last heroic attempt to stand, and failed. Instead, he slumped onto the cabin's beige carpet, unconscious.

A few minutes later, with the flight crew strapped in and wearing oxygen masks, the pilot executed an expert roll with the plane's door wide open.

The cabin door shut automatically at the touch a button, and the cabin re-pressurized. After a quick call to the satisfied client in Sao Paolo, the jet continued its serene ascent to 31,000 feet over the Mediterranean, as scheduled.

CHAPTER 53

The Cardinal's Requiem Mass was in Latin at Trinita Dei Pellegrini. Father Paul Corinth celebrated the Sung High Mass in the presence of the Pope, the first time in decades that a reigning pontiff had so graced a Requiem in the *Usus Antiquior*.

The old Baroque Church was filled to overflowing with Catholics and the curious. Every moment was recorded, to the exasperation of the media, by a battery of amateurs wielding smartphones and tablets.

The media were, in a word, overwhelmed. This Mass was like nothing they had ever witnessed. From the three celebrants in black brocaded vestments slowly appearing through a dense fog of incense, followed by rows upon rows of clergy and altar servers, to the reverent placement of the Cardinal's body on a high funeral bier, the Requiem with its slow, inexorable choreography, seemed an experience outside of time and place. And above it all, the haunting Gregorian chant cascading down from the *schola* in the tiny choir loft.

The congregation was a mystery, too. Mostly young and soberly dressed, they knelt on the cold stone floor with great devotion – fantastic visuals for the cameras, but quite perplexing. Why would young people care about a dead Cardinal? And this Mass, was it some new trend?

The striking young British woman from Reuters was intrigued. Determined to garner photos and quotes from photogenic young Italians, she at once zeroed in on Gina and Luca as they left the church.

"...and the nun had to come and get Carlo out of your *bedroom*?" Luca was laughing, shaking his finger at Gina in mock admonishment. He had to admit that once his sister had had a few days' rest, she looked stunning. Gina's golden skin and glossy brown hair glowed under her elegant ochre–and-sienna mantilla.

"Luca, I'm telling you now something you won't believe," Gina waved off his teasing, flashing her left hand with a quick sparkle of her new engagement ring. "I will go to that altar and marry him without sleeping with Carlo before."

"Why? You decide you don't need to take him for a test drive?" Luca was relentless.

"No, I don't need that," Gina answered him seriously. "And I want this marriage to be the real thing."

"Pardon, but do you speak English?" The reporter's Oxbridge accent interrupted them.

They nodded and waited politely while she explained who she was. In the interim, Luigi, Carlo and Valeria appeared and joined curious passersby eyeing the reporter interviewing the little group huddled on the front steps of the church.

"Why do I love this Mass?" Gina repeated the reporter's question, giving it some serious thought. "Because I am Catholic, and this is the highest expression of our Faith."

"And are you wearing that veil because it is a sign of your subjugation, as in Islam?" the reporter asked, pressing her massive microphone insinuatingly under Gina's nose. "Or is this some kind of rebellion against the modern world?"

To the reporter's consternation, Gina laughed outright.

"Yes, of course," she grinned disingenuously. "I am of course wearing this as a sign of subjugation – to our Lord. You should try it yourself. The Church is open to everyone."

Leaving the reporter speechless in her wake, Gina smiled sweetly and moved off with her family into the crowd bound for the funeral feast at the parish hall.

Once inside, they all sat down with the White family.

"Mama still doesn't understand why Gina wears the veil, and why we love this Mass," Luca explained to them in English. "She thinks it's some kind of elitist thing."

Gina was still smiling broadly, her hand covered by Carlo's. The chauffeur sat close beside her, quietly smitten, his big arm laid protectively around her chair back.

Patrick nodded. "Older Italians think that."

"I tell her, 'what about Pop; he is no elitist' but she won't listen," Gina said, shrugging.

"I understand her," Michelle interjected. "My generation was raised to believe that the Church was 'moving forward' and that the Latin Mass was a sign of being old-fashioned -- medieval, even. And the veils," she smiled, "we wore them to church when I was a girl, but they went out of style by 1970. Later on I heard some women talk about how they were a sign of women's 'oppression'."

Because Luca was translating, Valeria understood and began nodding vehemently.

"She says the Church needs to stay with the times," Luca translated.

"The Church," Patrick answered slowly, "is not like anything else in this world. She is timeless. She is the only thing we have which exists both in time and out of time. She has no need to 'keep up with the times.'"

"And 'the times' sometimes spin out of control," Dyson interjected. "We are in just such a period now. The political framework of Europe and America – the entire West -- is vulnerable. Families are failing to form in most of mainland Europe. Even in Italy, the heart of the Church."

Just then, Sister Mary Grace and Sister Benedicta arrived, followed by Father Corinth and the Bishop, both dressed in cassocks. In the crowded parish hall, people eyed the religious in their traditional garb with frank curiosity, which turned to surprise when they were greeted with enthusiasm by the American and Italian families.

Ignoring the startled looks, the Pirisis, the Whites, Carlo, the nuns and the clerics all sat down together at a massive oak table along one wall. Straightaway, the Bishop said grace and blessed the food, and everyone settled in to eat.

"Except here," Carlo resumed the conversation where they had left off. "Mr. White, you say that families are failing to form. We are making a start, here." He looked at Gina, who smiled radiantly up at him, her lustrous brown eyes filling with tears.

"Yes," she managed to choke out, and proudly displayed her ring for the admiration of everyone at the table. "And we will hopefully be the first of many to begin our family lives around the Sisters and their palazzo."

Her news was greeted by a round of applause and exclamations of joy. Luigi and Valeria solemnly accepted warm handshakes and congratulatory hugs.

"How did it feel to celebrate a Requiem Mass before the Pope?" Sister Benedicta asked Father Paul under cover of the joyous noise. He was sitting next to her.

"Of course, this was a Mass I never wanted to celebrate," the priest answered quietly. He looked tired.

"And this was a Mass that the Pope never thought he would have to attend, I'm sure," Sister Mary Grace offered sympathetically.

At this last, everyone grew quiet and eyed each other, at a loss for words. Their common loss and their experience at the palazzo days before hung in the air between them, a bond forged under fire.

"The Cardinal," Dyson cleared his throat, "apparently was part of the reason we were targeted by the Community."

This got everyone's attention. Dyson went on to explain what Carol in Boston had told him about how the Cardinal had suspected the Community of money laundering, and had secretly taped his last meeting with them.

"When the story broke about Father Pilar's raping the seminarian, and his subsequent suicide, of course they started looking for Patrick, and found him," Dyson said grimly. "And when he survived their poisoning attempt, and they learned we were working with the Cardinal, they decided that it would only be a matter of time before we pieced together the story and figured out what they were up to."

"Wow, they gave us a lot more credit than we deserved!" Sister Benedicta burst out in wonder, as everyone else shook their heads. "I would have never put that puzzle together!"

"Maybe not you, honey," Michelle said to her daughter. "But your dad and his lawyers might well have, especially with the Cardinal's knowledge."

"But you had no idea that the Cardinal had done this, right, Dad?" Patrick asked.

"No," Dyson admitted. "But someone credible inside the Community had definitely gone to the media with the money laundering story."

"So it was only a matter of time," Phillip said wonderingly, "before the whole thing blew wide open."

"Which it has," Dyson pointed out. They all nodded. The headlines and photos of Community priests in police cars had raced around the world on social media.

"And nobody has caught the Head?" Patrick asked grimly.

"No, he seems to have disappeared from the face of the earth after he left our Katy standing by the side of the road in the dark," his father answered.

"Probably I was the last person to see him," Katy piped up.

"Yes, baby doll, yes you were," Phillip hugged his daughter closely. How near he had come to losing her!

"But, what would the explanation have been when they found all of us, dead in the palazzo?" Michelle asked.

Dyson opened his mouth to answer, but Luigi interrupted. He had been following Luca's translation of the conversation closely.

"*Terroristi. Mafiosi.*" He shrugged. "*Oggi,* the bizarre is normal, everyday. A rich American and a Cardinal with a crazy scheme to stop abortion, killed on a country estate with their family and some Italians, too."

"The media would have moved on in 24 hours," Michelle said bitterly.

Everyone was silent. It was manifestly true.

"So," Dyson cleared his throat again, "the Cardinal wasn't a wealthy man. But he was completely committed to the idea of the Sisters' maternity home, which he privately referred to as '*Casa della Madonna.*' I think it's the name we should adopt."

This last was greeted with approval by everyone, and a restrained round of applause.

Dyson held his hand up for silence.

"Before he left Boston," he continued, "he apparently must have had some premonition that he might not return, because his personal affairs are very much in order."

Everyone nodded, waiting.

"In the days since he died, I have heard from many of the Cardinal's friends in America. He was a man much admired by those worked with him. I daresay he was an example of the finest America produces."

At this, Dyson swallowed hard and his eyes reddened. Next to him, Michelle squeezed his hand, hard. He gave her a small smile, took a deep breath and went on.

"He must have had been discussing the *Casa della Madonna* project with some benefactors who are extremely wealthy. When they heard the news reports, they contacted his secretary Carol, who then passed the calls on to me. Net, net, it looks as if *Casa della Madonna* will be well provided for, going forward."

Everyone burst into applause, beaming at him and each other.

"And now, your Excellency," Dyson continued, motioning for silence and eyeing the Bishop soberly. "Now I have something to ask you."

The Bishop looked apprehensive, but squared his shoulders and waited.

"Do you know that Italy's abortion rate is twice that of neighboring Croatia?" Dyson paused a moment, to let Luca translate.

"This is *Italy* – the center of the Catholic Church," Michelle echoed, her arm around Josh, who was occupying himself with a bowl of pasta.

The Bishop sighed, held up his finger and signaled for Luca to translate.

"I come from a small village on the Adriatic, near Bari," he began. "In the early 1990's, the ferries began to once again make the journey to Croatia from there. That was how a local priest and some nuns from Acri departed for Croatia – they were sent for the first time since the last War, to a land that had been occupied by the Communists for more than 50 years."

Beside him, Valeria was nodding, deeply affected. Luigi put his arm around her.

"They found the church that they were assigned to in ruins," the Bishop continued. "It had been used as a stable, and later as a parking garage. The roof was off, and the inside reeked of decay. But they set to work, with their own hands, to clean it out. After a few days of hard work, some of the children came to watch; the adults were still far too frightened to risk being seen with religious.

"After about a week, the children came bearing cool water and food for the priest and the young nuns. Little by little," he smiled at the memory, "the children showed the adults there was nothing to fear. After awhile, the adults appeared and began to pitch in, to help the religious with their enormous task. When the church was finally cleaned and painted, a man appeared, wanting to talk to the priest. He had the bell, he told him, with great solemnity."

"'What bell?' the priest wanted to know."

"'The bell, the bell! From the church tower!' the man said with great excitement. And so he led them all back to his family house. Outside, in the garden, they found the man's father, now grown old. The elderly Croatian then began to relate how, in the wake of World War II and the Communist takeover, his own father and he had spirited the bell from the church, knowing that the Communists would destroy the sacred place and melt the bell down for weapons.

"So, at great risk to themselves, the father and son had buried the bell deep in their garden, in the dead of night. And for all those long years under the ferociously anti-Catholic regime, when people were imprisoned for hiding a rosary under their bed pillows, no one breathed a word about the secret bell in the garden."

The Bishop sighed.

"So then everyone dug up the old bell, but of course after all those years in the earth, it was badly damaged. There were no specialists who could repair bells there, as you might imagine, so the bell had to be shipped to Italy on the ferry."

"Because," Michelle interrupted, "of course Italy still has artisans who repair bells."

"Si," the Bishop said to her and spread his hands eloquently. "Because of course this is Italy, and we have such things. But you see the old man would not leave his bell. So, we took the bell, and the old man, back with us to Italy, where the Faith had always been practiced – that Faith denied to his entire generation."

Everyone was transfixed.

"*We?*" Dyson asked.

"Si," the Bishop said, meeting Dyson's gaze squarely and then said in halting English, "I was that young priest, sent to Croatia."

There was silence, as everyone held their breath.

"And in the years since the Faith has come back strongly in Croatia, as of course the people were denied their ancient Faith for so long. Meanwhile, as you say," he waved in agreement to Dyson, "the Faith is dying here, along with our families. It is the Faith that has given life to our culture for so many centuries. And now, our culture is dying. "

"Why do you think that is?" Dyson asked, his arms folded.

The Bishop sighed.

"Because we – the clergy – have not wanted to fight with our people," he said sadly. "Italians want to be modern. Yes, yes, they appreciate their great patrimony of art and culture but to most of them this is academic. They no longer connect this with the Church that created it, that created them.

"And some of us in the clergy have known this for some time, but have been complacent. We could not imagine an Italy without the Faith, so no one raised any alarm bells. We just went along as before, relying on the families to transmit the Faith. Until now, when it is clear that there are not many families, as you say, being formed," he sighed.

"So what is lacking?" Dyson asked.

The Bishop looked around the table.

"What is lacking is what I see here," he said simply. "What I see in you Americans, and in Luigi. The Faith."

At hearing this, Luigi suddenly began to shake his head vehemently. "No, no, no," he protested, as tears stung his eyes. "*Non e vero*. I have no great Faith. I have failed in the most basic thing, the thing that my own simple parents gave to me. I have not passed it down. My children," and with this he sobbed aloud, "my children have been brought up ignorant of the Faith. I did not teach them."

Hot tears were streaming down Luigi's face as Luca haltingly translated his words. Valeria bent her head, too, tears silently flowing, her arm around Luigi's back. Luca and Gina stared at their parents in wonder.

"It's not just you, Luigi and Valeria," Michelle responded thoughtfully. "For most of my life, my faith was something I took completely for granted. I sent my kids to catechism class, and took them to Mass. But that was it. I just thought, somehow, that they would be Catholic. But now I wonder how Catholic they would have been, if all this trouble hadn't started."

"Parents should not take all the blame for this," interjected the Bishop. "We are guilty, too, all of us priests and religious. We have been too concerned with keeping the old walls of the Church up. We have let our people slip through our fingers."

The table was quiet.

"*We* will pass the Faith down to our children." It was Stacey who broke the silence. "Bishop, with all due respect, I have seen what earthly power men wield in the military," she said, and her voice held quiet authority. "I can tell you categorically that without the Faith, we are most certainly lost."

Beside her in his wheelchair, with Katy perched on his lap, Phillip nodded quietly. He gazed at his wife, and thought with a catch in his throat about how easily he could have lost her, his children, his dignity and his soul. Stacey had agreed to return to England with him for his convalescence; their flight was scheduled for a few days' hence. Phillip knew this was by the grace of God.

"And what is lacking also is Beauty," this from Gina, speaking in Italian and English, earnestly holding tightly to Carlo's hand. "*La bellezza.* If I had known the beauty of the Mass, of what the Church teaches, I would never have lived as I did."

"What is also lacking is the Truth," said Sister Mary Grace, her chin lifted. Beside her, Sister Benedicta nodded vehemently. "And the courage to teach the truth, and to reach out with mercy to all those who need us so badly."

"In Italy the Faith is like that bell hidden in the garden, your Excellency," Father Paul Corinth observed.

The Bishop nodded, and suddenly smiled broadly.

"And now it is time we dig it up, my friends!" he grinned at them, arms extended. "Now is the time! And we start, in Spoleto! What about you, Father Corinth, will you teach in my seminary? I closed it a few months ago, but I think it's time to re-open it."

Corinth smiled. "What should I teach?"

"If the Pope can spare you once in a while, we'll start with the Mass in Latin," the Bishop declared. "I think Italians need to improve our liturgical instruction significantly. I can think of no greater tribute to your American Cardinal, in fact."

"Which brings me to what I wanted to say, Excellency." It was Dyson, who had been listening without comment.

Everyone looked at him.

"Now that my financial support is not so much needed for *Casa Della Madonna*, I would be pleased to extend that support to help seminarians in your Diocese," Dyson was smiling broadly.

Everyone at the table burst into applause.

"And that brings me to something *I* wanted to say."

Everyone at the table turned to Patrick. He was standing beside Michelle, looking pale but determined.

"I would like," he said, clearing his throat nervously, "to be your first new seminarian."

He was smiling radiantly as he was overwhelmed by the cries of 'bravo!' and applause sweeping the table and engulfed in a tremendous hug from his suddenly weeping mother.

EPILOGUE

Rome, four months later

Luca darted nimbly down the Lungotevere, swerving to avoid the tourists who seemed to be everywhere in Rome's torrid summer heat. He had stepped off a city bus in a hurry. His new job at Dyson's company in Rome was hard to walk away from, and he was late for evening Mass at Trinita Dei Pellegrini.

As he stepped quickly over the super-heated cobblestones, Luca considered how lucky his sister was to be in beautiful green Umbria in her last months of pregnancy, attended by Luigi and the sisters. He was looking forward to the weekend, when he would drive Valeria there on Friday after work. He knew Luigi would immediately press him into service on the palazzo or its property, but he didn't mind. He liked learning about how to live in the country, and his father obviously loved teaching him.

Things had changed, that was for sure. He felt years older than he had been just a few months before – a man, really, for the first time. He shook his head, as he recalled his family's tense meeting with Marco, just a few weeks before.

It had been Valeria who initiated it. When Marco appeared in his salon doorway for his morning cigarette, Valeria had suddenly stepped out from the shadows into the sun's glare.

Standing directly in his path, in full view of his gossipy clientele, she had commanded him to take her into the back of his shop. To underscore her request, Luigi and Luca had also emerged from the shadows, arms folded, to stand silently behind her.

The men remained outside as Marco reluctantly complied with Valeria's request; he led her through the shop past the row of women sitting in their beauty parlor chairs. Silence followed them. When Marco and Valeria disappeared behind a flimsy wooden door, everyone waited, uncharacteristically quiet. The MTV screens flickered and the pop music blared, but hardly anyone made a sound.

"Don't say a word to me, Marco," Valeria asserted herself before he could speak. Her face was grim. "I'm here to talk; you're here to listen. You'll either listen quietly or all your customers out there will get to hear exactly what I'm gonna say."

Marco shut his mouth, and looked sullen.

"Now," Valeria continued briskly, "this won't take long. I got a busy schedule. First, Gina's having the baby. Second, you're gonna pay for her doctor's bills. She won't be going to no filthy public hospital. Third – and this is the part you'll love – you won't have to pay nothing else. She and the baby will be all taken care of, by the Church."

At this, Marco's eyes widened, stunned.

"That's right," she said, smiling coolly. "You're off the hook. That should make you happy, though God knows I don't think you deserve it. Now, here's what's going to happen. My husband and my son are waiting outside, and we are gonna go with you to the bank. No – no, no complaining. I know you got the cash. You oughta be happy this is all you gotta pay..."

In the end, Marco had gone with them, without a word. At the bank, he had withdrawn the amount that Valeria wrote down on a slip of paper, and handed the envelope to Luigi, who accepted it gravely.

And that was that. Except that Luigi was praying intensely for Marco, Luca knew. So he wasn't too surprised when one of the ladies stopped by to have coffee with Valeria a few weeks later, and revealed what everyone in the neighborhood was buzzing about – Marco had gone back to his wife. Yes, she'd confided excitedly, and with his tail between his legs, too.

A few days after this, Marco had approached Luigi outside their apartment building. The older man was packing his car to return to Umbria. The hairdresser looked humble, his hands folded in front of him.

"Mi *dispiace*," he said simply, not daring to look at Luigi.

Luigi's eyes immediately filled with tears. Straightening, he embraced Marco warmly.

"It is the good God who has done this," Luigi told Marco then, wiping his eyes. The younger man nodded, and embraced Luigi again, and that is how Luca found them when he appeared to drive his father to Umbria.

Luca sighed, and in passing took in the view of the hulking Castel Sant'Angelo – ancient Hadrian's Tomb used as the papal fortress for centuries. Meanwhile, his sister and Carlo were to be married a few months after the baby came, by the Bishop in Spoleto's magnificent ancient cathedral. After their marriage, they planned to live in the nearby village. Gina and the baby would be well cared for; Carlo's mother, overjoyed at the answer to her years of prayers, had moved into a small room in the palazzo. She would help Gina, plus cook for the Sisters and the women residents.

It wasn't only Gina and Carlo. When the Bishop's letter announcing the establishment of *Casa Della Madonna* was read at Sunday Masses throughout the Diocese, it wasn't long before the inquiries started trickling in. Sister Beatrice, recovered from her concussion, cloned the Sisters' website into Italian and the emails started arriving. Sisters Mary Grace and Benedicta, aided by local translators, were kept busy answering the inevitable hail of questions from anxious Italian women.

A few were suspicious; but when they learned that they could have their babies without fear, supported and protected, the women began to arrive. Some were young, others approaching middle age. Some were educated, others not.

All were comfortably housed in the palazzo complex, which had proven to be relatively easy to reconfigure into small separate apartments. A local Catholic hospital sent maternity nurses. Carlo's mother and Michelle teamed up to teach cooking and childcare. The nuns provided counselling and support for the women, often traumatized, coping with crisis pregnancies. The nearby village provided housing for the fledgling families begun at *Casa Della Madonna*.

And in the palazzo's chapel, serenity reigned, as the Blessed Sacrament was exposed and Adoration held every morning. Every evening they prayed a family rosary together, led by Michelle and Dyson. Father Paul Corinth came from Rome to celebrate Mass in Latin for everyone in the palazzo on Sundays. Sister Beatrice set up her small library, and with the aid of Luigi's translation, began teaching catechism and history to the curious locals, most of whom had no idea about their own heritage.

One hot summer Sunday afternoon, Patrick, Father Corinth and the Bishop arrived with a large cardboard box, which they carried into the palazzo kitchen where everyone was gathered.

Inside was a mysterious medieval statue, badly damaged, of a bishop crowned with a miter. The statue had no hands.

"Ah, Santa Sabinus!" Beatrice cried in instant recognition. Everyone looked at her and then at the statue, mystified.

"We found him in the seminary cellar," Patrick explained. "He must have been down there for years."

"Sabinus was an ancient Bishop of Spoleto," said the Bishop slowly. "A martyr, *si*?"

"Yep," answered Beatrice matter-of-factly. "When the edicts of Diocletian were published against the Christians in the year 303, all were forbidden even to draw water or grind wheat, if they would not first incense idols placed for that purpose in the markets and on street corners."

"On the street corners -- here? In Umbria?" One of the women asked, fascinated.

"*Si, certo!*" Beatrice answered easily, pleased with her burgeoning Italian. "Saint Sabinus, Bishop of Spoleto, with Marcellus and Exuperantius, his deacons, and several other members of his clergy were apprehended in nearby Assisi for revolt and thrown into prison."

"Prison? A bishop?" another woman echoed.

"*Si*, it happened all the time!" Beatrice explained matter-of-factly. "So, anyway the Roman Governor summoned them before him a few days later and required that they adore his idol of the god Jupiter, richly adorned with gold. The holy bishop took up the idol and threw it down, breaking it in pieces. The prefect, furious, ordered that his hands be cut off."

While the women were exclaiming indignantly about this, Fr Corinth's smartphone rang; it was Carol in Boston. He stepped outside for a moment and after a few polite exchanges, she came right to the point.

"Father, I have Father Donovan here for you," she said, and in a moment he was speaking with his old mentor. The ancient Dominican had something important to say, he told Corinth. He had had a conversation with the Pope himself, via Skype.

"I saw the Holy Father with my own two eyes!" he exclaimed, his voice hoarse with age, obviously delighted. "And what's more, he saw me! Right on the computer screen, just like on Star Trek!"

"Wonderful!" Corinth replied heartily, a smile lighting up his thin face.

"Yes, and he told me how good your work is, too, Father," the Dominican told him, suddenly quite serious. "He told me that you are a great, strong support for the Church. He said you were 'invaluable' -- I believe that was the term he used."

At this Father Corinth's heart suddenly expanded in his chest, and it took a moment before he could answer.

"Th-thanks, Father," he replied huskily. "H-how very kind of you to tell me."

"Not at all, my boy," the ancient exorcist said, his own voice shaky. "N-Not at all. You are a credit to me, and to the Cardinal, God rest his soul. And your work will continue to be valuable to the Church, God willing. God knows you are needed, as a teacher and a priest."

Luca was thinking about all of this when he spotted Tessa waiting for him on Trinita's familiar worn steps. She was English, born of Sicilian parents in London, now working in Rome and a new parishioner drawn to Santa Trinita Dei Pellegrini by the beauty of the liturgy.

Small and neatly made, today she was dressed in a light summer frock with a nipped-in waist that flared to a full skirt which stopped crisply at mid-knee. Her heart-shaped face was framed by glossy black ringlets, which she now swept carelessly beneath her glowing indigo lace veil.

Tessa was bursting with excitement as he arrived. Smiling softly, she did not allow him to embrace her, holding his hands down with her own.

"I have something to tell you!" she sang out, and without waiting for a response, announced, "Someone you know is joining the sisters' convent in Umbria!"

Shocked, Luca felt his blood run cold. Could this be? Was it possible that she had a religious vocation? Why had she not told him?

"W-what?" he asked, confusedly, and then, in an agony of despair. "W-who?"

Tessa was too excited to notice his distress.

"How *could* you not know?" she asked in mock severity. "Men are *so* clueless!"

Stunned, Luca could not speak, so he merely shook his head and looked at his feet.

"Luca!" It was Tessa's turn to be shocked, as the reason for his reaction began to dawn on her. "*Luca, ascolta!*"

With an effort, Luca composed himself and looked her in the eye.

"Luca," Tessa said calmly and deliberately, "the person who will be joining the Sisters is that British reporter who interviewed you and Gina."

"Wh-What?!"

"Yes!" Tessa was aflutter with the news. "Apparently her interview with Gina made her curious, so she started attending morning Mass here at Trinita Dei Pellegrini -- and that started her conversion!"

Luca's sudden relief and joy knew no bounds. He threw his head back in a hearty laugh, and scooped a startled Tessa off her feet. Hands on her slim waist, he whirled her in the air, much to the delight of passers-by.

To the bystanders' further enchantment, Luca set Tessa lightly on her feet and they kissed, sweetly.

Then Luca took Tessa's hand in his, and to the infinite wonder of the witnesses, tripped up the stone stairs and stepped through the ancient church door, just as the *Asperges* began.

The End